THE MERMAID'S BUBBLE LOUNGE

SEANA KELLY

The Mermaid's Bubble Lounge

Copyright © 2025 by Seana Kelly

Ebook ISBN: 9781641973113

Print POD ISBN: 9781641973434

NYLA Publishing

121 W. 27th St., Suite 1201, NY 10001, New York.

http://www.nyliterary.com

Titles by Seana Kelly

For
Harper & Grace
You make me proud every day

ONE

New Book, Who Dis?

A cat slinks by the empty nightclub. It's past closing and the employees have all gone home. Which is for the best as, he loathes the smell of mermaids. There's nothing to be done about it. He doesn't control where the doorways are.

A cat rubs against his leg. He's in the deepest shadows, under the eaves of the nightclub, away from streetlights. He bends to scratch the cat, hearing the faint thump of feet and paws on the sidewalk.

Lifting his head to the wind, be breathes in the scents: a human woman and a dog. Perfect. He picks up the cat. It stiffens but doesn't try to shred him. Perhaps, he thinks, the cat understands he's a fellow hunter, silent and lethal.

When the jogging steps approach, he puts the cat back down on the pavement. It runs forward a few feet, hisses at the panting dog, and then moves back beside the hunter. That couldn't have gone better if the hunter had planned it himself.

The dog pulls at the leash, half dragging his petite female owner across the empty parking lot. He's a strong, muscular breed. The hunter can see her straining. He enjoys her predicament.

The dog is stronger, though she is the one in charge. Moments like this call that power dynamic into question. In the dog's mind, he may have been allowing her to give him commands because she scratches and feeds him. When it comes down to it, though, he knows which of them is the stronger and fiercer.

The woman yanks him back. "Heel."

Even from here, the hunter can see her embarrassment. She's lost control. She'll have to get used to that feeling.

The dog growls, dragging her closer to the building. The cat steps forward again, hissing. The woman's shoulders droop. Nothing to fear here. Just a cat getting her dog worked up.

Suppressing a grin, the hunter waits until she's just a bit closer. She doesn't have his—nor the cat nor dog's—night vision, so she's missing some very important context clues.

The hunter waits, like a spider on a web. Just a little closer.

"Buttercup, come on. It's just a cat. We need to finish our run." She tries to pull him back, but it's no use. He has the hunter's scent and is far too intrigued.

The cat runs around the empty nightclub, but still the dog pulls the woman toward her death.

Brow furrowed, she stares blindly into the dark at the hunter's shins, trying to make out what her little Buttercup is growling at. The hunter will show her soon, but not yet. He's a predator, much like the cat, who enjoys playing with his food.

"What is it?" she asks, exasperated. "Is it food?"

She steps closer, and the hunter lets his eyes glow red in the dark. "It's most definitely food," he says. "Mine."

The poor woman is paralyzed with fright when his fangs sink into her neck.

TWO

We Now Return to Our Regularly Scheduled Programming

I t was disconcerting, waking to a big, furry head in my face. "I'm not awake yet. Go lie down."

Fergus wasn't one to be put off once he'd heard the change in my breathing and knew breakfast and a run were in the offing. I was about to give in when Clive's arm tightened around me, pulling me flush against him, his mouth on the back of my neck.

Tipping my head forward to give him better access, I said, "You're supposed to be sleeping now." My voice was breathier than usual. He had that effect on me.

His hand on my waist slid lower. "I'm not sleepy yet."

While his fingers explored, I reached behind me, took a hold of him, and squeezed. Clive groaned. My laugh was cut off by my own gasp. Lifting my leg over his, he opened me up, his clever fingers making me mindless.

Fergus blew out a breath, went back to his bed, and flopped down, recognizing he wasn't going anywhere any time soon.

"I thought you'd be...tired." I'd lost my train of thought for a moment.

He flipped us over, holding my hips up while pushing my shoulders down. "Not in the least."

Face in the mattress, I came apart almost at once, but he was just getting started. He worked my body like the Master vampire he was, and it wasn't long before my whole body felt like a million sensitive nerve endings readying for impact. He sped up, his hands on me, knowing the secrets to my body. Teeth gritted, I rode out the short-circuiting explosions happening everywhere, all at once.

When I was finally able to move, I slid bonelessly back to the bed and tried to catch my breath. Clive pulled me in close, so my head was on his chest.

"Stay a little longer, love," he mumbled. The sun had fully risen, and he was finally being pulled under.

Blowing out a breath, I gave myself a moment for my heart to slow down and then kissed his cheek. "Sleep well."

I got cleaned up, put on my running leggings and a tight tee, strapped on my axe and sheath for those nasty fae assassin encounters that occasionally popped up, and zipped on a thin hoodie. The dwarf's axe had been spelled to disappear when it was on me, only becoming visible when I pulled it out of its sheath. I scared fewer joggers that way.

Once my running shoes were on, I slapped my thigh and Fergus jumped up, ready to begin today's adventure. He ran down the stairs in front of me, no doubt heading toward his water bowl before something distracted him.

I rounded the bottom of the stairs and saw him staring into the den, his tail wagging. "What is it, buddy?"

And then I saw it too. Two black eyes shining in the darkest corner of the room. My hand went to my axe handle and then I heard his voice.

"So jumpy. If he's wagging his tail, why are you ready to chop off my head?" Vlad rolled his eyes. "You really need to pay closer attention to his body language." He put aside the book he was reading and tapped his knee.

Fergus galloped across the room, trying his best to fit his huge body on Vlad's lap.

"We've discussed this," Vlad murmured, pushing my eight-month-old Irish Wolfhound, who was already tipping the scales at one hundred and ten pounds, back down. A lap dog Fergus was not, to his everlasting disappointment. "You may sit at my feet, like a dignified and loyal hound. You may not sprawl on my lap."

Snickering, I filled up Fergus' water bowl. "Good morning, Vlad. I have to ask. What are you doing here? I believe we gave you my old apartment to stay in."

Looking every inch the lord of the manor, he sat back in the leather chair, his legs crossed and a hand resting on the top of Fergus' head. "You did. I've run out of my own books and have come to read yours."

"Run out? There are hundreds of books in that apartment." I grabbed Fergus' leash and he leapt to me, his body wiggling in anticipation.

Vlad smirked, using his knee as a bookmark. "I should clarify. I've read the few worth reading. I was looking for a *good* book."

Irritated, I headed to the front door with Fergus dancing around me. "Those are fighting words, vampire. You're lucky I have more important things to do right now." I snapped on my pup's leash. "Come on, little man. We don't have to put up with this disrespect."

I closed the front door on Vlad's chuckle, slid my phone into the hip pocket on my leggings, and began an easy jog. I needed to let Fergus warm up. Wolfhounds weren't long-distance runners, but he'd been my running buddy since we'd adopted him, so he was building up the endurance.

Turning right, we jogged, nice and easy, up the road, past ocean, bay, and Golden Gate Bridge lookouts. We bypassed a short gate, barring vehicles, and then sped along the Lands End trail.

This was basically our backyard, and he had favorite routes. I usually let him decide where we'd run. I just needed the exercise, being a werewolf and all. I didn't care where we went.

When we came out in Sea Cliff, I thought he was heading to Owen and George's, hoping for treats, but he just kept going, plunging us into the Presidio. I thought maybe he wanted to visit the stables and see the horses, but he kept going. When I saw the Palace of Fine Arts ahead, I made him veer off for a visit. Clive and I had been married here six months ago.

Not one to be dissuaded, he continued his run as the city began to wake. The bell of a cable car rang in the distance while we ran through the Marina District. For a minute, I wondered if he was headed to see the dragons, but he went right past Drake's Treasures, the jewelry store owned by George's family. George's sister Coco lived above the shop. Fyr and his wolfhound Alice lived in the second apartment.

Fergus had stayed with them while Clive and I were in Budapest. Fyr had mentioned that the owner of a coffee shop around here liked to give the dogs treats when they visited, so I thought that was where we were headed, but no.

We went through Marina Green and then Fort Mason. Fergus was a dog on a mission. He kept us on the roads next to the water, but he wasn't getting distracted by seagulls or the feral cats that liked to hang out down here.

When I heard the barking of the sea lions at Fisherman's Wharf, I figured that was what had piqued his interest. He enjoyed watching them sunning themselves on the wide raft the city had provided. Occasionally Fergus would bark back at our huge local colony of mostly male sea lions. They were a fat and sassy bunch, enjoying the fish the tourists tossed at them.

He wasn't headed to Pier 39, though. Instead, he brought us to the back of The Mermaid's Bubble Lounge, a fae-run nightclub. Something felt wrong. While Fergus pulled me toward the front of the building, I heard voices crackling over radios and saw lights flashing on cars.

"Excuse me, miss. You can't be here." A young cop waved his arm, directing us to go around the cars. "That way, please. This is a crime scene. We can't have you here."

"Jimmy," an older cop grumbled. "You don't have to give them your life story. Just move them along."

The young cop swallowed and nodded, waving me away again.

Fergus and I went around the patrol car. The smell of death, though, slowed my steps. I looked back and saw a woman on the ground, her head at an unnatural angle. She was dressed like me in running gear. Unlike me, she had two bloody bite marks on her neck, like a vampire had drained her dry without closing the wounds. *Shit.*

Fergus whined, not wanting to leave the woman behind. I was right there with him.

The older cop set up a screen, blocking the public from seeing the victim. Scents were hard to untangle at the wharf. There was just too much with the fish mongers setting up for the day, the coffee kiosks, the popcorn and churros carts, cars, people—washed and unwashed—beginning their day of sightseeing, restaurants cooking breakfast, other dogs and their people walking by. Through it all, though, the odor of death was strong, too strong for her murder to have been recent. My guess was she'd been dead for hours, probably killed late last night.

I wanted to talk with Clive, but he'd be dead to the world for hours yet.

Wait. I knew who was up. I pulled out my phone and dialed Vlad.

"Missed me already?" he answered.

"No. I'm at Fisherman's Wharf. There's a dead woman on the ground with two bloody holes in her neck."

I heard him move. "Get close. Do you scent a vampire? Anyone we know?"

"I can't. The cops have her blocked off. We've already been told to move on. If the cop didn't look so queasy, he'd probably be yelling at me for being this close."

"Check her color," he said. "Exsanguination will leave skin unnaturally pale, like a maggot's, and she won't have dark bluish or purple spots on the bottom of her body from normal blood settling."

I grimaced. "As lovely as all that sounds, they've put a screen up around her."

He cursed. "Just describe what you saw."

I closed my eyes and brought it back. "She's lying on the ground beside the Bubble Lounge's outside wall. She's wearing running gear like what you just saw me in. Her head's at a weird angle. The bite mark's obvious and prominent, on the side of her neck facing the street, not the building."

He made an irritated sound. "Eyes open or closed?"

My focus had been on that bloody bite mark and what it meant. "Let me think." I tried to see her in my mind's eye. "Open, but not wide open, if that makes sense."

"Yes."

"From the scent, I'd say she was killed last night," I told him. "And her clothes, they're the kind that have a reflective stripe down the sides for people jogging at night." I thought about that a moment. "Weird, though."

"What is?" he asked.

"It's just odd." More emergency vehicles arrived, so I walked Fergus to the side, near the fresh fish stand. The workers there were watching the cops too. "Most women don't go jogging late at night on their own."

"Perhaps her running companion is the one who attacked her," Vlad suggested.

I shrugged, not that he could see me. "I mean, anything's possible since we have no idea what happened."

"Or," he continued, "she felt secure because, like you, she was jogging with a dog, one who ran off during the attack. Regardless, you should leave. They'll start taking pictures of the crowd and it would be best if you weren't in those pictures. I'd venture to guess that Russell, as Master of the City, has connections in the police department and the morgue. We'll see what information he can get."

"And in the meantime," I said, "we'll hope like hell that this doesn't have anything to do with what it looks like."

"The Guild is in shambles," Vlad said. "We're not prepared to deal with my kind trying to come out to the world, so, yes, let's hope very hard that there is a mundane explanation for this woman's death."

THREE

Too Many Creeps

B y the time we arrived home, Fergus was dragging and Vlad was gone. I ran upstairs to shower before I went to work. I flicked on the lights in the bedroom. Clive wouldn't care. Seeing him, though, made me wish he was a day-walking vamp, like Vlad. I wanted to talk with him.

I leaned over the bed and gave him a kiss. "I need to talk with you when you wake up."

Maybe it had been a run-of-the-mill creep with a strange weapon who'd killed her. Maybe. I was worried, though.

They'd talked in Budapest about a contingent of vampires who wanted to come out to the world. They wanted the power and the fear. They wanted to be at the top of the food chain, with humans cowering in subservience.

Yes, vampires were inhumanly strong and fast. Yes, they were undead killers, but there were a shit ton more humans in the world than vampires. Vampire hunting would become an overnight craze. Apps would be created to locate nocturnes and destroy vamps. Hell, a whole cottage industry would rise focused on exterminating vampires. Humans might not have super-human strength, but they had the numbers and could hunt around the clock.

I didn't bother closing doors or trying to be quiet while Clive slept. If anything, he told me he enjoyed sometimes hearing me get ready. If his subconscious was close to the surface, he'd listen and feel like he was with me.

Wearing my usual jeans, running shoes, and a hoodie, I jogged downstairs to get breakfast for Fergus and me. Was it June? Yes, but it was also San Francisco. Today was cold and overcast.

I filled Fergus' food bowl and then made myself a large chorizo omelet. When he finished his breakfast, he ran out to the little doggies' room, aka the side of the house. I brought out my plate and a large glass of iced tea to have my meal al fresco on the patio.

A hummingbird hovered over the salvia along the back wall of the garden. Fergus, who'd flopped on the ground beside me, tracked it but couldn't be bothered to stir himself. In fact, he rolled over, using my foot as a pillow.

"It's your own fault. No one told you to run all the way down to Fisherman's Wharf." I thought about it for a minute. "Why did you?" I scratched the side of his head. "You ran there like you knew what we were going to find."

Knowing our property had wards on top of wards, I didn't worry about calling Russell and talking outside. Russell, the vampire Master of the City was sleeping, as all good little vampires were right now, so I left a message for him on his cell.

"Hi. It's Sam. I know you're sleeping, but when you wake up, can you look into a murder near the Bubble Lounge this morning —or, more likely, last night. Fergus and I were on a run and saw a woman with a bloody, vampire-bite-looking wound on her neck. I told Vlad and we're hoping you have people in human services you can contact for more information. Anyway, just wanted you to know. Sorry to give you bad news. Say hi to Godfrey and Audrey for me. Unless that's not a cool thing to ask the Master to do. In which case, forget I asked. Anyway, thanks."

I needed to learn how to bullet point my messages. Oh, well. I brought my empty plate in and rinsed it before putting it in the dishwasher.

"Come on, buddy. It's time for work."

Fergus jumped up and ran to the front door. He may have been tired but there was an endless energy reserve for the stuff he wanted to do.

I locked up, snapped on his leash again, and then we strolled across the road and through the green area between home and The Slaughtered Lamb before taking the stairs down to Lands End lookout. Humans on the stairs made it down to a promontory at the edge of the ocean. Supernaturals, like myself, were able to trip a ward and continue down the stairs, going underground to The Slaughtered Lamb Bookstore and Bar.

My bookstore and bar was built into the cliff face at the water line. Aquarium-grade glass kept the books dry and gave us a gorgeous view of the ocean and the hills in the North Bay. How, you might ask. Magical builders helped me create the world's most beautiful bookstore and bar.

We weren't open yet, so it was quiet. Bright morning light streamed in through the window as kelp bobbed in the ocean. I flicked on a few lights and then went to the kitchen to fill the pup's work water bowl.

Dave, my half-demon cook, had left me a plate of cookies on the island. Baking helped with his uncontrollable bouts of anger, and I was here for it. Truth be told, morning cookies were my favorite part of the day.

Today's plate had a note beside it that read *lavender chai cookies*. What? Normally, the lack of chocolate would be enough to disappoint me, but these sounded intriguing. I grabbed a bully stick for Fergus and then a cookie for me. I took a bite and stopped, closing my eyes, letting the taste settle on my tongue. De-licious.

We opened at noon, but I had arrived early so I could unpack book boxes. Cookies and new books. Did it get any better than this? Once I'd loaded all the new books on a cart and broken down the boxes, I grabbed two more cookies and headed to the bookstore.

Owen, my right-hand guy, Slaughtered Lamb manager, and

wicche extraordinaire, arrived at eleven thirty to get the bar prepped. He'd watch that side of The Slaughtered Lamb while I covered this side, adding the new books to our inventory.

Holding the new books, often reading the opening paragraphs, made me happy, but today my mind kept returning to that poor woman who had just been trying to go for a run. A good long growl vibrated through my chest.

Owen appeared in the bookstore doorway. "Everything okay? Did we get the wrong shipment?"

I shook my head and then explained to Owen about the dead woman.

"I'm sorry." He shook his head. "That's horrible. George made us waffles this morning and you had to start your day with death."

"It was worse for her." I dropped the book in my hand back onto the cart. "She was just trying to do the most basic thing, just living, and some bastard decided her life was his to take."

Owen nodded. "It might have been a female vampire."

"That doesn't make it better," I protested. "If this wasn't a human creep, we're dealing with a vampire who is broadcasting who they are and what they do to the human world. Neither scenario is good."

Owen leaned his elbows on the counter and stared out the window as waves crashed. After a moment, he said, "Is it wrong that I'm rooting for a human creep?"

I shook my head. "One of them is horrible, but we can hopefully help the authorities capture the guy. The other is indicative of a much bigger and scarier problem."

Owen and I sat with that possibility for a moment and then he said, "How about if I get you a cup of tea?"

Slumping in my chair, I nodded. "Thanks. I'd appreciate that."

He walked back toward the bar. "Oh, and don't worry about shelving all of those. Meri wanted more hours since she's on summer break. She'll be here at opening."

Meri was my newest employee. She was half-fae and a teenager. Her father was a merman who scowled at us from the ocean, keeping his eyes on her to make sure she was safe. His near constant presence embarrassed her, but I'd assured her that many of us would have loved to have a protective dad watching over us. Mine died when I was a baby and while hers often scared me, I still got a little choked up when I caught him smiling, watching her work.

I opened the wards at noon. A group of four wicches were the first down the stairs. They were here most days, so Owen already had cups and a full teapot waiting for them. They were funny older women who enjoyed teasing Owen and sharing stories. If any problems went down, though, they'd be the first to start throwing spells. The magical community respected and feared the crone wicches. They knew their own power and had lost all patience with—what they referred to as—nonsense.

A moment later, I heard light steps on the stairs and knew Meri had arrived. She came in with her hoodie covering most of her face and her hands buried in her pockets. Meri was inhumanly beautiful. She had long white-blonde hair, golden skin, and violet eyes. She was a stunner who often had to deal with stalkers, other teens and, more disturbingly, adults. Consequently, she hid beneath oversized clothing. As someone who did the same for almost eight years—trying to hide my scars—I totally got it. Usually, when she arrived, she'd take off the hoodie and get to work. Today, she kept it on.

"Hey, Meri. How's summer vacation treating you?" I dipped my head, trying to see under the edge of her hood.

Her shoulder twitched before she picked up books from my cart to shelve.

"Meri?" I kept my voice low.

She paused, her back to me.

"Is everything okay?" I went around the counter and stood beside her.

She didn't turn around.

"You and I are the only ones here right now with excellent hearing. The ones in the bar are wicches. They won't hear us. I can see that everything isn't okay." I stepped closer. "You can talk to me."

She finally turned and lifted her head. Her luminous purple eyes were filled with tears. "I wanted to walk today. My mom is working. Fyr always offers to drive me, but I know he doesn't start work for a few more hours. I didn't want to ask him to chauffeur me around." She slammed the books in her hands on a shelf to her left. "I have a license. I'm working here to save money for a car. I just didn't want to beg for a ride today, so I decided to walk."

"How far of a walk is it?" I was pretty sure I knew where this was going.

"Only about a mile," she said. "My mom and I live in the Outer Richmond District."

I nodded. She was right. That wasn't too far.

"This man started following me." She shivered. "I just felt these goose bumps on the back of my neck. When I turned, there was this man who's been watching me." She yanked her hood down. The braid of her thick blonde hair uncoiled and fell over her shoulder. "You know how I love gardening?"

I nodded. Meri had a gift for growing things. She'd created a display in the gardening section of the bookstore that was overtaking the bookshelves around it. We had a lush English tea garden along the back wall.

"I can't work in my front yard anymore. Whenever I go out, he shows up to stand on the sidewalk, stare at me, and try to start conversations." The anger from a moment ago was dissipating, leaving only despair. "My plants are dying."

"I'm sorry. Does your mom know?" Although as a human, I'm not sure what she could do.

She nodded. "Yeah. There's this detective we've worked with on other stuff." She meant other stalking cases. Meri's had to change schools countless times. "Mom called her to talk to her about this man. The detective said she'd ask patrol cars to regularly drive down our street but that means they drive by once a day. I mean, I appreciate it but that won't stop him.

"Anyway, I started walking to work and there he was, following me. It's a really beautiful day. I just wanted to walk to work. That's all."

"I know," I said. "It's not fair that you can't go for a walk without someone bothering you, but I need you to remember that you have friends here. You could have called me, and I'd have jogged to you and scared the hell out of that guy." I let my eyes lighten to wolf gold and my claws slide from my fingertips. "I would have enjoyed making him wet himself."

Meri almost smiled.

"Owen could have driven over to get you and hit the guy with a go-away spell. Heck, Fyr could have breathed fire on him. No more problem."

Her eyes glittered, considering that one.

FOUR

The Fear of Sam

"I can't take my sweatshirt off without having to explain to people what happened." Meri pulled up her right sleeve. She already had a dark bruise forming in the shape of a handprint. Rage overtook me. Leaning down, I sniffed her sleeve, caught his scent, and raced up the stairs. I knew she shouted something after me, but I couldn't hear it. My head was filled with a roaring white noise.

I was done. This on top of the woman this morning? I was at a breaking point. This shit had to stop.

When I hit the upper parking lot, I spun, trying to catch his sent on the wind. She'd said Outer Richmond, a mile. I went to the main road but couldn't find him. I did, however, get her scent, so I followed that back. She'd clearly lost him somewhere along the way.

As I was running down a very steep hill and wondering why she'd taken this far more vertical route, it occurred to me that she'd done it to lose him. Sure enough, at the bottom of the hill, I caught his scent. Turning to the right, I passed apartment houses and single-family homes. My head was on a swivel, trying to find the asshole who laid his hand on her.

Where the hell had he gone? There was no way he'd left the

area, not after getting close enough to grab her. He was waiting somewhere. At the end of the block, I lost it. The stink of a passing bus's exhaust was in my nose, overlaying his trail. I retraced my steps, blowing air out of my nose, before I pulled up my hood and shifted my snout.

Head down, I went back to the corner, found the trail, and started running again. I shifted my nose back. No need to scare the little old lady walking down the sidewalk. I didn't need the boost anymore. I had him now.

I passed a bodega and skidded to a stop. Senses on alert, I scanned the area. A moment later, a man walked out of the bodega holding a bottle of water. He looked to be in his fifties, with sallow skin and sagging jowls. His hair was thin and an unnatural black that looked like it came from a spray can. His narrow eyes darted up and down the street. He unscrewed the bottle cap, took a sip, and then walked a few paces back to the intersection so he could keep watch and spot Meri on her return route.

My fingertips tingled. I wanted my claws, wanted to rake them across this creep's throat.

A moment later, I felt Clive in my mind with me. *Darling, why are you so angry?*

Glaring at the back of the creep's balding head, I tried to use my words. *I know killing is wrong, but I'm having a hard time convincing myself of that right now.*

I felt him pushing himself to be more alert. *What's happening?*

I explained about Meri's stalker and the bruise. I knew he knew it wasn't only about that. I had a lot of pent-up rage about what had been done to me when I was a teenager. It wasn't the same. I knew that. It didn't stop me from wanting to punish this bastard, though.

If I could, I'd kill him for you so you wouldn't feel the weight of it. We both know, though, that you'd carry the guilt of taking his life.

I'd be saving Meri and who knows who else.

True.

I huffed out a breath. *Fine. I won't kill him.*

Darling, you don't have to kill him to put the fear of Sam in him. Go scare him. It'll make you feel better.

The creep took a gulp of water while he looked up and down the streets, not wanting to miss Meri. The thighs of his baggy jeans had a sheen, like he regularly wiped his greasy fingers on his pants. His faded black camp shirt smelled like it needed a good wash.

The jeans hung off his flat ass, but there was a bulge in the back pocket. Perfect. I moved up behind him and snatched his wallet. He spun around, face dark with anger. One look at my yellow eyes and sneer, though, and he was taking a step back.

"H-hey," he stammered. "What are you doing?"

I flipped open his wallet. "Vincent Lloyd. Balboa Street." When I lifted my gaze from his license, I enjoyed the fear I saw in his eyes. His scent turned sour. "Vincent Lloyd." I glanced down again. "A fifty-four-year-old man who likes to stalk and terrorize a teenage girl. That's you, right?"

His eyes jittered in their sockets. "What? Of course not." He shook his head, reaching for his wallet. "You're crazy."

I held his wallet just out of reach. Allowing one claw to poke out, I tapped his chest in time with my words. "I. Don't. Believe. You."

He flinched, his eyes getting rounder, as drops of blood dribbled under his shirt.

"You're a sad little man who spends his days fantasizing about a girl almost forty years younger, a girl who has no interest in you, one who has made it clear you scare her but still you stare and follow."

He shook his head, sweat beading on his oily brow. "I don't know what you're talking about." He tried to snatch the wallet out of my hand, but I growled, low and mean. His eyes began dancing again.

"And today, you put your sweaty hand on her." I reveled in watching him begin to tremble.

"No. That's not true. Whatever that little bitc—"

19

I didn't think. I heard the word being formed and my hand moved, slapping the shit out of him. He hit the ground, my handprint on his face.

Crouching down beside him, I was pleased to hear a whimper. "I need you to understand, Vincent Lloyd who lives on Balboa Street, that if you so much as look at her from behind your living room curtains, I will come back and tear your face off." I held up one finger with a razor-sharp claw at the end. "Do you understand?"

And there it was. The smell of piss.

His head bounced up and down.

I leaned in closer, letting my teeth elongate. "Later, you're going to second-guess yourself. You're going to think you remembered this wrong. You were taken by surprise. I couldn't have been this scary." I smiled, letting him see my teeth and then I picked up his two-hundred-pound body off the ground with ease, placing him back on his feet.

"When you begin to doubt what happened here and question whether anyone would really notice if you started following her again, think of me and remind yourself that there are things in this world you know nothing about, things that can end you in the most painful ways without breaking a sweat. Yes?"

He gave another jerky nod.

I tossed the wallet at his chest and he squealed in fear. I might have enjoyed that sound too much. I sprinted across the street and up the steep hill, out of sight. I needed him to understand that I wasn't human, that my threat was real.

When I turned the corner, I slowed down, trying to get my rage in check. I didn't want to scare Meri or the wicches in the bar.

You did that beautifully.

I flinched at Clive's voice. *I didn't realize you were still with me.*

Is it wrong that I'm feeling very aroused right now?

I laughed and shook off the last of the anger. *I want to give Meri one of your cars. She needs a safe way to get around. She shouldn't have to ask people for rides or risk walking around town by herself.*

Clive was silent for a moment. *None of my cars are appropriate for a teen with a new license. How about if we loan her the money to buy the car she wants.*

Oh, I like that. Okay. I'll talk with her when I get back. Thank you.

Of course. He paused again. *You should also talk with your cousin Arwyn. From what Declan told me when we were trying to put out that fire at her gallery, she's also dealt with stalkers all her life.*

I walked across the parking lot and started down the stairs to the lookout. *Good idea. And they both have a father who's water fae. Arwyn's other half is wicche, so there are spells she can do to protect herself. Meri's mom is human. Still, though, there's got to be some fae thing that'll keep creeps away.*

There was another long pause. *I'm sorry, darling. If this is sorted now, I really need to go back to sleep. I'm having a hard time focusing.*

Sure. I need to talk with you when you wake about something that happened at the wharf.

Hmm?

He was out. The worst part of these longer days was seeing less of Clive. Summer blew.

When I came down the stairs, Meri was waiting at the bottom, looking apprehensive. I patted her shoulder and then waved her back into the bookstore. Brow furrowed, Owen watched us go.

I had Meri follow me to the chairs by the window, motioning for her to sit. "I found him."

Her eyebrows shot up as she looked me over, her gaze setting on my hand. "You have blood on your finger."

I held up my hand to check and then let my claw slide out. "No. I have blood on my claw."

Emotions flashed across her ethereal face: worry, anger, and finally a tentative hope that took the place of the defeat she'd been drowning in earlier.

I told her everything.

She whispered, "You made him pee himself?"

Shrugging a shoulder, I told her, "I'm very scary, Meri. I keep telling you, but you never listen."

She giggled, as I'd hoped she would, her shoulders finally relaxing. "You really don't think he'll be out there when I go home?"

I shook my head. "I don't think so. What I want you to do, though, is call me—or Fyr or Dave or Owen—if you even think you might be seeing his shadow around a corner. I guarantee you, all of us would look at it as a treat to go rough that guy up." I glanced at my claw again. "Now you might be wondering, *Sam, why aren't you cleaning off that blood?* Well, I'll tell you. I want Fyr and Dave to have his scent. I want them to know who our enemy is. Okay?"

She nodded, eyes glassy with tears, and then she popped up and ran into the bar. She came back a moment later, carrying a clear bar towel. "Here. Use this to clean off and then we can put the towel in a baggie to keep it free from other scents."

"Great idea."

She left again before returning with a large plastic baggie. I dropped the towel in and she closed it up. "I'm going to go leave this on Dave's desk. He's usually the first to arrive. I can explain when he gets here."

"Good call." Watching her go, the tightness in my chest relaxed. She was taking control. She knew we were her weapons when she needed us, but she was the one in charge.

When she walked back in, she was grinning. "Fyr is going to be so mad that he wasn't the one to scare that guy."

I nodded. "Both Dave and Fyr will be pissed off they missed out. They'll look forward to that call so they can have their own fun." I didn't want her to second-guess calling for help or to worry she'd be bothering any of us.

FIVE

Vlad Really Knows How to Clear a Room

"Okay." I gestured to the chair beside me. "That takes care of one problem. The other is your need for a car, so you're not left vulnerable to stalkers."

Meri nodded. "I'm getting close. I saved the money I made working at the Bubble Lounge too."

"Clive and I want to help. We're going to loan you the money you need to buy a good, safe car now and you can pay us back a little every month."

Meri was already shaking her head. "I couldn't. I don't want—"

"So you know," I interrupted, "I opened The Slaughtered Lamb when I was your age. I'd lost my mom. I'd been attacked and was covered in scars. I had no family and no place to go. I was dumped in this city to stay with a woman I'd never met before but who they told me was a friend of my mom's. Clive loaned me the money to build this place, giving me a safe space to heal and a life I grew to love. We all need help sometimes. There's no shame in letting someone lend a hand."

After a long pause, she nodded, her lavender eyes beginning to sparkle. "I can get my own car soon?"

"Absolutely. You said you were close. How much do you need?"

She scrunched her nose. "Is seven thousand too much? That should cover it and be enough to pay the tax and license stuff they add on."

I patted her hand. "When Dave comes in, I'll have him transfer money from my account to yours. He does the payroll around here. He'll do it faster than me."

Meri's grin was so wide, I felt the last dregs of my outrage draining away.

Leaning back in the chair, I watched the ocean swirl against the window. "I know I'm—what—eight years older than you, but I just got my driver's license too. Clive, of course, bought me some ridiculously expensive vehicle I'm too scared to drive, so instead I use a small, safe sedan that doesn't make me feel too over-whelmed."

Meri nodded quickly. "I've been researching cars for a while. It needs to be small, so I can find parking. I don't want a manual. I had to drive one in driver's training, and I about had a heart attack when I had to stop on Bradford Street and then start again. Even the instructor was white knuckling it."

I swallowed. "I've never driven that one myself, but I was in the car when Clive drove it in one of his manual sports cars." I rubbed my forehead. "I've had nightmares about that one. It's like a forty-five-degree angle." I shook my head, not wanting the thought to become lodged in there. I didn't want another night-mare where the street got steeper and steeper while the car I was in tumbled backward to the bottom.

She held up her hands. "Never again. Anyway, there are car dealerships with used cars in Colma. Maybe my mom can take me this weekend to look."

"I don't know how you feel about this," I began. "You've never met Clive, since you usually leave before nightfall, but if hanging with a vampire doesn't bother you, I can ask him to car shop with you. The man knows everything there is to know about them and he'll help you find a good one."

She bit her lip. "Will you be there too?"

"Of course. If that wigs you out at all, Dave could do it too. You'll just need to brace for snarly cussing."

She rolled her eyes. "He doesn't scare me."

"Nor should he." My relationship with Dave was complicated, but that had only happened recently. For the last seven and a half years, he's been my red-skinned, black-eyed, grumpy uncle who hated everyone else but tolerated me. It still hurt to know things I wish I didn't, but I'd trust him to protect Meri. "If Dave goes with you, you're going to end up with a very loud muscle car. He can't help himself."

She laughed.

"Okay, and the last thing on the Meri agenda is to ask if I can have you speak with my cousin Arwyn. She's half water fae and half wicche. Like you, she's gorgeous and has had to deal with predators since she was little. Can I call her and have you talk with her? She might have suggestions that will help."

Meri sat up straight. "Really? I've talked with my Aunt Nerissa and my cousins at the Bubble Lounge." She stared down at her hands in her lap for a moment. "None of them have the same problem I do. I mean, some humans are interested and hit on them, but it's not…"

"It's not obsessive violence masquerading as devotion?" I asked.

She shook her head. "No. Do you really think your cousin could help me?"

"Only one way to find out." I pulled out my phone and dialed. Once I'd explained to Arwyn what was going on, I handed Meri my phone and went out to the bar.

Owen slid a cup of tea to me. "Everything all right, boss?"

I took a sip. "Mostly. Meri can tell you why I sprinted out of here, if she wants."

While he brewed a fresh pot of tea for the wicches, I drew a flagon of mead for Grim, my dwarf regular who'd been sitting on the last stool at the bar since the first day I opened. I heard his very distinctive thump-slide footsteps on the stairs. My human-sized stairs were too tall for dwarfs. Now that I was thinking about it, that might have been why he was always so snarly.

"Good afternoon, Grim. I hope you're having a good day." I slid the flagon to the last stool as he stomped across the bar and then hopped up on his seat. He grunted his acknowledgement and took a big swig.

I went back to the kitchen, got the rest of the cookies, and came out to offer him one. His bushy eyebrows crashed down, appearing offended by the question. He ignored me and took another drink. I strolled back to the other end of the bar as Owen was returning and offered one to him.

"Those are delicious," he said, taking one. "I had one earlier. I have to ask Dave for the recipe. Mom would love them."

More patrons started down the stairs and Owen and I got back to work. Although I opened at noon, we usually didn't see an uptick in customers until around two. I left Meri to cover the bookstore while Owen and I served the bar.

Dave arrived at four and Meri ran into the kitchen to let him know what was going on. She'd returned my phone at some point, thanking me for introducing her to Arwyn. Meri looked lighter and happier than I'd ever seen her. A weight had been lifted.

Around five, Dave came out to update the menu board posted outside the kitchen. Chili and cornbread tonight. Dave wore a glamour when he was above where humans could see him. Up there he was a muscular, bald Black man. Down here, he didn't try to pass for human. He was half-demon and he looked it, with dark red skin and shark-black eyes.

Leaning against the bar sink, he crossed his arms over his chest and quietly asked, "Was that really all that happened?"

The bar was crowded and noisy. As of right now, Dave and I were the only ones here with sensitive hearing, so our murmured conversation was private. "I wanted to kill him."

He nodded, not looking at me. "I doubt she even knows, but she has a talent, a fae trick, for getting people to care for her."

I turned to him, brow furrowed.

He moved a beefy shoulder. "She's a sweet kid. Like I said, I doubt she even knows, but I feel it when she's around. I haven't talked to Fyr about it—we're not close like that—but he is extremely protective of her." He glanced down at his shoes and then said, "I was watching him. The fact that he constantly volunteers to drive her around was making me uncomfortable. He's almost thirty and she's seventeen. I didn't know if his captivity as a child was screwing with his head and his idea of appropriate relationships, or what."

"Do you know something?" Fyr would be out of here today if he was preying on a teenager.

Dave shook his head. "Nah. The two of them have a brother-sister thing. I think her fae magic makes him more eager to look out for her. That's all."

I blew out a breath.

"I do think that's why she doesn't work at the Bubble Lounge anymore. Working for her aunt seems like the obvious place to be and I'd imagine her aunt can pay her better than you can. She talked about her cousins being jerks to her. My guess is they feel her magic, recognize it, and resent her for using it on them. I honestly don't think she even knows she's doing it or how to control it."

He smirked at me. "She tells me you're loaning her money for a car."

I dropped my head into my hands and heard him laugh.

Patting my shoulder, he added, "Don't feel bad. I only know because I offered the same thing, and she told me you'd beat me to it." He shook his head. "The kid does need a ride. She's giving off some kind of vibe that makes the weak-minded go nuts. It's not safe for her to be walking the streets. The issue is we need to find someone who can teach her how to control her magic."

"I connected her with Arwyn. Maybe she can work with her."

Dave nodded slowly, watching the waves. "Arwyn knows more about her wicche side than her fae side, but I don't feel the need to protect her, so if she has the same talent, she's learned how to hide it. Good plan." He turned and walked back into the kitchen.

When the sun began to set, Vlad walked out of the back and sat on a stool at the bar. The volume of conversations dropped the minute he walked through the kitchen door. Patrons watched him out of the corners of their eyes.

A table of wicches near the stairs got up, waving nervously at me as they headed up and out. I crossed my arms and glared at him.

"What?" he asked, as though he didn't know.

Another table quietly skirted around him and disappeared up the stairs.

"You are ruining my business," I hissed behind gritted teeth.

He raised his eyebrows at me and turned to the side to watch five more people escape. "I have no idea what you mean. I haven't done anything. I merely sat in your establishment. If your patrons realized it was time to go home, that's hardly on me."

"Will you be purchasing anything this time?" I asked.

Expression haughty, he replied, "Unless blood donors have been added to the menu, I think not."

Dave walked out, carrying a tray with bowls of chili and baskets of cornbread. He stopped, scanned the rapidly emptying bar, and then turned to Vlad. "Couldn't you have waited until after I served dinner?"

Vlad glanced over his shoulder at the nearly empty bar and then at Dave's tray. "I could have, but I was bored."

SIX

Let the Investigation Begin

"Remind me the next time I say I'm bored that spending time with the two of you is not the solution." Vlad stopped to scratch under Fergus' chin as he walked in the front door of our house.

"No one invited you," I reminded him.

"Nonsense," he said. "I'm welcomed wherever I go."

Clive closed the door with a huff of amusement. "If you recall, I did warn you that shopping for a teen's first vehicle would hardly be interesting." Dressed in charcoal slacks and a snowy white linen shirt—the man had a million white dress shirts—he looked too formal for an evening of wandering around car dealerships. That was my husband, though. He was a heartstopper, with dark blond hair, stormy gray eyes, and a face and body chiseled to perfection. He was also a thousand-year-old vampire who wore suits like a second skin. Vampires were a strangely formal lot.

Vlad leaned into his reputation and wore only black, all day, every day. He had dark shoulder-length hair that was perpetually tied at the nape of his neck and an oversized, rather ridiculous, mustache that somehow worked on him. Black eyes completed his Nosferatu look.

I let Fergus out into the back garden, and the men followed. It was a soft night. "Can I get anyone anything?"

Clive sat on the love seat and shook his head. When I glanced at Vlad, Clive chuckled. "Did you miss that, darling? Vlad kept wandering off to get himself a snack. He's fine."

I gave Vlad my squinty suspicious look. "I thought you and Cadmael promised to be good while you visited."

Vlad, sitting in a chair to the side, brushed dog hair off his trousers. "Don't be ridiculous. No one was harmed in the making of my meal. And they were as bored as I was, shuffling around with their tired, bloodshot eyes, staring at sticker prices they couldn't afford, lost in thoughts of mounting bills."

"He didn't take much from any donor," Clive said, "and he even slipped some cash in their pockets." He grinned at Vlad. "That was almost kind. Very unlike you, old man."

"I have no idea what you're referring to." Vlad glanced around at the outside wall around our backyard. "And you're certain our voices don't carry?"

"Yup. We've tested it a few times." I went back in to get myself a soda. When I came out and sat beside Clive, he was explaining to Vlad about all the warding the house had.

"And I happen to know that when Garyn was in the city, she sent people to break in. They couldn't. Even she—"

Clive, who had his arm around me, squeezed my shoulder to shut me up.

I turned to him. "He knows what I can do."

"Yes," Vlad said, "but he doesn't like it when you remind me." Fergus dropped his head in Vlad's lap and Vlad almost smiled as he began stroking the top of my dog's head. "I've told you before. I would never hurt your wife." Lifting his head to stare at Clive, he finally said, "It was my suggestion to kill everyone in Budapest who could have put her at risk. Surely that affords me a modicum of trust."

Clive's hand had gentled on my shoulder, his thumb brushing

back and forth. I felt his gaze on me a moment before he said, "I trust no one where Sam is concerned."

I opened my mouth to argue such an over-the-top comment, but Vlad cut me off. "No. He's right. We've both lived long enough —though he much longer than me—to know how common it is to be betrayed by those we trust."

"And trusting someone with my own life," Clive murmured as he leaned in to kiss my temple, "is very different from trusting someone with yours. It's your decision, though. I shouldn't have tried to silence you."

I kissed his jaw. *I don't have to tell him if it worries you.*

His hand moved from my shoulder to the back of my head, his fingers digging in and massaging my scalp under my braid. I turned to mush when he did stuff like that. *Tell him whatever you'd like, darling.*

I turned back to Vlad and then pointed over our back wall. "Garyn was on the roof of the house next door. Fergus and I were sitting back here. I felt her near and went looking. What she saw when she looked into our garden was—I don't know—like an oil slick in moonlight. And it was up there." I pointed into the sky. "Like we have a dome over our property, keeping eyes and ears out. Multiple of her vamps tried to jump over our walls. All of them were thrown back. We're safe," I ended on a smile.

"That's good." Cadmael's solemn voice behind me made me flinch.

Vlad raised an eyebrow at me, a smirk hiding beneath his over-sized mustache. "You have these gifts and yet you don't use them. You may not have been able to hear him engage the elevator in the garage, but you should have heard him leaving it and walking into your home."

Clive rubbed my shoulder in comfort, but he didn't argue the point. They were right. I had to be more aware of my surroundings, even at home.

"Oh, good," I said, my voice bereft of joy. "Cadmael's here."

When I saw out of the corner of my eye Clive's cheek lifting, I figured no one begrudged me my dislike of Cadmael. The man did try to kill me a few times. Granted, he'd been possessed by a psychotic fae at the time, but still. He'd also announced to a room filled with powerful vamps that my enhanced gifts made me a threat to all vampires, causing Clive and Vlad to kill everyone in the room before the information got out. So, yeah. Cadmael wasn't a favorite of mine.

In fairness, he'd been tracking me, a werewolf-wicche hybrid, since I was born, hoping I might be the one with a unique combination of gifts that could mean final death to him. Cadmael had been a Mayan warrior in life. He was very, very old and wanted his interminable undeath to finally end. We'd struck an agreement. He'd work with Clive and Vlad to rebuild the Guild, the ruling body overseeing vampires around the world, but if he ever decided he'd had enough and wanted an exit, I'd provide one for him.

We had a truce, tentative and uncomfortable as it was. Neither cared for the other, but we'd suck it up—if for no other reason than because we knew if either broke it, it would hurt the people we cared about.

Cadmael walked out to the edge of the patio and looked up into the night sky. It had been overcast most of the day, but it was clear now. Stars sparkled above us. Fergus approached the big man. Cadmael looked down, staring at my dog. Fergus' tail hung still as he took in the man whose stoic countenance appeared to be carved from wood. Finally, Cadmael's hand stroked the top of Fergus' head, causing the pup's tail to whip back and forth.

I turned to Vlad. "Did you tell them about this morning?"

He shook his head. "I thought it would be better for you to tell us all at once."

I did. They listened intently but no one said a word until I finished. Cadmael, who had taken the chair beside Vlad, tipped his head back, studying the night sky again. "This has happened before."

Vlad nodded. "There were a series of these kinds of obvious vampire attacks in Paris, Prague, Bucharest."

"Rio de Janeiro," Cadmael continued. "Mexico City, Chicago. We discussed it in the Guild. The Masters in each of those cities investigated, often with the help of the Counselor. None of them could find even one of the killers."

"I would say the Counselors were in on it," Vlad said, "had I not been the one to investigate the killings in Bucharest. There were five victims—all human—though a mix of genders, ages, and ethnicities. There were no clues and no scents, other than the dead humans and their pets."

"They all had pets?" I asked, sitting forward.

Vlad nodded. "Yes, but that wasn't the case in Paris or Prague. A few did, but not all."

"That could be correlated rather than causal," Clive said. "People walk alone at night when they're walking their dogs. They feel safe doing so, not realizing how many predators there are in the world."

"Humans walking alone at night are the perfect target for my kind," Vlad added.

Cadmael nodded. "Does this group have a wicche working with them? How are they hiding their scent?"

"Maybe a sorcerer?" I suggested. "Do the fae have the ability to disguise scent markers?"

Clive shrugged one shoulder. "I have no idea, though the fae seem capable of doing whatever they want."

Cadmael shook his head. "The fae are sickened by us. I can't imagine one wanting to help us kill undetected."

"There are only a few really powerful wicche families left in the world," Vlad volunteered. "We can get the Historians tracking family trees and looking for ones vulnerable to bribery or manipulation."

I raised my hand. "I know one of the families." I thought about it a moment. "Actually, I know a million wicches. Is it okay if I ask around, or am I not allowed to talk about these killings?"

Clive scratched his cheek. "I'd normally ask you not to say anything, but the wicches in this town love you and would share information with you that they'd never tell any of us." He looked at Cadmael and Vlad. "Opinions?"

Cadmael shook his head, but Vlad said, "She found the body. It would be natural, even expected, for her to discuss it with her friends in her own place of business." He turned to me. "You might even mention that you didn't scent a vampire, even though it looked like a vampire attack. Someone may explain to you how that could be."

"I don't like it," Cadmael grumbled.

"So what else is new?" I muttered. "Okay, so tomorrow while you all are sleeping—I mean while two of you are sleeping—I'll call Arwyn again to ask about Coreys who might be in league with rogue vampires, and I'll talk about that poor dead woman. Maybe I can find out about hiding scent trails. Oh, by the way, I left a message for Russell earlier today to see if he could get any additional news about our victim or the way in which she was killed."

"Hmm." Clive took his phone out of his pocket, swiped through screens, and tapped on Godfrey.

A moment later, we heard, "Good evening, former liege."

"Godfrey, my wife tells me she called Russell about a murder this morning. Have you learned anything yet?"

"Well, I'm not sure I'm at liberty to discuss this with you. Let me check with the Master of the City."

We heard an annoyed, *Godfrey*, in the background.

"It seems my current liege has given me permission to speak with you," Godfrey said.

"Hi!" I chimed in. "By the way, Cadmael and Vlad are with us right now."

"Ooh, clandestine meetings, eh? And we weren't invited? Maybe next time. How are you, Missus? Is our former lord and master treating you well?"

Clive rolled his eyes, but I laughed. "I'm fine and he's good. I've missed you, though."

"Of course you have. What's not to miss?"

At another grumbled, *Godfrey*, we heard a sigh. "Yes, sorry. The Master will speak with you now."

"Hi, Russell," I interjected. "I've missed you too."

"Thank you." Russell's deep voice made me smile. "And I you." It was almost like old times.

"Too bad we're not all together in your office right now. Is my bench still up against the wall?" When Clive was the Master, I sat to the side, not wanting to sit in the position of one of his underlings. After Clive stepped down, he shared my bench with me.

I could hear the smile in Russell's voice when he answered, "It is. And as I told you when you moved out, you will always be welcome here."

I sat back, grinning, as Clive rubbed my arm.

"Gentlemen and lady," Russell began, "I should let you know that the San Francisco nocturne will serve as host for the Guild's gathering. The Counselors are scheduled to appear in a night or two. When they arrive depends on the position of the sun when the plane lands. The Asian Counselor has yet to check in with us— she's more hesitant than the others. The South American and African Counselors have confirmed that they will be attending."

"Thank you, Russell," Clive said. "I know they'll be in good hands. We need to begin the process of rebuilding the Guild."

"Have they agreed to stay in the nocturne?" Cadmael asked.

"Again, all but the Asian Counselor have confirmed staying with us during their time in town."

"Hardly surprising she's hesitating," Vlad said. "Her partners were killed in Budapest."

"That was our take as well," Russell replied. "Now, as to the murder this morning, we've only begun to get reports. The autopsy was supposed to be performed tomorrow but we were able to get it moved up. What we know right now is that the woman, Emily Lake, was running with her blue Staffordshire Bull Terrier a little after two this morning."

"So late?" I murmured.

"That was our question as well, my lady," Russell said. "Apparently, she suffers from insomnia and on nights she can't sleep, she often goes for a run. She specifically adopted the Staffordshire so strange men wouldn't approach her. Friends reported that she and the dog were a great team and after she adopted him, she no longer had to worry about being accosted on a run.

"Miss Lake had apparently just returned from a work trip. She texted a friend she was jetlagged, which probably accounted for her run early this morning. I had two of my people go to the Bubble Lounge to investigate—"

"That would be Audrey and myself," Godfrey said.

"By all means," Russell replied. "Tell them what you found."

"Bugger all, that's what. Too many people had trampled over the spot," Godfrey explained. "It was impossible to pull apart all the different scent trails. I can tell you there was no bleeding vampire there—before us, that is."

SEVEN

Whispers in the Dark

"If I may, Sire?" Audrey asked. I hadn't realized she was there.

"Go ahead," Russell replied.

"We found some of her blood spattered about."

The vampires around me stilled at that.

"We caught the scents of countless humans, as Godfrey said. We found her scent and her dog's. There was even a faint feline scent, as well, but no vampire. Now, I'm not saying it wasn't a vampire kill," Audrey assured us. "The poor lass was drained of blood, and she had a bite mark in her neck. We have a copy of the on-scene report, though, and the bobbies—"

"Officers," Russell quietly corrected.

"Aye, the officers, they reported an identical wound on her inner thigh too. We don't have the autopsy yet, but a contact we have in the morgue confirms that there was a bite mark over her femoral artery as well."

"Really?" Vlad asked. "Out in the open? A neck bite can look like a lover's kiss to a passerby. The same can't be said for the femoral artery."

"Oh, now, I beg to differ," Godfrey interrupted. "And on a related note, I have sympathy for your dates."

I laughed. Most of living in the nocturne blew, but these three I missed horribly.

"The draining of a body is actually a lengthy process," Clive began. "The killing took place out in the open. Perhaps moving to the femoral was intended to speed it along."

"It doesn't make sense," Vlad said. "It's too much blood. Were there any other bite marks on her body?"

"I thought the same," Russell said. "Draining her body only makes sense if it was some kind of feeding frenzy, if there were a group of vampires feeding on her."

"Otherwise," Godfrey interrupted, "we could just look for a bloated, potbellied vampire who sloshes when he walks."

I heard a thwack and knew someone had smacked Godfrey in the back of the head.

"He's not wrong," Clive said.

"See?" Godfrey muttered.

"There are about five liters of blood in an adult human," Clive explained. "That's a ridiculous amount even if it was two vampires feeding together."

"Is that a thing?" I asked. "Is feeding together an aphrodisiac, or were these platonic blood buddies?"

Godfrey chuffed a laugh. "My new band name."

Clive sighed. "We're solitary hunters, but it isn't unheard of for us to pair up."

"Unusual, though," Russell said. "We're too territorial over our meals to share."

"St. Germaine," I reminded them. St. Germaine was a very old and very twisted vampire in New Orleans who enjoyed torturing and feeding off humans with a partner.

Vlad shook his head. "He's dead." He gestured to Clive. "I heard you handed him his final death."

I raised my hand. "That was me. In my defense, though, he was a huge creep."

"That he was," Russell agreed.

"Blood spatter," Cadmael said, getting us back on track.

I was waiting for him to complete the thought, but both Clive and Vlad nodded.

"Blood spatter what?" I asked.

"It's the way we feed, ma'am," Audrey responded. "If we're feeding from a live human, our lips are on them before our fangs break their skin. Spattering is wasted blood. Even newly turned vampires wouldn't lead with their teeth."

"Sometimes," Cadmael began, "our kind can develop a kind of dementia."

"And we're back to St. Germaine," I muttered.

Clive patted my knee and nodded in agreement. "It can be caused by old age or starvation, but often they are ones who never should have been turned and certainly should have been handed their final death when it became apparent that there was a problem and they'd be a danger to secrecy. In St. Germaine's case, Lafitte was too weak to deal with him and so turned a blind eye to what was happening."

"And sometimes," Cadmael continued, "that vampire lives in isolation, in mental decline, so no one is there to notice or do anything."

A chill ran down my spine.

"Part of the reason the Guild instituted nocturnes," Clive said.

"Yes," Cadmael agreed, "but there are still those who have not been scooped up by nocturnes. We don't have nocturnes in every city of the world, and not all populous cities are run by us. There are Masters of the City who are werewolves or bear shifters, jaguar shifters, wicches. It depends on the area and the most powerful faction in that area."

"If we do have a dotty vampire—or a pair—wandering around the world, it still doesn't explain why he doesn't leave a bloody scent marker," Godfrey interjected.

I had a thought. The three men with me all turned to me, so I supposed I made a noise, though I didn't recall doing so.

"Yes, my lady?" Russell said.

"Nothing. It was just a thought. Maybe there isn't a contingent of vampires stirring up trouble and trying to come out. Maybe what we have is a crazy guy killing people in an obviously vampy way. Other vamps are whispering about it, believing a secret group of them is gaining power and soon they'll be the supernatural rockstars of the world. Really, though, it's just one guy attacking humans unchecked because none of you guys knew you were supposed to be watching him."

They were all quiet a moment, considering.

"Let's hope that isn't the case," Vlad said, "because I don't know how we'd find him, especially if he doesn't leave a scent trail."

"Perhaps, my lady," Russell began, "you could check to see if there is anyone in the city who shouldn't be."

I popped up. "Thank you. I got distracted by the car shopping. I meant to do this earlier tonight. You guys are easier to see when you're awake. Talk amongst yourselves," I said. "I'll be back."

I went into the house and lay down on the couch. Fergus followed me and squished his body between me and the back cushion. I had to scoot over to make room for my giant pup or risk my circulation being cut off.

I heard the murmur of voices on the patio, but it was low and easy to ignore. Eyes closed, I looked for the blips in my head that meant vampire. The three on the patio were the brightest, which could have been proximity, but probably had to do with them being the most powerful vamps in town. There was another glut of dark green blips in the nocturne. I scanned the city, slowly search-ing. I found the red blips of the dragons and the light green of the fae, most of whom were in either the ocean, Golden Gate Park, or the Mermaid's Bubble Lounge. Having visited, I knew Nerissa and her whole staff at the nightclub were fae.

There were two vampires in Chinatown, one in North Beach, three South of Market where a number of bars and nightclubs are. After checking each of the six free-range vampires and recognizing them, I went back to the nocturne to see if there was someone new there. It took a while, but other than one mafia-type from New

York, the rest were ones I remembered. None of them gave off unhinged killer vibes. I mean, any more than a regular vampire.

I opened my eyes to Fergus' snores and Clive sitting in the leather chair opposite the couch, watching me. The patio door was now closed, and I didn't sense anyone here with us.

"Where did everyone go?" I whispered

Clive crooked his finger at me, his gaze dark and intent. I grinned, giddy bubbles running through me. I didn't think I'd ever get used to it. He was too perfect, too gorgeous. He made my knees weak. Doing my best impersonation of an eel, I slid my body over the edge of the couch, landing lightly on the floor and then crawling over to his chair.

"Yes?" Kneeling between his legs, I rested my arms on his thighs. "You called?"

His gaze traveled leisurely down my body before he crooked his finger again. "Closer."

Grinning, I stood and climbed onto his lap, straddling his hips. "Yes?"

He put his hand on either side of my face and drew me in for a kiss that had me forgetting my own name. The world tipped and I was dizzy. When I finally came up for air, I realized Clive had his hands on my butt and was carrying me soundlessly up the stairs.

He took me into our bedroom, closed the door, and pressed me up against the wall before taking my mouth again. Reaching down between us, I palmed him and squeezed. On a growl, he tossed me on the bed and pinned me beneath himself.

"Are we alone?" I whispered.

Lips quirking up on one side, he looked over his shoulder, first in one direction and then the other. "You tell me," he whispered back.

Wrapping my arms around his neck, I drew him down for another kiss, using part of my mind to check the house. Alone.

I flipped us over, sat up, and unbuttoned his fancy shirt before running my hands over his perfect chest. "Sometimes," I whispered, "I see you and my mouth goes dry."

He lifted his eyebrows. "Why are we whispering?"

"I don't want to wake Fergus. Now, shush. I'm telling you something sweet."

He nodded. "Right. Sorry. Do go on."

I fluttered my fingers near my stomach. "Champagne bubbles dance through my body and I get lightheaded. It doesn't seem real. This can't be my life. I didn't know I could love someone as much as I love you." Embarrassed, I traced my fingertips over his abdominal muscles. "I'm not explaining this right."

He rolled us back over and kissed me soundly before breaking it long enough to pull my shirt over my head. "What you seem to forget, my love, is that it's the same for me, but I had to wait longer."

He brushed my nose with his own. "You're my own little miracle. I trudged through ages, keeping sacred the vengeance in my heart and then out of nowhere you appear, pulling at my heartstrings. Scared, brutalized, alone, and trying so hard to keep your chin up and be brave."

Tucking a stray hair behind my ear, he kissed me softly, almost reverently. "Just because I cover it better doesn't mean I don't get lightheaded looking at you. You take my breath away."

He shook his head. "It's hard for me to make sense of everything that had to align in the universe for you to not only be put in my path, but to, against all reason, love me. Part of me is terrified that whatever twist of fate brought you to me will twist again and take you away." He rested his forehead against mine. "I wouldn't survive it. I wouldn't want to."

"Then I guess we're going to have to take good care of each other so neither of us has to face the world without the other," I whispered, my hands in his hair.

He lifted his head and kissed the tip of my nose. "Yes," he said, leaving kisses along my cheek, my jaw. "Until I am a pile of dust and a distant memory, I will cherish this gift."

His hand went under me and my bra disappeared. "I think it's time I show my appreciation for your gifts," he murmured, his hand caressing one breast while his kisses trailed down to the other.

Back bowing off the bed, I thanked all those forces in the universe that had conspired to bring us together. What this man could do with his mouth should be celebrated in epic poems. His stubble tickled my waist, and I couldn't control the giggle.

He looked up, eyes hot, and proceeded to use his fingers and tongue, and every part of his body to turn the laugh into a moan. When he finally settled between my legs, I was a panting, needy mess. Clinging to him like a spider monkey, I squirmed, trying to impale myself.

Clive rolled us, putting me on top, and I got to take control. Desperate, I braced myself on his chest and rode. Eyes vampy black, fangs pressing against his lower lip, he watched, one hand plucking and rolling my nipple, his other sliding down my body to where we were joined, making me lose my mind.

When I was close, he reared up and sank his fangs into my neck, pushing us both over the edge. I rode the aftershocks and him until he wrapped his arms around me and pulled me down, so I was sprawled on top of him, too boneless to move.

My heart was still galloping as he traced designs on my back with his fingertips. Finally, my breathing began to slow, but my limbs weren't yet responding. The circuits in my brain appeared to be misfiring.

"I got that you didn't find anyone when you were looking for the killer. I felt that. Did you see anything interesting we should know?" he asked.

I kissed his chest and snuggled in. "Were you seeing what I was?"

"Don't get too comfortable. I'm not done with you." His voice was deep and dangerous. "And, no, not really. I couldn't see what you were seeing, but I felt your disappointment that you weren't locating a suspect."

I stacked my hands over his heart and rested my chin on them so I could see him better. "I found all the usual suspects. There's a new guy at the nocturne, but he seemed fine. The dragons were where I'd expect them; the fae too. I can't see wicches or demons. Or humans, for that matter. Maybe we're looking in the wrong direction."

He took out my braid and ran his fingers through my hair, massaging my scalp. With a contented purr, I dropped my head back to his chest.

"It's possible," he responded. "If it looks like a duck and quacks like a duck, though, we still need to be investigating ducks. And as you know, demons and wicches have their own scent." He wound my hair around his finger. "I keep thinking about that necklace your mother spelled for you. It wasn't until after you lost it that your scent changed and notes of wicche appeared. We could be dealing with a vampire carrying a wicche's talisman."

He ran his hand up and down my arm. "How are you feeling?'

"Blissed out."

He tossed me to the other side of the bed and pounced. "Perfect. Time for round two."

EIGHT

Geez, You Again

The hunter leans over the side of the roof, watching a merman, reeking of the ocean and dressed as a human, exit the back door of the nightclub. He carries two large garbage bags to the dumpster. He tosses them, letting them thump against the open lid before they slide in. He checks his phone and then returns to the club, slamming the door.

Cats come slinking out of the night to hop on the edge of the dumpster and sniff. The hunter scans the area for lone humans. He sees one moving silently around the corner of the building. The wind changes direction, and he gets a whiff of vampire. Interesting.

The hunter tips his head, studying the bloodsucker, especially his facial hair. The vampire moves slowly. When he circles back toward the front of the nightclub, the hunter follows along, tracking him from his perch on high. It's odd how rarely people look up.

The vampire pauses right where that terrified woman met her fate last night. A second one joins him. He looks up but he doesn't notice his observer. And then a third. This one has light hair that reflects the moonlight. He crouches over the spot where the hunter discarded the woman's body.

The front door opens and the vampires disappear. The mermaid stench has the hunter rearing back. A tall woman ushers out her employees and locks the door. They walk to the far end of the parking lot and pile into three cars. *Once they leave, the vampires return. The hunter loves this stage of the game. The poor things have no clue who the hunter is.*

The hunter smiles. He should at least make it sporting, he decides, kicking a pebble. All three look up at the same time. The light-haired one goes around the back, while the other two stare up at the roof.

Where did the other one go? The hunter moves beside a large piece of machinery and looks over the side of the building for the light-haired one. A shadow blocks the moon for a moment, and the third vampire walks across the roof. He gets to the edge, glances toward the machine, and then drops to the ground where the other two wait.

After a quick conversation, they all head in different directions. The hunter wonders if he should follow, to see what they're up to, but then he hears it. Someone is rummaging in the dumpster. That's his dinner bell. He races to the back of the building and leaps, landing silently beside a man balancing on the dumpster's edge while he rips open a plastic bag and pulls out half-eaten food.

The hunter decides it would be rude to interrupt, so he moves to the deepest shadows by the back door and waits until the man has eaten his fill—before the hunter eats his.

NINE

Not Again

I woke to scratching at the bedroom door. Exhausted, I dragged myself from bed and opened the door. Fergus gave me a look that said I'd betrayed him, barring him from the bedroom last night.

He moved past me and curled up in his bed with a disgruntled *hmph*.

"I'm sorry, buddy. Mommy and Daddy were doing grown up things and you were snoozing on the couch." I scratched his tummy and he rolled onto his back, giving me full access while his big paws treaded the air.

"Should we run or snooze?" Hanging out with vampires was hell on sleep. At the word *run*, Fergus leapt up and pranced in a circle. "Okay. Let me get dressed."

As I was getting ready, I realized I had a message from Clive on my phone. I ducked my head back into the bedroom and saw my husband in bed. Odd.

I opened voicemail and heard, *Hello, darling. I'm leaving you an update, since you're sleeping soundly right now. Cadmael and Vlad went down to the wharf to check out where the woman had been killed. After you fell asleep, I joined them. I now understand Godfrey and Audrey's frustration. The scent trails are all there. I feel like I could map the entire attack and its aftermath, all except for the killer.*

We've split up now. I'm searching along the water's edge for anything out of the ordinary and finding nothing. I'll probably stay down here another hour or so and then I'll be home. Chances are you won't hear this until I'm home and you're awake. So, good morning, love. Stay safe today.

I leaned over the bed and dropped a kiss on his lips. "I love you too and I'll do my best." After slipping my phone in my hip pocket, I slapped my thigh and Fergus jumped up to race me down the stairs.

My phone began buzzing as Fergus went to his water bowl. I pulled it out and looked at the screen. Nerissa.

"Hello?" The woman owned The Bubble Lounge. What was she doing calling me a little after five in the morning?

"Sam, I need your help."

"Okay."

She blew out a breath. "It happened again. There's a dead man by the dumpster and he has two holes in his neck."

My stomach dropped. "The police won't let me near the crime scene. They ran me off yesterday morning."

"I haven't called them yet. I had cameras installed yesterday. They have motion sensors. After being alerted a maddening number of times and only seeing cats or tourists appear on the camera feed, I muted the alarms. I meant to unmute when we closed for the evening, but it was such a long, horrible day, I forgot."

"I understand."

"I finally remembered and looked." She paused, the silence charged. "I saw the killer and he looks familiar. I just—I need someone like you, someone trustworthy, to check the scene. I'll send you the video clip as well. The body could be found at any time, though, so I need you to get to the club quickly."

"On my way." I disconnected, grabbed Fergus' leash, and headed for the elevator down to the garage. Fergus was confused

48

but followed.

When the elevator doors opened, I looked over a sea of expensive automobiles. Clive had a weakness for them. I went to the safe and sturdy sedan I usually drove, letting Fergus into the back seat. The drive down to Fisherman's Wharf was easy this early in the morning. I had to use a parking garage and then Fergus and I ran a block to The Bubble Lounge.

Hopefully the lack of sirens and flashing lights meant that no one had stumbled upon the body yet. We hopped over the chain blocking the entrance to the parking lot and headed around the side. I pulled my hood up, hiding most of my face, and then shifted my snout. Head down, I parsed through the scents, finding Clive, Vlad, and Cadmael among all the humans and fae.

Fergus whined, pulling at the leash. He knew there was a dead body nearby. I smelled it too. Head down, I followed the scent to the back. Clive had walked along this path.

I made Fergus sit and stay. He whined, but one growl from me shut him up. The dead man appeared to be living rough on the streets. His clothes were filthy. The stench of his long-unwashed body overpowered almost everything else. In death, muscles relax and bodies release waste, so I was sorting through those smells as well, looking for the killer.

The dead man had been on or in the dumpster, no doubt looking for food. There was the smell of cats all throughout the area, though that specific scent was focused on the dumpster. And Clive again, faintly and underneath the death.

As with the woman, the latest victim was on his back, staring sightlessly up at the sky, a prominent vampire bite on his neck. I leaned in as close as I could, to study and sniff the wound. Trails of dried blood marked a path from the bite to the collar of the man's jacket. Closing my eyes, I tried to sort through every single scent, looking for one that didn't belong.

The bark of the sea lions jolted me out of my daze. I had to call it in. I had no idea how long I'd already been here and whether or not one of the fishing boats had noticed me. I quickly took pictures and then a video, in case that helped.

I moved to Fergus, put my hand on his head, and dialed nine-one-one. Fergus was looking up, staring at the roof. As I spoke with the dispatcher and was told to stay until police arrived, I stared up too. Pointed ears appeared, and then the bright eyes of a cat looked over the edge, staring down at us.

Shaking my head, I finished answering questions. When I disconnected with the police, I called Vlad.

"What?" His bored voice helped settle my nerves.

"There was another attack last night. I'm first on the scene. I just called the authorities and was told to wait."

"Where?" he asked.

"The Bubble Lounge again."

He cursed. "Quick. Take pictures of everything and send them to me."

"Already ahead of you. I'm sending them now." While they sent, I continued, "I searched all around the building. Besides you, Clive, Cadmael, Godfrey, and Audrey, there isn't another one of your kind around."

"The images are coming through now. Get me a picture of his hands."

I did and sent them. Vlad was quiet, looking through all the images, I assumed.

"What's the matter with his neck? Is that a trick of the light or was his neck cleaned?"

Crouching down, I studied the area and then took a video. "This man hasn't had access to a bar of soap in a long time. His face and hands are coated in a kind of oily grime. The side of his neck where he was bitten, though, is in a patch of clean."

"Interesting."

Sirens wailed in the distance.

"Send me everything," Vlad instructed, "and then delete all the images and the record of this phone call. Stow your phone out of sight and look frightened when they arrive. You have a legal address now. Give them that, tell them you're feeling sick, and then ask if you can leave. You're an innocent witness who found a scary thing. Remember that."

Car doors slammed and boots pounded on the pavement.

"Gotta go," I whispered and did as he said before sliding my phone back into my hip pocket. *Shit.* If they patted me down, they were going to find the axe on my back. *Shitshitshit.*

Fergus and I moved back to where it felt like an innocent human might stand. When the cops came around the corner, I jumped and held up the hand not clutching Fergus' leash. A cop stared at me, so I pointed a shaking finger toward the body to the side of the dumpster.

Another cop waved me to the side of the building and asked to see my ID. I explained I was running and not carrying one. I gave him all my info and explained what I saw.

The older cop from yesterday came around the corner and squinted at me and Fergus. "You were here yesterday too." His voice dripped with suspicion.

I nodded, my eyes wide and hopefully projecting fear. "We run down here a lot. Fergus likes visiting the sea lions." Right on cue, the sea lions began barking and Fergus gave a quiet woof in response. "We were cutting through the back because I didn't want to run past where that poor woman was." I scratched behind Fergus' ear. "He smelled it first and pulled me over. I've never seen a dead person in my life. And then two in two days."

I leaned over and kissed the top of my pup's head. "Sorry. We're not running down here ever again."

"Big dog," the first cop said. The older one had already dismissed us and was headed back to the dumpster.

"Irish Wolfhound. He's eight months old, though, so he still has some growing to do."

The cop held out a hand. "Is he friendly?"

"Oh, sure." I gave Fergus some slack so he could say hi to the cop. "I wouldn't have a giant dog I couldn't control."

He asked me a few more questions and then let us go. Fergus

and I ran back to the parking garage and headed home. I'd lied to the cop about a few things. One of which was I did have ID on me; I just didn't want to have to give him any more information than was necessary. As I didn't want to be pulled over leaving the scene of a crime in a car after I'd told officers I was running, I was overly careful on the drive home.

Once I parked, I sat in my car, trying to shake off the nerves. A hand rapped on the window, causing me to yip in fright and Fergus to bark and growl.

Vlad's face appeared in the window, rolling his eyes. I threw open the door, hoping to hit him, but he was unsurprisingly fast. Fergus scrambled over the seats so he could get out right beside me. Now that he knew it was Vlad, he was squirming, looking for pets.

Vlad waited for us at the elevator. "Are you coming?"

The door opened and Vlad went in, with Fergus dancing around him. I followed, hitting the button for the first floor. The door slid to the side and Fergus raced to his food bowl, even though I hadn't filled it yet. He clearly just wanted to make sure I knew where my priorities should be, helpful dog that he was.

Vlad flew to the darkest corner of the room, behind a bookcase.

"Dude, are you moving my furniture?" I scooped kibble from the food bin and dropped it into Fergus' bowl. He began inhaling it at once.

"Were you concerned about your guests' comfort, you would have done this yourself, instead of forcing me to erect a lightless place for myself."

Shaking my head, I refilled the water bowl. "We gave you a comfortable, lightless place to stay. It's my underground apartment. No one told you to come into our house during the day."

Unlike yesterday, it was bright and sunny today. I opened the back door so Fergus could go out when he was done eating. The window in the dining room was across from the den, so I closed those curtains, making the den darker. Once Fergus came back in, I drew the curtains around the back door as well.

"The video is helpful," Vlad said from his fortress of inky blackness.

Oh, that reminded me. I pulled up my texts and tapped the video Nerissa had sent me this morning of the killer. The cameras were good, but it was dark, the only light coming from distant streetlights. The man I saw this morning hoisted himself up on the side of the dumpster and was pulling open bags. Something flashed in front of the camera and then a man was standing behind the victim. I could only see his shoulder, the back of his head, an ear, and a bit of his jaw. He waited while the man ate something. The killer was completely still. Was he breathing?

When the man slid down from the dumpster, his knees buckled, but he clung to the side until he was standing on his own. The killer moved into the frame, spun the man around, grabbed him by the neck, and pulled him to his mouth.

Horrified, I watched as the poor man stared straight ahead, showing a disturbing lack of alarm. Had he been put in a trance? Faster than I would have thought possible, the now dead man was being dropped to the ground. The killer turned toward the camera before leaping up and out of the frame.

Heart racing, I backed up to watch it again. When the killer turned toward the camera, I froze it. Vlad.

TEN

Scars for the Win
_____

"**W**hy is your heart racing?" Vlad's dark eyes peered out at me from the corner.

Darling? Are you all right?

Not sure. There was another killing. I just came from there and checked the video Nerissa sent of the murder. It's Vlad.

Do you know where Vlad is right now?

Yep. He's staring at me from the corner of the den.

I'm coming.

No, you're not. I'm fine. I went back to the dining room and opened the curtains. Vlad hissed in the corner. I invited Clive into my mind, so he could see what I was seeing. His brain felt sluggish, but I knew he was intent on the video in my hand.

I played it again.

Ask him where he went last night after we parted.

"Clive wants to know where you went last night after you all split up."

"Why? And what's on your phone that has your heart racing and Clive listening in?"

"Don't be a dick. Just answer the question." I didn't want to believe it. I thought of Vlad as a friend. This didn't make sense.

54

I don't think that's him, darling. The height looks off and the hair isn't quite right. Play it again, just from when the killer arrives.

"I searched the piers," Vlad responded. "There were some faint vampire trails, but they seemed to be normal feeding patterns in crowded, tourist-filled areas. Nothing the Guild needs to concern itself with."

"And then what?" I pushed while hitting play again.

The flash.

He dropped from the roof. When we were there, we all heard something up there. I even went up to investigate, but I didn't see or sense anything unusual.

What's usual for a roof, I wondered.

He was slow to respond. The burst of energy he had felt at my heartbeat was disappearing. *Birds. Lots of cats down there.*

Yeah. I saw a cat on the roof too.

Wait. "Have you answered me yet?" I asked Vlad.

"I didn't want to interrupt you plotting with Clive. Now tell me what is on your damn phone?"

"We're not plotting and how do you even know he's talking to me?"

"Your facial expressions always give it away. You need to work on that," he replied, though I'd mostly stopped listening. There was too much going on.

Look, Clive said in my head. *The hair is wrong. Vlad wears his hair in a short tail. This one's hair is a few inches longer.*

Could that be the perspective from a camera above?

I don't think so. And look at his size compared to the dumpster. I wasn't really paying attention to it when I walked around back last night, which means the size felt appropriate for The Bubble Lounge. Go back. How easy was it for the homeless man to climb on it?

"What is going on?" Vlad demanded.

I waved my hand at him. "Shush. We're busy over here."

Darling, get your laptop so we can see the image bigger.

Good call, but my laptop is over where Vlad is.

The was a long pause and then Clive said, *Show him the video. It's not him and he might have more ideas. I don't trust my brain right now to pick out the salient details.*

Okay, good. That's where I was leaning too. I closed the dining room curtains.

"Does this mean you're no longer afraid of me?" he asked from the corner. He sounded bored, but I could hear the hurt.

"I need my laptop. It's on the end table beside you."

He held it out and I took it before sitting on the carpet beside his chair. Fergus dropped down, resting his big head in my lap.

"Kinda in my way," I muttered, powering on the computer and pulling up my texts. "Nerissa, the owner of the Bubble Lounge, is the one who called me this morning about another dead body. She installed cameras around the periphery of her nightclub yesterday, so she has video of the killing."

"And the killer looks like me," he stated.

"How did you know?"

"Why else would you be panicking?" He crooked his finger. "Let me see it."

I tapped on the video and then handed him back the laptop.

I wanted to see that, Clive said in my head.

We will. Vlad seemed hurt that we were suspecting him, so I wanted him to see why.

Clive was quiet, so I assumed he agreed with me, but then he said, *You're incredibly sweet. How did I get so lucky to find someone concerned with vampire feelings?*

"Hmm." Vlad leaned forward, staring at the screen.

"Did he just drop into the frame?"

Vlad nodded slowly, his eyes glued to the laptop screen. A moment later, he reared back as he tapped the trackpad. "Well," he finally said. "I understand why your heart raced." He glanced over at me in the dark. Werewolf night vision was handy when dealing with vampires.

Pointing at the screen he said, "This isn't me. I can't explain it, but this isn't me. After I left Clive and Cadmael, I searched the piers and then ended up at a bar. I thought it was a biker bar, but I recognized pretty quickly it was a gay biker bar, which is only a problem because this mustache gets me hit on in a lot of gay spaces. Your dragon bartender was there, but it was the other bartender I was interested in. She's not human. She's—"

"Stheno," I told him.

He stilled. "You know her?"

"She's a good friend of mine. Tell me, though, are your intentions honorable?"

"Of course not," he said, as though talking to a child.

"Perfect. Hers are never honorable either. I'll be your wingman, but first we need to figure out the killer part."

"Right." He looked down at the screen and then turned to me again. "What is she? I didn't recognize her scent, and it's driving me crazy."

Grinning, I said, "That's for her to tell you. I keep my friends' secrets."

"Some wingman," he muttered.

I held my hand out. "Can I move it to the coffee table? Clive wants to see it too."

He handed it to me and I placed it on the low table beside me, thinking Vlad could see it easily from the chair. Instead, he sat on the rug beside me. I backed up the video and we started it again.

When the victim hoisted himself up on the side of the dumpster, I paused. "Clive thinks the killer is too tall to be you. He's basing that on the height of this dumpster."

Vlad pointed to The Bubble Lounge's back door. "Standard doors in the US are just under seven feet."

Six foot eight, Clive confirmed.

"That being the case, this dumpster is probably five and a half feet tall," Vlad continued.

I thought about it. "That makes sense. The mermaids in their human form aren't super tall. Nerissa is tall, but she wears high heels, and I doubt she's the one dumping the garbage."

I hit play again and we watched the killer drop into the frame.

"Clive also says his hair is too long." I jumped up, annoying Fergus, and moved back so my perspective on Vlad matched the camera. I turned on the end table lamp, my gaze jumping between the screen and Vlad.

"He's right," I said. "The hair in the video is a little longer. Also, the shirt is wrong. His has a normal collar. Yours has a band collar. This is some fancy, designer shirt, isn't it?"

Vlad looked down at what he was wearing. "My tailor made this for me sometime in the late nineteenth century."

"And it still looks this good?"

"I take care of my things," he said, still staring at the screen. "The ear is wrong." He tapped the killer's ear. "Mine has a scar." He turned his head to the light. "I barely avoided a sword cutting my throat that day."

There was a notch in the outer shell of his ear, a notch the killer didn't have. We continued the video.

Wait, Clive said at the same time Vlad tapped the mousepad. "Did you see it?" Vlad asked me.

"No, but Clive did. You both saw whatever you saw at the same time."

Some of us carry handkerchiefs to wipe dirty necks. Sweaty, unwashed skin taints the taste of blood, Clive explained.

"He moved his hand over the man's neck, but he wasn't holding anything." Vlad ran it back for me. "See? Nothing in his hand, but the man's neck is clean. You sent me a video of that clean spot earlier."

Wicche? Clive suggested.

"Perhaps a sorcerer," Vlad mused.

"I can ask Dave if he thinks it's a demon. They can shape-shift," I said.

I was sure there was something on the roof, Clive told me.

"Clive says he was positive there was something on the roof."

Vlad nodded. "We all sensed something up there. Did he see anything at all?"

Clive thought a moment and said, *Only a small black cat leaning against the HVAC unit for warmth. Perhaps the killer has a chameleon-like ability to blend his appearance and scent into his surroundings. I might have walked right past him.* I could feel Clive's frustration but wasn't sure how to help. We were all grasping at straws.

I passed on what Clive said, and Vlad shook his head in annoyance before starting the video again.

When the victim was dropped on the ground and the killer turned toward the camera, Vlad stopped it again. "We can't drain humans that fast."

"Oh! The eyebrow's wrong." I leaned forward and pointed at the killer's left eyebrow. "Yours has a break. Another scar. His is smooth and connected."

When I arrived, Cadmael and Vlad were talking, Vlad's right side was to the building. Perhaps the killer didn't see him head on and so couldn't recreate the scars he hadn't seen.

I passed on Clive's observation and Vlad stopped to think before nodding. "He's right. My head was down when I was going over the spot where the first victim had been killed, looking for scents. Afterward, we moved away from the building to check the surroundings. I had my right side to the building. Cadmael, his left. When Clive arrived and investigated, Cadmael and I were still talking."

"So, the next time he kills," I began, "and we know there will be a next time, will he look like Vlad again or will it appear as though it's Cadmael or Clive? He's seen all three of you." I texted Nerissa back, letting her know it wasn't Vlad—key details were wrong—but it had to be someone who could glamour themselves to look like Vlad. I let her know we would keep investigating and asked for any information she might have on possible killers.

I had a news notification on my screen. I would have ignored it, but I saw the word *vampire,* so I clicked on it. "Uh-oh. The media has picked up the story and there's an article in the Chronicle: *Vampire Killer Strikes Again.*" I turned to Vlad. "That can't be good."

Especially not when we have vampires from around the world ready to converge on us.

"We're not going to be able to keep this quiet," Vlad said. "Not with what's left of the Guild arriving in two days."

ELEVEN

Have You Met Me?

"I mean, technically, almost half of the Guild is already here investigating," I reminded them. "You guys are on top of it."

Vlad stayed on the floor with me but leaned back against the chair he'd been sitting in. "The problem is that it doesn't make us look terribly competent. How is it there's a vampire—or group of vampires—killing in this city but we have no clues?"

"Oh. You're either dumb or in on it. Is that it?" I asked.

Vlad nodded.

Unfortunately, he's right. We'll need to discuss this with the rest of the Guild, but given what we know, we won't come off well in the report.

"Okay, but Vlad said the same thing has been happening in a bunch of major cities and that other Counselors were involved in those investigations. They didn't figure it out either. How does this make you guys look bad?"

"They did, though," Vlad replied. "Remember? They said a contingent of vampires who want to come out to the world are staging these killings as a first step. So either this is a completely isolated incident that coincidentally bears a striking resemblance to other murders, or those other Counselors were wrong."

"Geez, you guys aren't infallible. Are they really going to get their knickers in a twist that their theory proved to be incorrect?" Vampires were ridiculous.

"Have you met us?" Vlad asked, his eyebrows raised. "My question is this: has the killer glamoured himself to look like me for all the killings or did he change his look tonight after we visited the first crime scene?"

"Oh." I grimaced. "Have you pissed someone off recently?"

He gave me a long look. "Again, have you met me?"

"Okay, well, I have to go get ready for work. I think you guys need to stake out the Bubble Lounge tonight, though." I paused. "Wait. Those killings in Romania that you investigated—did they all take place in the same spot?"

Vlad considered. "No. They were in the same neighborhood, though. There probably wasn't more than a few blocks between them all."

I nodded. "Like Jack the Ripper." I got up and moved across the room. "They never identified that guy either. Maybe he's still out there, killing people."

"He was named *the Ripper* for a reason. He didn't drain them of blood; he sliced them up and removed organs," Vlad reminded me.

"Yeah, but the bodies were still drained of their blood. It ran out on the streets instead of being consumed. Maybe he's got some kind of blood fetish," I suggested.

"Now that does sound like us." Vlad took my laptop and moved back to the chair.

I shrugged. "It'd just be cool to solve that one."

"Clive knows. You should ask him."

"What!" I ran across the house and up the stairs, Fergus on my heels. Bursting through the bedroom door, I dove on the bed and rolled into Clive.

Do you really know who Jack the Ripper was?

If I tell you, what will we have to talk about in twenty years?

I kissed his cheek. *Come on. Please!*

Clive chuckled in my head. *Vlad was having you on. I was nowhere near Whitechapel in 1888. Sorry, darling.*

Bummer. I took a shower and got ready. By the time I was headed back downstairs, Fergus shot out of his bed and raced past me. Vlad was no longer in the den. He must have gone back to the apartment through the folly. The dragons were almost done building it and they didn't seem as angry as they initially were about working for a vampire.

They didn't even seem to mind that Cadmael was living in the section of the folly that appeared to be a tropical island. Clive said Cadmael, a vampire who was over two thousand years old, spent all his time lounging under the stone ceiling that had been magicked to look like bright sunshine in a clear blue sky. Clive and Vlad also loved the folly for much the same reason: experiencing what felt like the sun after ages in the dark.

I wanted to finish processing the new books before we opened, but the mayhem of the morning meant I wasn't as early as I'd intended. Still, I got a fair amount done before I heard Owen coming down the steps.

"Hey, boss." He went to the book cart to peruse the new titles, looking well-rested and content.

"You look good," I told him.

He glanced up, ready to make a joke, and then stopped himself. "Thanks. I'm really happy." He reached for my hand and squeezed it. "Sometimes it feels unreal. I love him so much, Sam. I didn't know I could have this. I just"—he shook his head in wonder—"how did we get so lucky?"

"Your parents must be proud. You snagged yourself a rich doctor." I moved the stack of books I'd finished to the shelving cart. "I bet your mom brags about you every chance she gets."

Owen laughed. "You know her well. My cousins tell me she often lets drop how spectacular our house is or some wonderful thing George did for me."

His mate George was a very kind and extremely good-looking

dragon shifter. There weren't many dragons left in the world, but those still around were loaded. Dragons and their treasures. George was a veterinarian working with large exotic animals at the San Francisco Zoo. He bought a mansion for Owen and himself in Sea Cliff, an enclave of the extraordinarily wealthy. Their house was right on the water, with a view of the ocean and the Golden Gate Bridge.

"Which reminds me," Owen began. "I'm supposed to invite you and Clive for dinner Saturday night."

"We'd love that, but we can't make it this Saturday. What's left of the vampire Guild is coming to town for meetings in—wait. Am I allowed to tell you that?" *Shit.*

"I didn't hear a thing," Owen said.

My phone buzzed in my pocket. When I took it out, I saw a text.

Vlad: No. You're not.

I shouted, "Quit eavesdropping, you creep!"

Owen paled, whispering, "Is Vlad listening to us?"

"It appears so. Anyway, Clive and I are busy, unfortunately. Can we get a raincheck on dinner?"

Owen nodded, glancing over his shoulder warily. "Sure. No problem. I'll get to work now."

"I'll go with you. I need to ask you about a couple of killings." I followed him behind the bar and started cutting lemons and limes while he prepped the espresso machine and checked the beer taps.

By the time I finished explaining the whole situation, he was sitting on the stool I kept behind the bar, shaking his head.

"No scent at all?" he asked. "I mean, a wicche could clean a scene, covering over all the smells, but to leave everything *but* the scent of the killer?" He shook his head. "I wouldn't know how to do that. Let me ask my mom. She might know if it can be done."

I added cherries to the cocktail garnish cups. "If Hepsibah or Lilith or any of the crones are in today, I'll ask them too."

Owen nodded. "Check with Dave. Maybe it's a demon thing."

"Maybe." I went back to the bookstore and before too long I heard Grim's distinctive step coming down the stairs. We were open.

Thirty minutes later, I walked back into the bar to see if I had any powerful wicches in yet and instead saw Meri skipping down the stairs.

"Owen, did Sam tell you? I got a new car!" She held up her keys.

He high-fived her. "What kind did you get?"

"I only wanted electric," she told him. "So I wasn't sure if I could afford anything." The salesman we had last night had kept trying to steer her toward sporty, sexy cars. It turned out I didn't need to worry about her being taken advantage of. She firmly told him what her requirements were, and he tripped over himself trying to make her happy.

"She ended up negotiating an excellent deal for herself," I told him.

Meri beamed. "I bought a brand-new Leaf. It was the least expensive of the EVs. I was annoyed it didn't come in green, though. It's a leaf." She rolled her eyes. "I got blue, so it's like the ocean. Mom met us at the dealership so she could co-sign the registration and stuff. And she called this morning and got me put on her insurance, so I drove it to work. No more begging for rides."

She was grinning ear to ear, and the bar somehow felt brighter. "Oh, and Sam, I haven't seen that guy again. I was working in the front garden, and I didn't see him creeping around. Thank you!" She looked out the window, spotted her dad, and pointed to the ocean entrance in the far corner of the bar.

While Meri told her dad all about her new car—I assumed, since I didn't speak mermish—I headed to the table near the stairs where Hepsibah, Lilith, and Rose were sitting with their cups of tea. All three women had to be in their eighties, at least. When I sat at their table, Rose stopped mid-sentence, and they all turned to me as one. "Yes, dear?"

"Ladies, I'm sorry to interrupt, but I had a wicche question and knew you three were the ones to ask."

Rose sat a little straighter, but both Hepsibah and Lilith just raised their eyebrows and waited. They weren't falling for flattery. I told them about the killings. Lilith and Rose looked horrified, but Hepsibah nodded as though she already knew. When I was done, I asked them the question I'd asked Owen about covering the scent of one individual.

Rose shook her head, but Lilith and Hepsibah shared a look and then Hepsibah said, "White wicches, no. If you're dealing with a sorcerer, it's possible."

Dave's heavy boots began to pound down the stairs.

Hepsibah pointed to the staircase. "That's who you should ask. If it's a wicche, it's done with demon power. My guess is that it's a demon."

"What's a demon?" Dave asked as he walked around the back of the bar and poured himself a tumbler full of cinnamon Schnapps.

I thanked the women and followed Dave into the kitchen, hopping up on the counter, ready to launch into the story again.

He held up a hand to stop me while downing his Schnapps. He put the empty glass in the dishwasher and said, "I already know. Russell called me last night and I went to the Bubble Lounge. There was no demon involved."

My shoulders slumped. "Are you sure? Maybe it was a sorcerer using a demon's power to mask his scent."

He leaned against the counter and crossed his beefy arms across his chest. "Could a demon do it? Yes. Did a demon do it? No. It's not about scent for me. My nose is almost as sensitive as yours, but that's not what I needed for this. Demons leave a meta-physical trace around anything they touch. It wasn't there."

Well, shit.

I pulled out my phone. "He killed again in the middle of the night." I pulled up my text app and hit play on Nerissa's video before handing him my phone. "Clive, Vlad, and Cadmael went to see if they could pick up a scent to identify the vampire. The killing took place after the three of them visited the nightclub."

Unlike Vlad, Dave had no reaction. I only knew the video had ended when he handed my phone back to me.

"It wasn't Vlad," I told him.

"I know." He rubbed his hand over his bald head. "The hair is too long and the ear is wrong. It's damn close, though. Vampires can't glamour their appearance. Are we sure it's not fae?"

"We're not sure of anything, other than you saying it definitely isn't a demon. I went over the crime scene early this morning before I called the cops and didn't catch any fae scent other than the merpeople who work at the club."

He blew out a breath. "I'll go back and check again after work. There's no point going now. The cops are probably still there and I'll have too many tourists with cameras to avoid. I want to get up on that roof."

TWELVE

Back Away from the Bars and No One Gets Hurt

"Clive said they all heard something on the roof. He went up to look around but didn't find anything. He's wondering if the killer can hide in plain sight."

Dave pulled a covered plate from the refrigerator. "I made those seven-layer bars you like. I was going to leave them out on the island, but Russell's call distracted me." He slid the plate along the counter, so it bumped into my hip.

I stared down at them with hearts in my eyes. Shaking his head at my baked goods devotion, he went into the cold storage room. These bars were my favorites. There was chocolatey, caramely, graham crackery, toasted coconutty deliciousness in every bite.

"Owen!" I shouted.

He burst through the door, a look of alarm on his face, and then I held up the plate.

"Gimme, gimme, gimme," he chanted. "It feels like my birthday anytime he makes these." Owen picked up a bar with reverence before taking a bite and closing his eyes in bliss.

Dave returned with his arms full of vegetables. "You two are ridiculous. Go eat those somewhere else. You're in my way."

My eyebrows slammed down, but I was too busy savoring my

bite to talk. Once I'd swallowed, I warned him, "You're trampling on our religious rights. This is a holy experience for us. Back off."

Ignoring us, Dave went back in the cold storage room.

Owen's gaze went to the door to the bar. "I guess we have to offer some to other people, huh?" His expression clearly said he wanted me to disagree with that preposterous idea.

I held the plate close to my chest and growled.

Grinning, he said, "Okay. Good."

We ate in silence, content to share the moment, but then Meri pushed in. Owen and I flinched guiltily. If I could have, I would have hidden the plate. Don't judge me!

As it was, I recognized I had to offer her one. I held out the plate. "Dave made seven-layer bars, if you want one."

She studied them a moment and then wrinkled her nose. "No thanks. I hate coconut."

Owen and I recoiled at her words, until we remembered that meant more bars for us.

"Can one of you come back to the bar?" she asked. "Rose wants a cocktail, and I don't know how to make those."

Owen nodded, wiping off his fingers and following her. I took advantage of being alone with a plate full of bars and had a second one.

"You're going to give yourself a stomachache," Dave grumbled as he washed the veggies.

"Mind your business," I muttered, taking another bite. I glanced around the kitchen. Fergus normally followed Dave in here when he arrived, hoping for handouts. "Have you seen my dog?"

Dave gestured to the dark doorway into my old apartment. From here, it looked like a black rectangle between cabinets. It was a ward. It kept most people out of the apartment that had been my home for seven years, the apartment Vlad was now using.

I resisted the urge to hide my plate of treats somewhere no one would find them and went back into the bar. Owen was studying his phone. He glanced at me and waved me over.

"Mom says she doesn't know of any spell that can cover just one scent among many," he told me.

I grabbed Grim's tankard and refilled it. "Yeah. Hepsibah said the same."

"I thought of something, though." Owen moved closer. "Benvair is coming over tonight for dinner." He watched the ocean crash into the window wall for a moment, lost in thought. "You should join us so you can ask her. She may have an idea. We eat at seven, though. Benvair is a stickler for eating on time. It'll still be light then, though, so it would need to just be you, not Clive."

I squeezed his arm. "Thank you. That's a great idea. And don't worry about Clive. I can tell him later."

"Good. I'll let George know we'll have one more." He pointed at the bookstore. "Ready to switch?"

I nodded and waved him off. "Oh, wait. Do I need to dress a certain way?" Benvair, the matriarch of the Drake clan and George's grandmother, was a terrifying woman. Elegant and powerful, she was a Black woman with perfect skin, high cheekbones, and beautiful dragon green eyes. She dressed impeccably, making me feel perpetually shabby in her presence.

Owen grimaced. "She expects us to dress for dinner. George and I wear slacks and dress shirts—no ties—and Coco usually wears a skirt or a dress. Coco hates it, but it's easier to just put one on than deal with Benvair's disapproval. Fyr joins us when he can, but as he mostly works nights, that's not often. We've been adding Sunday brunches to the weekly dinners so we can include him more, which he really appreciates."

I nod. "A dress. Okay. I can do that. Thank you for the invitation."

"You bet." Owen went into the bookstore and I started collecting empties in the bar.

The afternoon went quickly, as people started getting off work and coming in. When Fyr started his shift at five, I told him I needed to leave by six today so I could go home and get changed.

Fyr seemed to take everything in stride. I suppose after one has been abducted and imprisoned for years, needing to work the bar by yourself hardly qualified as a problem.

He tucked a clean bar towel into the waist of his jeans and drew far more glances than the act deserved. He'd been working here for months but still drew attention because he was gorgeous. He was a mountain of a man with long blond hair he mostly wore tied up in a bun. Picture Thor and you had Fyr. He nodded to the people at the bar, rolled up his sleeves, and got to work mixing drinks.

Fyr's first name was actually George. All dragon families apparently have one George per generation. It's a nod to St. George, who supposedly slayed a dragon. It'd been explained to me that St. George was himself a dragon shifter. The famed battle was just him fighting with his brother. The humans celebrated one brother pretending to kill the other brother. Dragons continued using the name because they thought it was hilarious that humans were so stupid.

"It's good that you're getting changed. Not that you don't look nice," he quickly corrected. "It's just that Grandmother Drake has certain standards." He glanced at my jeans and sneakers. "Coco regularly gets scolded for wearing boots to dinner."

Fyr was the last of his family of dragons. He grew up in Wales and was kidnapped as a child, like George's twin brother Alec. Both had been held captive for too many years by a vampire who liked to feed on other supernaturals. When we ran into Fyr in England in December, he decided to move to San Francisco to be near the Drake clan. There were so few dragons left in the world, family lines were blurred to include all.

"What about you? Do you get dressed up too?"

He scratched his cheek on a grin, and I could have sworn I saw a blush. "Oh. Well. Not really. It's not fair and we all know it, but Alec and I can get away with anything." He stuffed his hand in his pocket. "She's so happy to have us back safe and sound that she never criticizes anything either of us does. It drives Coco nuts that she gets slammed if her grandmother doesn't approve of the length of her skirt, but I can show up in jeans and boots and I just get a hug and a kiss."

Laughing, I shook my head as I filled a pint with a lager.

"It's not right," he admitted. "I feel bad, but not bad enough to dress up."

A little before six, Fyr nudged me toward the stairs. "I got it," he said. "If I need any help, I'll ask Dave to come out."

"Great. Thanks." I waved to any who were looking in my direction and then gave a short whistle for Fergus. He came running out of the bookstore, where he no doubt had been taking a nap, and met me at the stairs.

On the quick jog home, a gray cat kept pace with us. I was waiting for Fergus to pull at his leash, wanting to chase the cat, but he didn't seem to notice. He was intent on getting home and getting his dinner.

The house was dark, of course. "Vlad, if you're here, say something. I'm about to open some curtains."

Silence.

Okey-dokey. I opened the curtains as I made my way through the house to the kitchen. To be on the safe side, we'd had the windows treated to make looking in extremely difficult, but they still let in light, which was what I wanted.

Fergus sat by his bowl, waiting for me. When I filled a glass with water and drank it down, he nudged his food bowl, making it scrape against the floor.

"Yes. I know. You want to be fed. I was thirsty. I—damn it! I left the bars at work. Shitshitshit." I texted Dave.

Me: Can you put the plate of bars in the cold storage room? I forgot to grab more before I left.

Dave: Already gave the plate to Fyr. Since he has to work alone tonight, I decided he needed them more than you.

A grinning demon emoji popped up and a growl started deep

in my chest. "I'm going to beat that guy, Fergus." I filled the pup's bowl with kibble, adding a few leftover pieces of salmon I had in the fridge. While Fergus ate, I plotted my revenge against Dave. It would be long, tortuous, and bloody.

My phone buzzed again. Dave sent an image of the plate on the bottom shelf in cold storage.

> Dave: I did offer him one, but he declined. He said he didn't like coconut. Is that a fae thing?

> Me: Odd. That's a weirdly specific dislike for all fae. Anyway, I'm glad. I didn't want to have to hurt you. Getting between a werewolf and her food is never a good idea.

I opened the back door for Fergus and then ran upstairs. Sea Cliff wasn't far. I had time for a quick shower. I leaned over the bed and gave Clive a kiss before diving into the bathroom.

After I was clean and mostly blown dry, I went to the huge closet to find a dress. What would Benvair find appropriate?

"Wear the sea glass green silk," Clive said.

I spun to hug him. "What are you doing up already?"

He held me tight, rubbing his nose against my temple. "I missed you and wanted to see you before you went out."

I breathed him in as well. "How'd you know I was going anywhere?"

Tapping my head gently, he said, "You're thinking quite loudly. Dinner with the dragons, eh?"

I gave him a quick kiss and pulled the green silk dress over my head. Clive was there to hook the button at the back of my neck. I checked the mirror. It was a tank dress, with delicate stitching and tucking at the waist on one side, giving the skirt the illusion of movement.

Clive wrapped his arms around me, resting his head on my shoulder. "Lovely is too weak a word. You make my cold, dead heart yearn to beat again."

"Aww, you sweet talker." Turning in his arms, I lost myself in a kiss before rearing back with a gasp. "What time is it?"

He glanced over my shoulder at the clock on the wall. "Six-forty-five. Why?"

I raced back to the bathroom and gave my eyelashes a few swipes with the mascara brush, put on a tinted lip gloss, and then realized I was still barefoot. Thankfully Clive was standing in the doorway of the bathroom with a pair of strappy sandals, some earrings, and a handbag.

I kissed him again, grabbing the items in his hands. "You're quite the lady's maid." I sat on the bed and strapped on the sandals and slid in the earrings.

"I prefer valet," he corrected.

"Tomato, tomahto." I threw my keys, lip gloss, and phone in the small handbag and stood before Clive, my arms out. "Will I pass Benvair's inspection?"

"You look gorgeous," he said, ushering me toward the elevator. "Stop on the first floor and grab a bottle of wine from the fridge. I tried to get it for you while you were doing your mascara, but the curtains are open downstairs."

"Oh, shoot. Sorry!"

He gave me a quick kiss and ushered me into the open elevator car. "Don't be late."

I shot out on the first floor, closed all the curtains, made sure Fergus was in and closed the back door, grabbed a bottle of wine, and was back in the elevator in record time. Fergus seemed confused, but he was stretching out on the couch as I headed down to the garage.

THIRTEEN

Not Feeling Too Welcome Right Now

The drive was short, and I was able to find a place to park right across the narrow street from Owen and George's home. I checked the clock on the dashboard. Four minutes. Perfect.

You couldn't see much of their home. It was hidden behind a wall covered in ivy. I went through the garden door, followed the path through their lush, fragrant front garden, and was knocking on the door before seven.

Owen opened one of the large double doors and gestured me in. When I handed him the wine bottle, he kissed my cheek and whispered, "You look perfect."

Waving me forward, he led me through the grand marble entry, down a few stairs, and into a great room with cathedral ceilings and a window wall looking out over the ocean and Golden Gate Bridge. Waves pounded against the rocks at the property's edge below. They had a patio off the lower level that ran out to steps leading into the water.

George and his brother Alec regularly swam in the ocean. It was one of the ways they were trying to help improve Alec's strength and endurance after being held in a small cell for twenty years. The last time I saw Alec, he was looking more like his twin and less like a death camp survivor. He was on his way. Healing the outside, though, was a lot easier than healing the inside. Take it from me.

The home was elegant, without the dark, austere quality of Benvair's mansion. Hers had dark, smoky gray walls and black wood floors, giving her house the appearance of a luxurious dragon's lair. Owen and George's home was lighter and more open, with creamy walls, blond floors, and furniture in off-white, ocean blues, and greens. It was a calm and restful home, which was probably one of the reasons Alec lived here with them. Owen said Alec had the lower level to himself, and while he used to hole up down there most of the time, he was now spending more and more time up in the light with the others.

In the great room, Benvair sat in a high-backed chair beside the marble fireplace. Regardless of it being a weeknight and her only having walked a few doors down to her grandson's for dinner, Benvair was, as always, perfect. She wore a deep charcoal gray pencil skirt with matching heels, a gorgeous fire-red silk blouse, and had large rubies at her ears.

"Good evening, Benvair. It's lovely to see you again." I tried not to fidget in her presence. Tried and failed. "I hope you don't mind my joining your family dinner this evening."

Benvair, the queen of pregnant pauses, scrutinized me from head to toe and then took a sip of her red wine. "Of course. This is Owen's home as well. He's free to invite...others."

"I'm grateful," I told her.

Coco, wearing a simple black skirt with a white button-up blouse, sat alone on a bench near the window. As I was keen to put some space between Benvair and myself, I crossed the large room to greet Coco.

"I wanted to thank you for helping to take care of Fergus while Clive and I were out of the country."

She waved away my thanks. "That was all Fyr. I just kept them company sometimes when he went for coffee."

"If only Fyr could have had the night off as well," Benvair said, "so he could be here this evening."

"Sam." George came out of the kitchen with a pained look on his face. He'd heard his grandmother and gave me a hug. "You look beautiful. I'm so glad you were able to join us tonight. Now that we're done moving in, we want to have friends and family over more often."

"You'll need to finish furnishing the house," Benvair told him.

Owen came out of the kitchen with two glasses of wine, one for him and one for George. "Sam, this wine is delicious. Thank you."

"I'll let Clive know you liked it. That was his suggestion."

"I believe I gave you my interior designer's contact information," Benvair continued, not allowing the discussion to be derailed by wine talk.

George wrapped his free arm around Owen. "You did, Grandmother. Thank you, but Owen and I are enjoying doing it ourselves. It's slower this way, but everything in the house is something we picked together, which means more to us."

Alec walked out of the kitchen and for the first time, I felt like I was seeing double. The transformation was incredible. When we'd freed him from that dungeon six months ago, he'd been skin and bones. He couldn't stand on his own, let alone walk. Now, he was almost as tall as George. Thinner, still, but he looked healthy and thriving in his faded jeans and a blue button-down oxford shirt.

Tears rushed to my eyes. "Alec," I whispered. "Look at you."

"Sam, how are you and Clive?" He walked over and gave me a big hug. Unlike most dragons, Benvair especially, Alec didn't have a problem with vampires. Yes, Aldith had kidnapped and fed on him for twenty years, but Clive, Russell, and Godfrey had found him and battled an army of vampire and fae soldiers to rescue him. He would never not be grateful for his freedom.

"He's good. Thank you for asking. And he will be so happy when I tell him how great you're looking."

Alec went to Coco and took her empty glass. "Sam, Owen tells us you're not a wine drinker. Would you like some iced tea? That's what my sister and I are drinking."

"I'd love that. Thank you," I said.

"Good." He waved me forward. "Come with me and you can help me carry the glasses back."

He was giving me an escape hatch, and I took it. The kitchen was filled with wonderful, spicy smells and looked like it should be featured in an architectural magazine. They had white cabinet uppers and soft teal lowers. The countertops appeared to be a sparkling white quartz. A massive island in the middle of the room had teal leather stools on one side and a deep prep sink on the other. There was even an eat-in nook on the far side of the kitchen, right in front of the huge windows.

The massive head of a black jungle cat came up from the nook bench and snarled at me. Alec dropped the glass he was holding on the counter and moved in front of me, with his hands held up.

"No, Jade. This is our friend." He went to the black jaguar and crouched by her head, murmuring something to her. Glaring at me with luminous green eyes, she gave a deep, guttural roar that sounded strangely like sawing.

"Forgive me," I said. "I didn't mean to startle you." I'd completely forgotten. Owen had told me that Russell and Audrey had rescued a jaguar who had been imprisoned by a lone vampire in the attic above Meg's penthouse, downtown at the Palace Hotel. Meg was one of the Furies. She'd been coming to my bar since it opened, but she'd been strangely absent recently. It was starting to worry me.

Owen had said the jaguar was covered in scars and had yet to shift to her human form. Russell had given the traumatized cat to George, hoping his gifts as a veterinarian would help her. "And I'm sure I smell like vampires. I'm sorry. I shouldn't have come into your home."

She was dangerously beautiful. Her jaguar rosettes created a black-on-black pattern in her fur. It was heartbreaking, though, to see all the breaks in her glossy fur where her skin was scarred and burned. I knew the vampire who'd done this to her was dead, but I wished I could reanimate him and kill him again.

Alec stood and the jaguar came to her feet. She gave me a

reproachful look and leapt over the back of the seat to stalk down the hall.

Alec turned back. "I would have warned you if I'd known she was in here. She hadn't been a minute ago. She doesn't normally come up when we have visitors. I think she caught your scent and came to investigate." He picked up the glass he'd dropped and pulled two more from the cupboard. He filled all three with ice and then pulled a pitcher from the refrigerator, pouring tea into each of our glasses.

Alec looked pointedly at me as he handed me my glass. "It's okay. Jade is strong and she's healing. She wasn't expecting you to walk into her space, but she still stayed in control. She warned you away from her. She didn't attack you. She was in control and protected herself."

He may have been staring at me, but he was talking to Jade.

"She's doing a lot better than I was after my attack," I said, hoping she was listening. "I was covered in scars, didn't trust anyone, and hid underground in my bookstore and bar for seven years. If you ask me, she has the heart of a warrior."

I thought I heard a chuff of air from down the hall. It was so faint, though, I wasn't sure. Alec smiled and then tipped his head toward the living room. Apparently, he'd heard her too.

When we went back out, they were all sitting silently, no doubt listening. George was beside Owen, his mouth at Owen's ear. Wicches didn't have the enhanced hearing all the rest of us did.

"Here you are, Coco." Alec brought his sister her glass and then sat on the bench beside her. "What are you making us for dinner, George? It smells good whatever it is."

Alec's message was clear: Everything is fine. Please resume your conversation.

"Lasagna," George told him. "The way you like it." He turned to me to explain. "Alec loves when I do a layer of pesto within the layers of tomato sauce."

"He also does three times the meat, which I appreciate," Alec added.

"That sounds amazing. I'm glad I'm here on lasagna night." I sat on Owen's other side on the couch and took a sip of iced tea, my gaze falling on Coco. I worried about her. She was George and Alec's older sister. Though she had been only ten when the twins were eight, she seemed to have taken on the full responsibility for Alec's abduction. No amount of reason could lift the burden. When she'd gotten older, she'd tried to numb the pain and guilt with alcohol, but she'd eventually dragged herself back out of the bottle and was sober now.

Alec was still recovering. He suffered from panic attacks and had a hard time leaving the house, but he was healing and getting stronger. George, too, was thriving having his twin back, no longer sleepless and ravaged with guilt for being the one who made it out of those woods that day.

Coco, though, watched Alec's every move with such concern in her gaze that it broke my heart. Alec bumped her shoulder with his own and murmured something to her. She smiled, but it dropped from her face when he turned away. Her stolen brother may have been back, but it didn't look as though she was ever going to let herself off the hook for how that vampire had tortured and broken him.

George's phone buzzed in his pocket. "Why don't we move to the dining room and Owen and I will bring in dinner."

Alec patted his sister's knee and then went to his grandmother, offering his arm and an escort to the dining room. Coco and I followed. A huge, round cherry wood table dominated the room beneath a coffered ceiling. A mural filled the far wall. Instead of sitting, I went to study it.

"Owen, when did you have this done?"

He stepped up beside me. "What do you think?"

"It's incredible. Wait." I touched the wall. "Is this wallpaper?"

He nodded. "Remember I told you my family used to be artisans in ancient China?"

"Yes, but you said they made teapots and cups." I stepped back to take in more of the scene.

"Right, but we had painters in there as well. This painting has been treasured and passed down for centuries. I told my mom we were having a hard time deciding what to do in the dining room and she commissioned one of my cousins, who's a graphic artist, to duplicate the painting.

"My parents have the original. It's small, maybe eight by ten. My cousin had to digitize it and then sharpen the image enough to have it fill a wall this size. The nice part is that now every family member has a print of the original to hang in their home. And thanks to Mom, we have this mural."

The painting was of an ancient Chinese village on a misty mountain in the clouds. The other walls had been painted a deep green. They played off the colors of the painting while disappearing from notice. The mural demanded all the attention.

"Wow," I breathed. When I turned, I realized the others were waiting for us to sit down. "Sorry."

The circular dining table filled the large dining room. Although there were only six places set tonight, it looked as though it could easily fit twelve.

"Perhaps we could eat before the food gets cold," Benvair scolded.

I sat quickly and tried to blend into the background. George served up steaming slabs of lasagna and then we passed bowls of roasted asparagus and garlic bread.

The food was delicious, but I had a hard time focusing. My gaze kept drifting back to the artwork on the wall.

"I believe you had a question for me. Did you not?" Benvair asked, making me flinch. "Isn't that the reason you're joining our family dinner?"

FOURTEEN

The Face in the Mirror

I swallowed quickly and then took a sip of iced tea. "Yes. Of course." I glanced at everyone eating. "It's about the two killings at Fisherman's Wharf, though. I don't want to spoil anyone's dinner."

Benvair waved away the concern. "We're all adults here. I hadn't heard about a murder." She turned to George. "Had you?"

He nodded, swallowing. "I did from Owen when he got home from work. I hadn't heard anything earlier."

Benvair turned back to me. "Start at the beginning."

Looking longingly at the food I wanted to eat, I put down my fork and explained what had happened the last two nights at the wharf.

Benvair turned to Owen, so I snuck a quick bite of lasagna. "This isn't something wicches can do?"

He shook his head. "According to Mom and a few crones at work, no."

"Hmm." Benvair nodded. "Lydia would know if it could be done."

I didn't know why her simple statement made my throat tighten. I'd been worried, I supposed. I didn't want Owen to be treated like a second-class citizen in his relationship. Benvair believed dragons were the greatest creatures in the realms, so I worried that Owen, being a wicche, was given the kind of verbal slaps I was getting tonight. Benvair's complete confidence that Owen's mom Lydia clearly knew everything there was to know about wicchecraft settled my heart.

Owen, who was sitting beside me, reached under the table and patted my leg. I swore, the man was an empath.

"I checked with Dave about demons," I told them. "He said one could, but he'd checked The Bubble Lounge, and one didn't. Apparently, he doesn't need to rely on scent. Demons leave some kind of trace that other demons can see, which is interesting."

Benvair took a sip of her wine. "And now you're wondering if a dragon did it? No. We don't kill that way and we'd never kill innocents like that." Red fired in her eyes.

I held up a hand. "No, no. I wasn't suggesting that. I was looking for your insight into the killing. Vlad says vampires can't drain a body that quickly."

"How do they know the bodies were drained?" George asked. "Does Russell have the autopsy report?"

I shook my head. "Not that I know. We spoke to him last night about the first killing. He was able to get the autopsy moved up, but they didn't yet have the report. The nocturne has an informant in the morgue, though, who described the body as drained."

"You mentioned a video," George said. "Can we see it?"

"Sure." I pulled my phone out and started to hand it to him.

He shook his head. "Just hold up your phone. We'll be able to see it fine."

Since Owen didn't have enhanced vision, I stepped behind my chair so the angle would work better for him. Tapping the phone screen, I pulled up the video, hit play, and then held it for all of them to see.

"This is the second victim?" Owen asked.

I nodded. I knew when the killer dropped into the frame because all the dragons blinked and Owen flinched.

"Why wait?" Coco murmured. I questioned that as well. Why had the killer waited for the man to eat before he attacked?

When all the dragon eyes moved to my face, I put the phone back in my pocket and took my seat.

Benvair took a sip of wine. "I haven't seen him, but I've heard that you brought Vlad back from Europe with you."

"We did. This isn't him, though. We analyzed the video this morning. The killer's hair is wrong and he's too tall. Vlad has scars on both his ear and his eyebrow from all his battles when he was human. Both scars are on his left side. Clive says Vlad had his right side to The Bubble Lounge when they went to investigate."

Benvair nodded, deep in thought.

"So, the thought is that the killer was hiding when Clive and Vlad went to investigate," George said. "Is that it? The killer saw Vlad and glamoured himself to look like him for the second killing?"

Shrugging a shoulder, I said, "That's our current theory. The killer either doesn't have a scent or he knows how to hide it because we couldn't find it."

"What did you find?" Alec asked.

"Based on the first murder and what appeared to be a vampire bite on the woman's neck, we all assumed it was a vampire. Clive and Vlad went to investigate. They scented no vampires. I went the next morning when Nerissa called. I was there before the cops. I went over both crime scenes, in the front and back of the club. The only vampires I scented were Clive and Vlad. There were lots of different merpeople scents, which makes sense, as they work there. There were a million human scents, as it's in a tourist area, and lots of cats, who are there for the fish."

"Did Clive and Vlad go together?" Benvair asked.

I thought a moment. "No. Clive was with me. He met them there."

"Them?" She inquired.

"Oh." *Shit.* "Yes. We have another visitor staying with us. They went together and then Clive met them there."

"And who's that?" she inquired.

"I'm pretty sure I'm not supposed to be talking about that. Vlad made himself known by coming into the bar." I tapped my forehead. "I've got a lot of secrets swirling around in here and I try to keep them."

Owen swallowed a bite of bread and asked, "Is it possible the killer was a wicche before he was made a vampire? I mean, is that a thing?"

I considered Vlad, a vampire who was a day-walker because of his wicche mother. "Yes. It's a thing. I think that's why certain lines of vampires have enhanced gifts. Clive has superior mental skills, as do the others in his line. Other vampires could have different enhanced gifts."

"Can fae be turned?" Coco mused quietly, looking down at her plate.

Benvair glanced to the side, taking in her granddaughter and then returned to her plate and her own thoughts.

"I don't think so," I told Coco. "The vampires always talk about how incompatible their magic is with the fae."

Benvair nodded. "The fae are life. Vampires are death. I can't imagine any member of the fae sitting still and allowing a vampire to turn them."

I took a sip of iced tea. "And I'd assume the moment they died, they'd end up back in Faerie, where I can't imagine the queen allows the undead to wander."

Owen grinned at that.

"All right," Benvair said. "Given he has the ability to create a glamour, our killer is a supernatural, but he's neither a wicche, a demon, nor any kind of shifter—"

"Wait." I didn't realize until I'd done it that I'd interrupted Benvair. Oops. "It could be a shifter who's also part wicche or part fae." I turned to Owen. "Wicches can glamour."

He nodded. "Sure, to greater and lesser extent. Just like with vampires, some wicche families have a gift for glamour." He changed his eye color to lavender, like Meri's, and then changed it back. "I can do little things, like changing hair and eye color for short periods. I couldn't change my entire body to mimic someone else's, though."

I turned back to Benvair. "I'm sorry. I interrupted you. You were saying?"

She looked as though she was deciding whether or not to let it slide. Thankfully, she continued her thought. "So, it seems as though we're looking for a vampire with enhanced gifts, a shifter with a magical lineage, or a member of the fae."

"One who doesn't have a scent trail," I added.

Tapping her finger on her lips, she considered. "The fae rarely remember they have noses. They are magical beings who can do almost anything. Scent is beneath them. Shifters sniff. The fae are too good for that," Benvair snapped. "The idea that one not only thought about his scent but did something to cover it seems far-fetched to me."

"And whatever it is," I said, "it has the ability to hide in plain sight. Clive and the other vampires heard something on the roof. Clive went up and found nothing—didn't see, didn't sense, and didn't smell anything out of the ordinary. Can you think of any type of being who can do that?"

Alec growled low in the back of his throat. We all turned to him. He shook his head as though trying to dislodge an unwanted thought.

"I remembered something." He gestured to my plate. "You eat while I talk."

I didn't need to be told twice.

"I'm not good with time," Alec began. "I was down in that cell forever. Maybe a few years ago, I was awake while everyone around me slept."

"Why?" Coco asked, her food forgotten.

He stared at the fork in his hand for a moment, clearly uncomfortable. "I was in a lot of pain. I'm good at disassociating, so normally I could still sleep, but not that time. Anyway, I knew the sights and sounds. I knew when guards changed shifts, when *she'd* come down, when food was delivered. It was quiet. Well, no. It was never completely quiet. There were snores, and grunts, and farts, but it was a down time when nothing was happening. Most slept. Some zoned out.

"I was on the ground, staring down the dark passage between cells, trying to force my mind past the pain when he appeared. I hadn't heard him coming down the steps. Even vampires make some noise: the grit of dirt on the soles of their shoes, something. I'm never surprised. Living as I was, I became hyperaware of any movement, any sound around me. He didn't walk down those stairs. I know he didn't.

"The silhouette of a man appeared at the end of the row, a shadow in darkness. He stopped at each cell, seemed to study who was inside, and then moved on soundlessly. When he got to mine, I turned my head and looked up."

Alec swallowed, his anxiety rising. "He was emaciated. Eyes sunken. Lips pulled back from blackened teeth. What stood out to me, though, was that his skin was dark, like mine. Most of the vampires and fae I saw were white—well, fae are usually more gold or sometimes green, but you get what I mean. This guy had skin like mine.

"He stared down at me, shook his head, and then moved on. I watched him. When he got to the cell with the troll, he roared, just like a troll does, and then smashed the cell bars. The troll in the cell shot out into the passage, roaring and bouncing off the bars, racing for the stairs. Other cells were broken open and more prisoners ran or limped out. The guards came and it was chaos, people getting beaten bloody, but also prisoners running out.

"My cell was at the end of the passage. No one came near it. No one broke it open. I just watched the brutal beatings from the stone floor of my cell." He paused. "What I just realized is that the face he'd shown me as he looked down at me was my own. I hadn't seen myself in a mirror since I was eight. After I was rescued and we were in Drake keep, I saw myself for the first time in twenty years and I panicked. It was the same as that man who'd started the riot. He'd stared down at me that night, wearing my face."

FIFTEEN

And to Think, I Used to Love Churros

Coco made a sound. It was a whine so quiet, I doubt Owen even heard it. Benvair reached out and took her grand-daughter's hand.

Alec, still lost in the memory, stared at the table. "I don't know what he was."

"Could you identify his scent?" George's gaze cut back and forth between his siblings.

They were all trying to pretend like everything was okay. It wasn't, but just like Alec had tried to normalize Jade's snarling, George was trying to communicate that remembering was okay, that Alec was safe now.

Alec shook his head. "My nose had been broken. I couldn't smell anything."

Coco made the sound again and this time, it broke through Alec's memories.

He turned to her and gave her a sad smile. "I'm fine now." He leaned over and kissed her cheek. "Grandfather would have said it was character building."

Benvair cleared her throat and told him, "No. He wouldn't have."

Alec wiped his mouth with his napkin and stood. "I'm going to get dessert. Owen and I made it last night." He motioned to his sister. "Come help me."

After they left, we were quiet, lost in our own thoughts. Benvair stared up at the ceiling and blinked before reaching for her wine.

George went to the buffet on the side of the room to retrieve the wine bottle, then filled Benvair's glass before splitting what was left with Owen.

"I'm sorry. I shouldn't have done this." I'd ruined their evening. I'd expected to see anger or disgust in Benvair's eyes, but I found neither.

"Nonsense," she said. "If this creature is here, we must find and destroy it."

Alec returned, carrying a plate of chocolate eclairs, with Coco behind him carrying the plates and forks.

While she passed them out, Alec said, "Owen knows I love chocolate, so he's been teaching me to cook desserts." He glanced at his grandmother. "Don't worry. I'm starting to learn how to cook real food too, but I prefer the desserts."

"You made these?" I asked in wonder. "They look delicious."

"Hope so," Alec said. "Remember, George, when we were little and Cook made eclairs at the keep?" He glanced at Benvair, smiling. "George and I stuffed ourselves. We must have eaten twenty of them. Cook was so angry when she went into the kitchen and they were all gone."

George laughed. "Yes. You had us bring the dogs in so we could plausibly blame them for eating all the treats."

"That was you?" Benvair acted as though she was outraged to have been deceived, but I could see the relief in her posture, in her expression. Talk of the twins and their mischief was far better than picturing Alec stolen away from them, alone, and in pain.

"Owen supervised—"

"Barely," Owen interrupted. "I sat by the window and read."

"You helped with piping the pastry," Alec clarified.

George and Alec ignored the forks and picked up the eclairs, polishing them off in two bites before reaching for seconds.

"Mmmm, heaven. You know," I said, "if you wanted, you could come to work with Owen. I'm sure Dave could teach you some new recipes."

Alec nodded and swallowed. "I'll think about it."

Good evening, darling.

I looked out the doorway and across the great room to the windows. They were dark, the bridge lit up in the distance. *Hey, you. Are you at Owen and George's?*

Yep. We just had dessert. And I may have learned something about our possible killer.

Good. It sounds like it was a successful dinner. I don't want to interrupt your evening. I'm just letting you know that Cadmael, Vlad, and I are headed down to the wharf to stake out The Bubble Lounge.

Perfect. Here's hoping you catch the bastard.

I turned back to my hosts. "Clive and his friends are going to the wharf to stake out the scene."

"Actually," Alec said, "I'd like to do that too. I want to see if there's something there I recognize."

There was a charged silence. No one wanted to tell Alec not to go, but everyone was worried, especially after that story.

Benvair nodded decisively. "Yes. That's an excellent idea. I'll go with you. I want to know what's going on." She stood abruptly. "We need to change. I'd suggest all black. I'll be back in a few minutes and we'll drive downtown. All right?"

So many emotions played across Alec's face. He knew what she was doing, and he appreciated her care. "Yes. I'll get changed too."

"It seems only fair," George reasoned. "Grandmother and I gave two of the bastards who were manipulating Fyr the dragon's kiss. It's your turn to do violence with Grandmother."

Benvair's smile was razor sharp. "I enjoyed that." She patted her lips with her napkin. "I'll be back shortly." She strode out of the dining room and out of sight.

When the front door opened and closed, I slumped in my chair. Owen laughed.

Alec rose and turned to his sister. "Will you be here when I get back?"

She paused, so George answered for her. "She will be. We're going to make some popcorn and watch a show while we wait for you."

Coco looked between the twins and finally nodded. "I guess I'm watching a show and eating popcorn."

"Good." Alec disappeared, heading down to his floor. Owen, George, Coco, and I cleared the table.

"Do you want to stay, Sam?" Owen asked.

I shook my head. "I want to get changed and head down to the wharf too. I'll take Fergus with me as cover."

"Be careful," George said, leaning over to give me a kiss on the cheek. "The first woman was running with her dog."

"True, but I have three vampires watching my back. I'll let you guys know if I learn anything."

I said my goodbyes, grabbed my handbag, and headed out to my car. Benvair was on her way back, dressed all in black.

"Goodnight and thank you," I said quietly.

She nodded. "It's good for him, you know." She paused at the garden door and then looked back at me. "Going out. Confronting what scared him. These are all good signs. Know this, though, I will never let anything like that ever happen again, not to any of them. I'll burn down the world before I let any of them be hurt like that again." Her eyes flashed red in the dark.

"Good," I answered.

When I got home, I found Fergus lying in his bed as the elevator doors opened. "We never got to exercise this morning. Feel like going for a run?"

He bounded up and was dancing around my feet as I changed out of my fancy dress and into running gear. Once I had my hair up in a braid, I slid my phone into my hip pocket and headed for the elevator.

Fergus liked to sit his butt on the car's back seat, with his front paws on the floor, so his head could rest on my shoulder as I drove. When I hit red lights, I'd scratch under his chin. Vlad had said that the Bucharest killings hadn't taken place in the same location. I wanted to check out all the piers, so instead of the parking garage near the wharf I'd used last time, I parked in The Viper's Nest parking lot with all the motorcycles.

Since I was leaving my car here, I figured I should stop and say hi. The bouncer on the door looked ready to stop Fergus and me but then he recognized my face and waved us through.

The music was loud and colored lights flashed in the darkened bar. Some patrons were dancing in the middle of the room, a few were making out in booths, but most were standing around, talking and laughing. I headed to the end of the packed bar, near the rotating pie display case on Stheno's side. Some muscle-bound guy was handling the other end of the bar, which made sense, as Fyr was at The Slaughtered Lamb tonight.

Stheno, one of the three gorgons sisters you might remember from Greek Mythology, glanced over. Her initial annoyance at someone trying to order a drink from behind the pies disappeared.

"Hey, kid. What are you doing here?" Her gaze drifted over my clothes and Fergus. "Since when do you run late at night?"

I leaned in and whispered, knowing she'd hear me even over all the noise, "Do you know about the killings at The Bubble Lounge?"

She nodded, pulling a slice of coconut cream pie out of the display and sliding it to where I was standing. She reached under the bar and found me a fork. Two desserts in one night. Score!

"It looks like a vampire killing, but we're pretty sure it's not. Clive, Vlad, and Cadmael are down here, staking out the nightclub. I was planning on checking out the area, undercover with Fergus."

Stheno's brow furrowed. "The first victim was a woman running with a dog. I don't like this idea." She filled a glass with water and put it next to the plate as I took a bite.

"Mmm, Dave is so good at these."

Some men were waving, trying to get Stheno's attention, so while she filled drink orders, I finished the pie and then shared what was left of my water with Fergus.

She took the empty plate from me and put it in the dirties tub under the bar.

"Don't worry. There are three vampires within a mile and a half who'll be there if I need them."

"That's not helpful if he hits you in the back of the head before he drinks your blood." She shook her head. "As your former bodyguard, I say just go upstairs, lounge on my couch, and monitor the area from there." She tapped her head. "You don't need to be in it."

"I tried that after the first killing. I didn't see anything problematic and then he killed again a short time later. And the attacks have been in the wee hours of the morning. It's not even eleven yet." I shook my tense shoulders. "I can't see or smell important clues from your couch—though I do appreciate the offer."

She tipped her head to the side, her long coils of curly hair seeming to move on their own. "I don't like it. You're a grown up, I suppose, so do what you want, but I don't like it."

"I can protect myself," I reminded her.

"Against what, though? We don't know what we're dealing with yet."

"I'm not jumping into a pond filled with piranha. I'm going for a run in an area where there are three vampires and two dragons. Benvair and Alec are here as well."

She waved me off. "Fine. Go. I'm busy." She went back to talking with customers and filling drinks.

Fergus got some pets on the way out and then we were jogging through the parking lot and running along the Embarcadero, past the piers. We passed other dog walkers and couples strolling. The Ferry Building was lit up, a family on the steps, taking pictures. Small bars were dotted along the piers, some quiet, others with people overflowing into the parking lot, laughing and drinking.

We passed a man running with his dog in the opposite direction. His dog pulled to get close to us, but Fergus kept going straight because he's a good and smart boy. I had to leap over the top of the damn dog who'd cut in front of me. The stupid runner was grinning when his dog blocked me and then looked shocked when I kept going. Geez. Let people run. I'm not out here looking for a date.

I went through a stretch that was quiet. I didn't see anyone on either side of the road, so I checked and found three green blips and two red ones clustered together. "We have less than a mile before we can take a break, buddy."

Maybe half a dozen piers later, Fergus slowed, lifting his head to the wind. He'd smelled something. He slowed even more and then stopped near a shuttered churros stand. The tourists were gone for the night, so the stand had been closed up. Something, though, drew him to it.

Clive, Fergus is very interested in a churros stand less than a mile from you, on the Embarcadero.

I'll find you.

I felt him running, so I pulled Fergus back and took a sniff myself. Fish, ocean, vermin, cats, and cinnamon sugar. I wasn't sure what had attracted Fergus. A rat ran along the side of the pier building, but Fergus didn't notice. He whined, trying to get close to the boarded-up stand. With a yip, followed closely by a low growl, he strained against the leash.

Clive stepped out from behind the stand. I blew out a breath, annoyed that I'd gotten myself so worked up. He reached out a hand to Fergus, who growled, showing his teeth.

"That's odd. Dogs normally like me," he said in a voice that was not Clive's.

SIXTEEN

Don't Mess with My Dog

A chill ran down my spine. I breathed in deeply, a fake smile on my face. "He's just protective." Whatever this was, the scent was all wrong. It was neither human nor vampire. *He's here and he's glamoured himself to look like you.*

He beckoned us forward. "He probably smells the dog treats I keep in my stand. Come around back and I'll get him one."

Fergus backed up until his quivering butt was touching my legs. He didn't want me going to the Clive look-alike. I patted his flank. We were on the same page.

"No thank you."

The fake Clive was suddenly in front of me, his hand clamping Fergus' snout closed like a muzzle. He leaned in, leering, and then his nose scrunched up in distaste. "What have you been—"

My claws slid through the wrist of the hand holding my dog. Fergus yelped and shook off the severed hand still wrapped around his nose. The killer's eyes went wide and then swirled in black and gold. Fae.

Staring at his forehead to avoid being mesmerized, I reached for my axe. His stump went for my arm before he remembered he had lost his hand. While he worked through his new reality, I plunged my claws into his chest. He leapt back instantly, his head turning toward where I felt Clive approaching. Snarling at me, he spun and raced down the pier.

The real Clive ripped the axe out of my hand and gave chase. I dropped to my knees to check on Fergus. While I held him, I scanned the wooden planks we were on, looking for the severed hand. It wasn't here. Perhaps it had just appeared in Faerie.

When I tried to touch Fergus' snout, he whined and pulled his head away. "I'm sorry, little man. I'm so sorry he hurt you." He leaned into me, his body quivering. I scratched behind his ears. "You were so brave, trying to protect me."

He sat, and I rubbed my hands up and down his sides until the shaking subsided. I felt Clive moving up behind me and then my axe was being returned to its sheath.

"I lost him." He rested his left hand on Fergus' head. The pup flinched, sniffed his hand, and then leaned in to Clive's touch.

I felt Clive's hurt, that his own dog had been taught not to trust him. I pulled Clive down where Fergus could sniff his face and hair and then I reached for the right hand he was holding behind his back.

"It's nothing. You know I heal quickly."

I sighed. He was right, but I hated that he was in pain and hiding it. My axe was fae made and vampires couldn't touch fae metal. It burned their skin.

"What happened?" Benvair's voice made me jump. Dragons were every bit as quiet as vampires.

Clive and I stood and walked to Benvair and Alec, who waited on the sidewalk. I explained what had happened and Alec went to the churros stand, sniffing around the back.

He came back a moment later, shaking his head. "I don't smell anything recent, just the humans who work here or visited, and some mice."

I kept a hand on Fergus's shoulder as he leaned into me. "Can he mimic scents the way he mimics faces? Is that why we aren't finding him?"

Benvair and Alec's gaze cut to the side. She patted her grandson's arm, but she was staring into my eyes. "I'll check. Perhaps I'll find a familiar scent." The lightness of her voice didn't match the severity of her stare.

When I started to turn to see where Benvair was going, Alec grabbed my hand and kept me where I was. Clive stilled, but neither of us turned. There was something behind us.

"I'm sorry you missed dinner tonight," Alec said to Clive, though he seemed to be focused over Clive's shoulder.

"Yes," I said, not wanting Clive to speak. "I was sorry about that as well. It was a lovely dinner." *If he hasn't heard your voice yet, he won't be able to mimic it.*

I understand.

"Perhaps another time," I said to Alec. "Our friends made lasagna, asparagus, and garlic bread. It was all delicious." If this thing was human, he'd know something was up because this conversation was so blandly stilted, it was painful. "Our friend here also made us dessert, which was amazing."

Alec's gaze returned to me for a moment, one side of his mouth kicking up. He understood I didn't want to use his name if we were being overheard. He lifted his head and inhaled deeply and then, staring over our shoulders, shook his head. "Next time you'll have to tell me what your favorite dessert is so I can make it for you."

A ball of fire erupted behind us. Before I could react, Clive had Fergus and me across the street, away from the weak glow from a distant streetlight. We watched the pier where we'd been standing. A few minutes later, Alec and Benvair crossed the street to us.

Voice so low, even I had trouble hearing, Alec said, "He can mimic animal shapes as well. There was a cat slinking up the side of the pier building. It ignored a rat that ran right past it."

"Yes," Benvair said. "That's what caught my attention as well. I feigned interest in the food stand so I could get closer to him. He didn't smell like a cat." She thought a moment. "More like a rat, actually, though it was quite faint."

"Wait," I interrupted. "When Fergus was pulling me toward

the stand, a rat ran past us and Fergus didn't even turn his head. Maybe he was slinking around, looking for his next victim as a rat and when Fergus and I showed up, he turned himself into one of the last people he'd studied: Clive."

"I was, perhaps, thirty feet from him," Benvair said, "when he turned to watch me. As I didn't want a killer wandering around town with my face, I burned him," she said. "Unfortunately, though, I didn't kill him. He ran, his body scorched. He was fluctuating between shapes and then he just disappeared. I hurt him—I know that—but I didn't kill him."

"Better than I did," Clive grumbled. "I chased him but, as with you, he disappeared."

"The cat," I murmured.

Clive nodded. "Yes. I just realized that as well. When I went on the roof of The Bubble Lounge, I saw a small cat hiding behind the air conditioning unit. He was up there, watching us last night."

"If he can appear to be anyone or anything, how will we ever catch him?" It felt like we were farther from an answer than when we started. "We can't sniff the entire city until we find a cat or maybe a rat or—Oh. That's how he disappeared. He probably shifted into a cockroach or something and dropped between the wooden planks of the pier."

Clive rubbed a hand up and down my arm. "We'll figure it out."

"We're going to go home now," Benvair said. "If you think of a way we can help, let us know. I, too, will put out feelers. Someone has to know what it is and how to kill it."

"He's fae. His eyes swirled black and gold when he was trying to mesmer—wait," I said, grabbing Clive's arm. "Blood. Did you see blood on him? I cut off one of his hands and buried my claws in his chest."

Clive lifted my hand to study it. The claws were gone, but I still had some blood under my fingernails. "We need to preserve this. Dave may be able to find him through the blood."

I glanced down at Fergus. "I was so worried about him being

hurt or my needing to comfort him, I was petting him and probably rubbed off the blood on my hands. Stupid."

Clive kissed my forehead. "Stop. One thing you are not is stupid."

"But the blood, the injury." I glanced between Benvair and Alec. "You both scented him. Did you smell blood?"

They both shook their heads. "And the cat wasn't missing a paw," Benvair informed us.

I blew out a breath. "So, he heals when he shifts? Shit."

"But," Alec said, "you cut off his hand and made him bleed. If he bleeds, he can be killed."

"Indeed," Clive agreed. He turned to me. "Where did you park?"

"Stheno's place."

Clive took the leash from me. "I'll drive you home. Try not to touch anything. We'll call Dave in the car." He turned to Benvair and Alec. "Thank you for coming out tonight. We'll keep you informed. And Alec, you're looking quite hale. It's good to see."

Alec tipped his head to Clive and then he and his grandmother walked in the opposite direction, back to their own car.

We started to walk, Fergus' leash in Clive's left hand.

"Can I see?"

He knew what I wanted, so he lifted his right hand. It was still red, with small sections of skin missing. "By the time we get home, it'll be back to normal. Not to worry, love."

"My neck is just sitting over here, doing nothing."

The look he gave me made my knees weak. He leaned in, brushed his nose against my temple, breathing me in, and then kissed my neck. When his fangs slid in, my eyelids drifted closed. Each draw inflamed my body. When I felt his tongue, I knew he was closing the bite wound.

"Thank you, darling."

I reached for his hand. The redness was mostly gone. Only the spots where new skin was coming in still looked tender.

He held my hand and pulled me along. "I'm fine and I don't

like leaving you here exposed longer than necessary. You hurt him. You and Benvair are the only ones who have accomplished that. I want you out of this area."

We jogged back, made it to the car quickly, and then Clive tapped the in-dash screen to call Dave.

"What?" Dave sounded especially snarly, which made sense. We'd probably woken him up. He got up early now to bake.

"Sorry if I woke you," Clive responded.

There was pause and then Dave asked, "Why are you calling me on Sam's phone? Where is she?"

"Here with me," Clive told him.

I leaned forward. No idea why. "Hi, Dave. My phone is the one paired with this car."

"Okay," he grumbled.

Who knew Dave didn't trust Clive? That was a new one. "Remember that thing killing people we talked about?"

"Yeah."

"I'm pretty sure he's fae. He has the swirling eyes they do, and he can shift between people and animals."

"Sam stabbed him, so she has some of his blood under her nails," Clive informed him. "We're hoping you can use that blood to track him."

We heard grumbling and the sound of movement before the call clicked off.

"I assume that means he's coming." I held my hands fingers up in my lap as Clive drove us home. "We need to make sure it's Dave before we open the door to him."

"I was thinking the same," Clive said. "We'll need to impose security questions on our friends."

I thought about it a moment. "We need to text them the question when they're at the door. We don't want them giving out private info when a grasshopper could be overhearing. Which reminds me." I lifted my right hand and spoke into the queen's ring on my pinky.

"Hello. It's me. Sam. We're having a problem. There's a person here who is killing innocents. He's doing it in a way that looks like a vampire, but he's not one. He has swirly fae eyes—black and gold—and he can shape-shift into people he sees or into animals. We don't know what he is or how to stop him. Any help you can give us would be greatly appreciated." I dropped my hand and then quickly lifted it again. "Thank you. Over and out."

Clive shook his head on a grin.

SEVENTEEN

Eww

"The wards on the house cover the garage door, right?" That was all we needed. I didn't want a shape-shifting cat to sneak in when the garage door opened.

"They do." Clive reached over and rubbed my knee.

I used my knuckle to tap the screen, calling Vlad. It rang once.

"Yes?" Vlad's voice was barely audible.

"Hey. Clive is with me. We're driving home. Fergus and I ran into the killer. He definitely appears to be fae. He can shift between human and animal, healing his wounds as he shifts. Just giving you the heads-up."

"We wondered why Clive disappeared. I wasn't looking forward to telling you that we'd lost him."

"Benvair, matriarch of the local dragon clan," Clive began, "burned him when he was in the shape of a cat. She said he ran from her, charred but fluidly shifting shapes before he disappeared. As Sam said, shifting seems to heal him. She cut off his hand, but when he shifted into the cat, he had all four feet."

"So," Vlad said, "he can be hurt but he also has the ability to heal at will. That should make killing him a challenge."

"Indeed," Clive agreed. "We also have the last five Guild Counselors not already in San Francisco arriving either tonight or tomorrow night."

"Coincidental or planned," I wondered aloud.

"If we didn't know that Aldith conspired with the fae king," Clive said, "I'd say it was coincidental. Now, though, I have no idea."

"I have to go," Vlad said. "Cadmael is motioning to me. If you need to get a hold of me again, text. I'm on a stakeout." The click was loud and clear. So too was the implied eyeroll.

Clive turned up our street and then drove under the rising garage door. He parked in my usual spot, opened my door so I wouldn't have to touch anything, and then the back door so Fergus could jump out. Clive unsnapped the pup's leash and led us to the elevator.

He took us to the first floor, as we were waiting for a visitor. Fergus ran out, straight to his water bowl. I went to open the back door and bumped into Clive, who took care of it.

"Have a seat, darling. We don't want you touching anything."

I was too wound up to sit, though. I went to the window and looked out for Dave's muscle car. Instead, I saw a black bird smash into the ward around our house. It dropped to the sidewalk and then stood as a cat. It gave its fur a quick shake before sitting, his gaze trained on the window I was looking out of. *Shit.*

"Clive?" I called.

"I saw." He moved in behind me, wrapping his arms around me. "Be right back."

He was gone out the back with my axe. A moment later, I saw him streak through the yard toward the cat, who shifted back into the black bird and was high in the air when Clive leapt, swinging the axe.

When Clive landed, the axe in his gloved hand glinted in the moonlight, blood-free. A moment later a full-throated engine roared around the corner. Clive stepped up onto the curb as Dave parked and got out. They spoke and then Dave and Clive were looking up into the sky. Clive headed for the front door, Dave behind him, so I met them, opening it.

"Hey."

Dave nodded as he walked by me. "Your new friend followed you home, huh?"

A chill ran down my spine as I noticed two eyes glowing from under a bush across the street. I closed the door and locked it, feeling sick to my stomach.

Clive returned the axe to my sheath and then pulled off the glove.

"Smart thinking," I told him.

Slipping the glove in his pocket, he wrapped his other arm around me. "I got the idea from Vlad. I didn't have it with me at the wharf, but I won't make that mistake again."

Dave was sitting in the den, so I went to close the back door. Clive pushed me toward the den and closed it himself.

"It doesn't matter anymore," I said, feeling the weight of our misses tonight dragging me down. "We know where he is, and we can't catch him."

He rubbed my back, leading me into the den. "Let's see. All information is helpful."

I sat on the couch beside Dave. He held out his hand for mine. Holding it steady, he focused on the blood under my fingernails.

"Claws," he grumbled.

I shifted that part of my body so my claws shot out. He knew to keep my hand pointed away from him. Again, he scrutinized them.

I felt something soft and hot on the tip of my middle finger, but it was gone before I even registered it. He'd dropped my hand as his eyes closed. The fingers on his right hand moved, almost in a faint echo of a forgotten spell.

Glancing at Clive, I found him glaring at Dave, his eyes vampy black. What?

When Dave finally opened his eyes, he was glaring right back at Clive. "You think I enjoy this? You asked me."

"That was before I knew you were going to lick my wife's finger." Clive was seething.

"Claw," Dave corrected.

Eww, that was what I'd felt? "Okay. Everyone stand down," I said mostly to Clive before turning back to Dave. "Did you learn anything?"

Dave collapsed into the cushions, resting his head on the back of the couch. He was reminding Clive that he was no threat. At least right now in this situation, he wasn't.

"Yeah," Dave said. "Definitely fae. I think I know what he is, but I'm not sure." He stretched his legs out and crossed them at the ankles. "He—"

My phone buzzed in my pocket. Who would be calling me so late? I checked the screen. Just a number, no name.

"Hello?"

"Hello, yes, is this Sam?" The voice sounded familiar but I couldn't place it.

"It is."

"Oh, good. We've spoken on the phone before, my dear."

Clive mouthed *Bracken.*

"Is this Bracken?" I asked.

"How clever you are! Yes, I'm your great-uncle Bracken. I just received a call from Arwyn. She said she had a dream about you being in trouble and thought I should call you. She wasn't sure why. She just thought you needed my help. So, what can I do for you?"

I put it on speakerphone and glanced between the men, both of whom shrugged *why not?*

"We could use your help. Thank you." I went through what had been happening and Dave's certainty that the killer was fae.

Bracken was silent. I glanced at Clive, who motioned handwriting back to me. I had excellent hearing, but Clive's was better. He could hear Bracken writing through the phone.

Bracken muttered quietly to himself. "Yes, yes. It's the only thing that makes sense. Well, given what you've told me, I think you might have a pooka on your hands."

Dave blew out a gust of breath and nodded. "That's the fucker's name. I couldn't come up with it."

Bracken paused.

"Oh, sorry! I forgot to tell you that both Clive and Dave are with me."

"Ah. I see. I remember Dave's voice now. It's good to speak with you again and I would still like to interview you. At your convenience, of course."

Dave rolled his eyes. "I'm kinda busy."

"Of course you are." Bracken responded, not the least bit put off by a snarly demon. "I'd be happy to go to you. I just purchased a new vehicle and would enjoy the drive."

"Yeah. Fine. Whatever," Dave rumbled.

"Splendid." Bracken cleared his throat. "Samantha, if this is a pooka in the human realm, I'm afraid we're in quite a lot of trouble."

I looked between Dave and the phone. "Okay, but what *is* a pooka?"

"Quite right," Bracken said. "I'm getting ahead of myself. A pooka is a malevolent fae spirit. He's a chaos agent."

"Wait," I interrupted. "A *spirit*? As in something ghosty that I could influence?"

"Unfortunately, no," he said, "though that would be handy. They often use the term spirit when describing a pooka because, I believe, no one is quite sure what the pooka's natural state is. It changes depending on who or what it's trying to devil. The odd thing is that pookas normally cause trouble. They don't kill. Some stories even cast them as agents of good. The fact that you, presumably, have one in the human realm, killing in the guise of a vampire, is really quite outside the bounds of what they normally do."

"Is there a special significance to killing in the style of a vampire?" Clive asked.

"Well, although he's killing now, his *raison d'etre*, as it were, is to cause mischief, chaos, problems. There were, I believe, quite a few vampire deaths in San Francisco a month or so ago—"

"How do you know that?" Clive asked.

"I have my ear to the ground, don't I?" he responded. "I heard rumblings, was interested, and began to research. Now, from what I've heard, the human authorities never found any of the dead. I was told that if bodies were left behind, they were disposed of before they could be discovered. This could be the pooka deciding that vampire victims should be found, so he'll make them himself."

"But that makes no sense," I interjected. "That was vampires warring with other vampires. They weren't killing innocents."

"We did have some in town feeding off humans," Clive said so quietly, I had trouble hearing him. "We'd need to ask Russell if any were killed."

"Russell?" Bracken asked.

Clive blinked, surprised he'd been overheard by a wicche.

"Yes. He's the Mast—"

Clive shook his head at me. Oops.

"Um, he's a vampire," I lamely finished.

There was more scribbling. Even I heard it that time.

"The Master of the City is a vampire named Russell," Bracken mumbled to himself.

I cringed and mouthed *Sorry* to Clive.

"I wonder if he'd allow me to interview him?" Bracken continued to mutter and scribble. "That's interesting, isn't it?" he said in a more normal voice. "Is he choosing to kill in that style because it is the vampires who lead the city? It's rather embarrassing, isn't it? The vampires are in charge and yet there's nothing they can do about one of their own who is a rogue. That's just the sort of chaos a pooka would feed on: vampires running around, trying to find what isn't there."

"Benvair said—"

"Benvair," he interrupted me. "Benvair. How do I know that

name?" He was mumbling to himself again. "Dragons!" he shouted, clearly just remembering. "She's the head of the Drake clan. My, you do know some very important people, don't you? Sorry. Please continue."

One side of Clive's mouth kicked up. My great-uncle was an interesting one.

"Benvair said when she breathed fire on it in its cat form, it was charred black but fluid. She thought it disappeared, but I'm thinking it shifted into something smaller and went between the wooden slats of the pier."

There was the sound of tapping. Dave mimed tapping a pen on paper. I nodded. Right. That was probably it.

"I think you're right, my dear. I've never heard of pookas having invisibility gifts."

We were all quiet, lost in our own thoughts, and then I asked, "Why the wharf? The vampire nocturne—" Clive shook his head again. "I mean, their nocturne is nowhere near the wharf. Why is he hunting there? I mean, it's a tourist spot, but there are lots of tourist spots in this city."

"You said the nightclub was fae-owned, didn't you?" he asked.

"Yes, but Nerissa, the club owner, is trying to stop him. He's bad for business."

"Tell me about the club, please?"

I did. I told him everything I knew, including that I'd fought a powerful vamp in there a few months ago. I wondered if Bracken had a wicchey gift for drawing out information. When he asked me a question, all I wanted to do was answer him in as much detail as I could. It was weird.

"Hmm. Sometimes—though they are loathe to admit it—when a large group of the fae are all together, they can inadvertently create a doorway into Faerie."

I thought about that mirror in the Wicche Glass Tavern, the fae bar in Colma that Bracken's sister, my great-aunt Martha had owned. It had a doorway into Faerie, one I'd used.

"If the pooka isn't connected to anyone at the club," he continued, "it's possible he just happened upon the doorway and is using it to create a little chaos."

Great.

EIGHTEEN

An Unpleasant Walk Through the Folly

"Let me do a little research," Bracken said. "I'll get back to you once I have something helpful."

"Thank you," I said and disconnected.

While Dave and Clive discussed the pooka possibility, I went to the dining room window and looked out on the dark, empty road and park beyond. I didn't see anything at first. The trees were blowing in the wind off the ocean, but I didn't see—there it was. A black cat sitting by the trunk of a huge tree, right between me and the bar entrance. *Shit.*

"Hey, Clive?"

Not a moment later, he wrapped his arms around my waist. "I see him."

"Oh. That statue cat over there?" Dave asked, looking out the kitchen window.

"Yep." It gave me the creeps.

"I know this is a big ask," Clive began, "but I need you to change how you get to work. No more running across the green and down the stairs. You and Fergus can go through the folly."

"And no jogging," Dave added. "It's too dangerous until we figure out how to kill him."

"And is there a reason the menfolk think they have a right to tell me what I can and can't do?" I was trying really hard not to be annoyed.

Clive kissed my ear. "Sorry, darling, but he has clearly taken an interest in you. He spoke to you, planned to kill you, and instead you cut off a hand and stabbed him in the chest."

I looked over my shoulder at him. "You just tried to slice him in half with my axe."

"Yes, and I missed." He tightened his arms around me. "I don't like it when deadly creatures take an interest in you."

Dave chuffed a laugh. "Pot. Kettle."

I gave him a dirty look, not that he noticed.

Clive kissed my neck. "That's my fear. Did my taking an interest in you alter the path of your life to a far more deadly one?"

I turned in his arms. "My sorcerer aunt was trying to kill me long before I met you. Then there was my—what—half cousin who attacked me. My life was messed up B.C. Before Clive." I went up on my toes and kissed him.

"I'm out of here," Dave muttered.

I broke away. "Wait. Not the front door. It's too obvious. If he wasn't watching when you arrived, there's no need for him to see you now." I pointed to the back door. "Go out that way, hop the wall, and then come around the corner, like you're leaving someone else's house."

"Yes," Clive said. "We'll watch from here. See if he moves."

Dave changed directions. "Fine." He left and a few minutes later jogged around the corner, got into his car, and drove away.

When I looked back at the green area for the cat, my heart stopped. The silhouette of a large, muscular bald man now stood beneath the tree.

Clive pulled me away from the window. "Please, love. Don't go out there. I'm bloody useless fifteen hours a day in the summer. Until we figure out how to deal with this thing, I need you to stay away from him."

I rubbed my hands up and down his arms. "Yeah. I can do that."

He kissed me. "Why don't you go to bed now. You need sleep. I'll contact Cadmael and Vlad. There's no point in them standing around the wharf when we know he's across the street."

I nodded and slapped my thigh. "Come on, Fergus. Let's go to bed." Unfortunately, it took a long time for me to finally fall asleep and when I did, I was plagued with nightmares about the pooka wearing my likeness to attack others.

I woke to my phone alarm buzzing. I rarely ever needed the alarm; I usually woke early on my own. Not today, though. I didn't think I finally slept peacefully until Clive came to bed right before dawn. Consequently, I was exhausted and pissed off that this damn pooka was having a grand old time being a murderous psycho. Asshole.

After dragging myself out of bed, I got cleaned up and dressed. Half asleep, I held onto the rail and made my way down the stairs. Fergus went to his water bowl and then sat, waiting for his food bowl to be filled.

"You look like hell."

I jumped, my heart stuttering to a stop before galloping out of control. Vlad sat in the darkest corner of the den, watching us. "What the flip, dude? Unlike some, I actually need my heart to work. Stop scaring the shit out of me."

I could swear I saw a smirk under that giant mustache. I remembered my dreams and took my axe out of the sheath as I moved toward him. "Tell me something only you and I know."

Tilting his head to the side, he watched me. "Oh, yes. Of course." He had Vlad's Romanian accent. "Clive and I killed every member of the Guild in Budapest."

I replaced my axe. "Shh. We don't need that getting out. Next time, pick a less top-secret detail." On an eye roll, I went back to the kitchen to feed Fergus.

I needed to eat something too, but I wasn't feeling great. Worrying and nightmares had messed with my appetite. I opened the back door for Fergus and then scanned the refrigerator for anything I thought my stomach could handle. Maybe I should have soup for breakfast.

I closed the fridge and then turned to the kitchen window, pushing up a slat of the closed blinds, letting in a shaft of sunlight. I scanned the front of the house and the green across the road.

There was no cat that I could see, but there was a woman sitting under the tree reading. A man jogged past, adjusting his headphones. And older man walked his dog up the road, moving past where I could track him. Was he any of these people? The dog, perhaps? I stared at the tree and saw a squirrel facing this direction. Was that him? Had he killed again last night?

"I thought werewolves needed to eat often," Vlad said from his corner. "Why aren't you eating?"

Ignoring his question and the sick feeling in my gut, I said, "He could be anyone. How—how do we kill something that can look like anyone, that can shift to heal whatever we manage to do to him?"

"Will we arrive at the answer to that question faster if you're tired and weak from hunger?" he asked in reply.

I shook my head, still staring out the window, and remembered why I felt so sick this morning. I'd had a dream where Clive approached me, but he was a little off. There was something not quite right. I'd thought he was the pooka and had swung for his head with my axe. There was a look of pain and shock and then a pile of vampire dust dropped to the floor at my feet.

When I woke, I assured myself Clive was fine. I knew he was sleeping, but I couldn't shake the horror of what I'd done in my nightmares. "How do I know who the bad guy is?" My stomach twisted, remembering the look of hurt and betrayal on my husband's face before he turned to dust.

"You should probably get something to eat, and we can discuss it," Vlad said.

Fergus trotted back in and I closed and locked the back door, closing the curtains so we were plunged into full dark. I went back to the kitchen, deciding Vlad was right. I pulled a few meat sticks out, took a bite, and slapped my thigh.

"Let's go to work, bud."

Vlad was suddenly blocking me. "You can't go out there. As you said, we have no idea which guise he's currently wearing. It's not safe for either of you."

I shook my head. "Real nice. Bring Fergus' safety into it to get your way. We're not going out the front," I told him. "We're heading in through the folly."

"Oh," he said, walking across the room to pop the door for the elevator. "Why didn't you say so? I'll go with you."

We took the elevator down to the garage and walked past a showroom of sports cars.

Vlad gestured to all the very expensive vehicles. "Does this concern you?"

I shook my head. "Clive loves cars. He told me that when one is as old as he is, it's easy to lose interest in everything. He calls these his weakness, but they're what bring him joy, so why not have as many as he wishes? I want him to be happy."

Vlad made one of his thoughtful *hmm*s. "Has he purchased one since you moved in?"

I paused to look around the garage. "I don't think so." I pointed to the insanely beautiful and expensive Mercedes-Maybach. "He bought me that one when we got married. I have yet to drive it." I shook my head. "I'm terrified of scraping it up. If I ever got locked out and have to sleep in the garage, though, I'm heading straight for that back seat. It's so insanely luxurious."

We went through the heavy metal door into the folly. On this end, it looked as though we were walking into a cave, the walls roughhewn, the ground appearing to be packed dirt. The tunnel twisted and turned before the first of the folly worlds opened up.

The smell of salt air and the roar of the surf filled the tunnel. Fergus ran onto the island, the ocean hitting the shore in the distance. He dug in the sand under the tall palm trees before running back to us. The dragon builders were magical. Did it make any logical sense that there was a huge, mountainous, tree-filled island with a vast ocean under our house? No, it did not. Was it here anyway? Yes, it was.

I knew that was not in fact a sunny blue sky above us. I knew I could turn a dial back in the tunnel and this sunny midday sunshine would fade into purple twilight, stars beginning to glitter in the sky. It was hard to believe it, though, as I stood here, smelling the salt air, feeling the ocean breezes and the sand beneath my feet.

This was where Cadmael stayed, lying on the beach under the sun for the first time in over two thousand years. Cadmael wasn't a day-walker, like Vlad. He was more like Clive. He was old and powerful enough to get up during the day, if need be, but his natural daytime state was rest.

We continued down the tunnel, eventually coming to the end, leading into Canterbury, England, one thousand years ago. Closest to the tunnel was the village center and the cathedral. Then there was a tavern, some cottages, and eventually fields and Clive's old family farm.

The builders had lately completed this world. Clive and I had sneaked in to explore last week when the dragons weren't looking. Holding my hand, we had walked to the village, while he told me stories of his childhood. The folly allowed me to see and feel his life, a life so far removed from mine as to seem like a fairy tale, but now he was able to share it with me. I'd never be able to thank the dragons enough.

Fergus sniffed at the meat sticks I had in my hand that I'd forgotten all about. I gave him one and Vlad made a *tsk*ing sound.

"What is with you and food today?" I asked.

"You don't take care of yourself," he said, sounding angry. "You're a wolf. You should be eating far more than you do. And what were you thinking going jogging in an area where he'd just killed a woman jogging with her dog?" He walked on, fuming. "You know he's terrified of losing you, don't you?

"You go on about his cars bringing him joy," his tirade continued. "And you don't even realize that he stopped buying them when he found you. They were a distraction from endless night. You are his love, his joy, his reason for upending his undeath so you wouldn't have to live in a nocturne filled with vampires who make you uncomfortable. *You* are his weakness. And you—you race into danger and don't take care of yourself!" He was shouting by the end, and I felt it like a punch in the gut.

NINETEEN

I'm Not Feeling Hopeful

We continued through the folly in silence, eventually entering the Shire, the first of the worlds the dragons had built. My mother had introduced me to Tolkien when I was a child. Every time I walked through the Shire, I felt close to her and to the world I had escaped into when we were on the run.

I didn't respond to Vlad right away. I wanted to think about his words and his anger. Vlad had lost his beloved wife, a werewolf, so I understood the rage over what he saw as my carelessness.

"Do you know my story?" I finally asked.

He glanced at me, one shoulder twitching. "Bits and pieces."

"I'll give you the condensed version," I told him as we walked down the center path of Middle Earth. "My mother was a Corey wicche and my father a Quinn wolf. Star-crossed lovers that neither family accepted, though the Quinn side was far more hostile."

"Werewolves," Vlad said, as though that explained everything, and perhaps it did.

"My grandfather, Alexander Quinn, hated wicches and wouldn't stand for his son marrying one. He banished my father after he married my mother. Not long after I was born, my dad was killed." I turned to Vlad. "I still don't know the story there. I think anyone who might know is dead. Anyway, my assumption is that my mother's sister Abigail killed him. She was a sorcerer, jealous of my mother's magical talent, and incensed about my mother sullying the pure Corey line with a werewolf abomination.

"One of my first memories is her trying to drown me in the tub. My mother smashed a vase over her sister's head, grabbed me from the tub, and ran. I spent the rest of my childhood on the run, my mom trying to keep us a few steps ahead of her sister, trying to keep me alive. My mother was a very strong and gifted wicche, but this took a toll on her. She used much of her magic to keep us hidden. When that didn't seem to be holding, she made me a pendant, pouring her magic into it, so that she could keep me away from her sister. It dampened both my wicche and wolf natures. I had no idea we were magical, no idea she was a wicche, until last year.

"Money was tight. We stayed in rundown rentals in seedy parts of town. Sometimes we stayed for a couple of months and I started at a local school, but more often than not, Mom felt her sister closing in and we were running in the middle of the night again."

I stopped at a pond, taking in the beautiful green hills, the doors to the hobbit houses in the distance. "When I was seventeen, Mom said it was time to go again. I wanted to stay. We'd been there a couple of months and graduation was coming up. I was hardly ever in school long enough to complete courses, but I was smart, worked hard, and did well on tests. It was stupid, but I wanted this one thing."

I shook my head, staring into the water, angry with myself all over again. "I wanted to graduate. I wanted one normal thing. Mom gave in—I rarely ever asked for anything. Abigail found us. Mom hid me in a closet, using her magic to keep me from her sister's notice. Abigail called up her demon to cut my mother to shreds. I couldn't move, but I watched it happen, unable to help.

"I was alone after that. I didn't know anything about my

mother or father's families, so when a man found me and told me he was my father's brother and he wanted me to live with him, I went. I didn't know what else to do. He took me to the Santa Cruz Mountains, to his pack grounds.

"It was okay at first. I didn't know about werewolves. I thought they were just outdoorsy people. One night I was attacked. Taken. I woke blindfolded and chained in a shack in the woods. Sometimes he was a man, sometimes a wolf. I was raped and beaten, cut, bitten, slashed. It lasted forever. Or a day and a half, depending on whether or not you were the one being tortured. When I was found, my uncle didn't know what to do with me, so he sent me to San Francisco to stay with a wicche he said was a friend of my mother's.

"Clive told the supernatural community that I was under his protection—not that I knew that at the time—and he eventually helped me plan and open The Slaughtered Lamb. I hid. For seven years I hid in my bookstore and bar, too afraid to engage with the world. It was only last year, a little less than a year, that all the craziness started again. That pendant my mother made me when I was a child was destroyed and Abigail found me."

I picked a flower by the pond's edge, marveling at how realistic it was. "I've been running and hiding most of my life." I met Vlad's gaze. "It's still hard for me, but I won't do it anymore. I won't hide, hoping the scary things leave me alone, because I end up missing all the good things too. I wouldn't have Clive if I hadn't come out of hiding. I wouldn't have my home, Fergus, my friends.

"Clive understands all of this and as much as it may scare him, he encourages me to stand on my own two feet and fight what comes at me. He'll be there right beside me, but he won't hide me away again. So, while I understand your concern, and I thank you for it, I won't retreat and let everyone else take all the risks. I may not be a day-walking vampire or a two-thousand-year-old Mayan warrior, but I do have unique gifts that make me useful."

I moved back to the path and he followed me, continuing our walk. "I normally eat more, but I had really upsetting nightmares and my stomach is tied in knots today. I went out last night because I'm not defenseless. I've been trained in hand-to-hand combat and know how to use my axe. I'm better able to fight this monster than a human. We needed information, so I went in search of it. Regardless of what you think of my abilities, I'm neither weak nor stupid. If I hadn't gone for a run, we wouldn't know anywhere near as much as we do now. You all would probably still believe it was a contingent of vampires who want to come out to the world."

I shrugged. "Be angry, if you'd like, but you're not the boss of me."

Vlad didn't respond, but he walked beside me. By the time we made it to my apartment, I expected him to stop. He didn't. He followed me into the kitchen. Dave was already there, his head in the refrigerator.

I turned back to Vlad. "What are you doing?" I pointed at the door to the bar. "The sun is right on the other side of that swinging door. What are you, a daredevil?"

Dave had turned at our arrival and was now leaning against the counter, watching us.

Vlad tipped his head toward Dave. "Get out your axe and ask him a question."

Shit. I hadn't stopped to consider— "He's not wearing his glamour. The pooka wouldn't know what he really looks like."

Vlad nudged me and I rolled my eyes, pulling out my axe, pointing it at Dave. "Who's your dad?"

Dave looked back and forth between Vlad and me. "You know who my fucking dad is. How do you know this little asshole isn't the killer?"

I blew out a breath and returned the axe to its sheath.

The kitchen door swung in, Owen and bright sunlight entering the kitchen. I shouted as Dave moved to block Vlad, but then we both realized he wasn't there. I ducked my head back through the ward into my apartment. Vlad was sitting on the couch, a book in his hand.

Shaking my head, I turned to tell a very confused Owen that everything was fine. "It turns out that when faced with fiery death, vampires are quite fast. Anyway, how are you?"

Owen looked between the two of us and then shook his head, no doubt deciding it wasn't worth asking. "I'm fine, but last night sounded insane. Did Benvair really let loose a plume of fire out in the open?"

I tipped my head from side to side. "Sort of, but not really. Did she breathe fire? Yes, she did. Out in the open? Not so much. We were on a deserted pier, behind a churros stand. I mean, someone could have been looking out their window at the exact right time to see it, but it's doubtful."

"Crazy," Owen said. He turned, scanning the counters. "Are the bars gone?"

"Oh!" I grabbed Dave's arm. "Tell me you saved the last of them?"

He went to the fridge. "You two are nuts." He pulled out the plate and slid it onto the island. Owen and I fell on them like hyenas.

After I finished one and claimed a second one, I paused. "Owen, do you know anything about pookas?"

He finished chewing and then swallowed, shaking his head. "What's a pooka?"

I told him about our conversation with Bracken last night and then told Dave about the pooka stealing his likeness.

"Great," Dave grumbled.

Owen looked longingly at the last bar and then checked the time on his phone. "We need to open." He pushed out into the bar while I finished the second one. I eyed the last bar, wondering if I had it in me.

Dave picked up the plate and put it back in the fridge. "No. You're going to make yourself sick. Go to work." He shooed me away. "I'm busy."

Fergus stayed with Dave, hoping for handouts, while I went to the bookstore to finish processing the new books.

It wasn't long before Meri showed up, all smiles. She stowed her bag and then went to work shelving the new books. We'd been working together for a while before it occurred to me. Meri was half fae.

"Meri?"

She looked up from shelving the new psychology books.

"Do you know anything about pookas?"

Flinching, she dropped the books in her hands. "Pookas?" she whispered.

I nodded. "What do you know about them?"

She glanced over her shoulder and then out the window into the ocean as she came behind the counter to stand right beside me. "You should never talk about them," she whispered. "They're evil."

I remembered what my great-uncle had said. "I thought they were mischief makers, chaos agents, not evil."

She looked like she was afraid we were about to be attacked. "That was long ago and in Faerie. The ones that made it into this realm..." She shivered. "My father used to tell me about them when I was little. You know, like, *You better do what your mother says or the pooka will steal you.*"

"So they're something the fae use to scare their children?" I asked.

She shook her head. "They're real. I asked my father about them—I used to have nightmares—and he said when the pookas arrived in this realm a few hundred years ago, they didn't start out killing. Humans are easy to kill, though, and their emotions are so much stronger than the fae's. Pookas got a little drunk off it. It wasn't just chaos. There was grief and anger, fear and suspicion. It was exciting and they began to crave it, like a drug.

"The queen's guard came to this realm to hunt them down. Pookas could not be trusted to live amongst the humans. It's not just that they have no concept of right and wrong, it's that they don't care about secrecy. Humans learning about—or even guessing at the existence of—the fae just adds to the confusion and fear. They terrorize a community, glut themselves, and then move on to do it all again."

A chill went down my spine. "If we have one now, I assume that means the queen's guard couldn't hunt them all down." If Algar and his warriors couldn't do it, how were we supposed to?

TWENTY

Scuttlebutt

_____

M eri's gaze went to the window. She waved and then pointed to the bar. "That's my dad. Let me ask if he knows how to fight them." She ran off and I was left wondering how we could possibly corner and kill a powerful shape-shifter.

Owen brought me a cup of tea. "Hey, boss. Looks like you're almost done with this order."

I nodded and took a sip.

"The scuttlebutt around town is that we have vampires visiting soon." He looked apprehensive. "It won't be like last time, right? No battles in the streets?"

I moved a finished stack of books to the shelving cart. "No. It shouldn't be." I glanced up. "Whose scuttlebutt? I thought it was super hush-hush?"

He grinned and waggled his eyebrows. "I have my sources."

"But how would George know?" I asked.

Owen gave me a disgruntled look. "Listen, sister, I've lived in this town a lot longer than you. I know people." At my blank stare, he rolled his eyes and said, "Fine. Dave told me."

I pulled the last stack of books out of the shipping box and Owen began to break it down. "How did he—" I remembered that someone at the nocturne had asked Dave to check out the crime

125

scene at The Bubble Lounge. If that someone was Godfrey, he probably would have blabbed. "Never mind. Dave knows lots of people too."

Meri returned from the bar, looking dejected. "He says he doesn't know of any way to stop them. He thinks there were originally three pookas free in this realm. He heard that the queen's guard captured two of them."

She bit her lip. "The thing is, though, they really are seen as a kind of fae boogeyman, so he doesn't know what's real and what's made up. He said, though, that he might know someone who does."

Her expression brightened. "I told him everything you've done for me—getting rid of that man and helping me buy a car. I think he's decided he owes you. If he can, he'll find the answer."

I put down the book I was inventorying. "You know you don't owe me anything, right? No one's keeping score."

She gave a quick shake of her head. "You don't know my dad. He won't stand for being indebted. Chances are he won't learn anything you don't already know, but it's worth him trying, right?"

"Absolutely." I reached out and squeezed her hand. "Please thank him for me. We need all the help we can get."

"Good," she said on a decisive nod before picking up a stack of books and continuing to shelve.

Owen and Meri ended their shifts at the same time, so he was able to walk her to her car. So far, the creepy stalker hadn't returned. I didn't want to dim her joy, but I did remind her before she left to keep an eye out. Obsession was pretty powerful, even in the face of fear.

Fyr, Dave, and I worked the evening shift. I'd go home soon, but not yet. The sun wasn't down, so Clive was still sleeping. Working helped to distract me from our current problem.

At a little after nine, Fyr left to start his shift at the Viper's Nest, and I went behind the bar. It was a quiet night. There were only two occupied tables, with five people in total. Two were drinking beers and the other three had a fresh pot of tea. Dave would take over for me when I left, but for now, he was baking in the kitchen.

I was sitting on my stool behind the bar, a book in my lap, but I couldn't focus enough to read. I watched the dark water smash against the window, the sky purpling, and I worried that he was out there now, wearing a stolen face and plotting his next kill.

I was so distracted, I didn't realize we had two more people in the bar until a pair of strong arms wrapped around me and I felt a kiss by my ear. Glancing past Clive's shoulder, I saw Vlad sitting on a stool. Unfortunately, the other patrons noticed him too. They had a good healthy fear of Clive, but they also seemed to recognize that he'd never attack them. They did not give Vlad that same trust.

"Good evening, darling. How has your day been?"

I stood so I could hug him properly. "I'm okay. Just worried," I said into his shirt. "It's better now, though."

He kissed the top of my head.

I looked up at the sound of Dave's heavy boots. He shoved a meatball sandwich on a plate at me.

"I already ate."

"So eat again," he grumbled, heading back to the kitchen.

I glared at Vlad, who seemed unusually interested in the state of his pristine shirt sleeve.

"Don't play innocent. I know this was you."

Clive rubbed my back. "You've been putting in a lot of late nights. No point in wasting food."

The concern in Clive's gaze made me pick up the sandwich and take a big bite.

"Darling, we need to go to the nocturne. Visitors have arrived."

I waved to the last of my customers heading up the stairs.

"The thing is," Clive continued, "the pooka knows where we live. I don't feel comfortable leaving you home all alone."

I swallowed a second big bite. "We're warded up. I'll be fine."

"Yes," he said, his hand on my back, "but wouldn't you like to visit Russell, Godfrey, and Audrey? I know they've missed you."

"You should probably bring the dog too," Vlad put in. "Just to be safe."

I took another bite while I glared at the interfering busybody. To Clive, I asked, "Would it make you feel more comfortable if I was in a nocturne filled with bloodthirsty vampires?"

Grinning, he gave me a kiss. "It really would."

"Fine. It's not like I have any customers left anyway." They followed me back to the kitchen. I rinsed off the plate and put it in the washer. "Dave, the mustachioed one cleared us out again, so you can head home whenever you want."

He nodded, crouched in front of the oven, staring through the glass front. "I have some baking to finish. I'll leave when I'm done." He paused. "Are the wards closed?"

I set the wards with a thought. They were tied to me. "They are now." I led the way into my apartment, where Fergus was lying on the couch, his feet up in the air. "Come on, buddy. We're going to go visit Daddy's vampy friends."

"That word." Clive took my hand and we ran back through the folly to our home, Fergus at our heels.

Once there, I got cleaned up, made up, and stood in the closet, considering. I wanted to make a good impression for Clive but also wanted to fade into the background for me.

"Clive?" I knew he was in the sitting area of our bedroom, waiting for me.

"Yes?"

I ducked my head out and saw him scratching behind Fergus' ears with one hand while he texted with the other. He put the phone down and looked up at me, waiting.

"What's the protocol? You're not the Master anymore, but now you *are* a Counselor. Which is higher up the chain, right?" I glanced over my shoulder into the closet and then back at him. "I mean, am I even meeting the bigwigs? Do I need to dress like I used to for formal gatherings, or will I just head straight to Russell's office?"

He lifted an eyebrow. "Do you honestly believe I would shuffle you away somewhere hidden and not show you off?" He stood, tutting as he moved to me. "Wear whatever you want. You don't need to follow our protocols. You know that." He gave me a kiss.

His eyes went vampy black. "You know what I've missed?" His hands settled on my hips. "How about your leathers?"

Grinning, I pushed him away. "Nuh-uh. We'd never make it out of the house." I went back into the closet. "Besides, those were destroyed in New Orleans."

Proving he is an excellent hunter, he walked past me and went straight to the drawer holding a pair of battered leather pants. He gave me a look that had me unbelting my robe.

"We don't have time for this," Vlad shouted from downstairs.

I slammed my eyes shut, hoping to hide from the embarrassment.

"Bugger off and wait in the garage," Clive snarled, wrapping his arms around me and nuzzling my neck.

"No way," I whispered. "They can hear everything. Go go go. I'll figure it out." I pushed until he finally relented.

"I'll go kill Vlad and then I'll be back," he grumbled.

"If you kill him, you'll just have to find yet another replacement." I surveyed all the dresses I had—and there were a lot—looking for the right mix of understated and chic. Ugh. I just wanted to be comfortable and look decent. Was that too much to ask?

I was leaning toward a summer-weight little black dress but then remembered how cold the nocturne was. Clive put up the heat for me, but I wasn't there anymore. Vampires didn't feel the cold, so they didn't bother. Poor Norma, the human liaison who worked during the day, had a space heater in her office.

I found a garment bag hanging in the corner that I hadn't noticed before. It looked as though Godfrey was still shopping for me. For the longest time, I'd thought Clive had been picking out my new clothes. Apparently, it was Godfrey—and occasionally Audrey— who enjoyed shopping for me. At least they had good taste.

It was a long, knit column, with thick, uneven bands of horizontal color in sea green, teal, silver, violet, midnight. It would definitely make more of a statement than I'd intended, but it was so pretty and soft.

I tried it on and then chose a pair of midnight blue stilettos to go with it. I looked in the mirror, trying to decide. It was very body conscious, form-fitting from my neck to my calves, but I was also completely covered. I put on the blue diamond earrings that matched my wedding ring and found a small handbag that matched.

When I went into the bedroom, Clive was back in the chair waiting for me. He moved toward me, his gaze seeming to eat me alive. And then I was crushed against him, and he was kissing me like our lives depended on it.

Eventually, he drew back. "You look gorgeous, love." His hand brushed up and down my back. "I haven't seen this one. It's perfect on you." His eyes lit with mischief. "My only complaint is this high neck."

It hit the underside of my jaw. One of his fingers pushed it down to trace my throat before he leaned forward to kiss it. When he pulled back, his eyes were dark.

"Come, love," he said, taking my hand. "We should go now."

Fergus popped up from his bed and followed us to the elevator. We went down to the garage, where we found Vlad and Cadmael standing beside the Mercedes-Maybach. The body of the sedan was dark green with a silver hood, roof, and trunk. It was a sleek work of art that cost six figures and I was scared to death of wrecking it.

"Your lovely wife sung the praises of this one and now I'd like a ride." Vlad said, smirking at my discomfort.

Clive lifted the hand holding mine, kissed my wrist, and walked me to the back door, opened it, and helped me in. The leather was buttery soft. Instead of one back bench, there were two seats that felt like a sumptuous cloud and a leather recliner had a love child.

I sat and swiveled in, reclining back into a cozy leather cuddle. Granted, the axe on my back kind of wrecked the whole soft-as-a-cloud thing. When Vlad opened the opposite door, Fergus jumped in, trying to find a comfortable place to sit between Vlad and me. He settled his butt on the floor, with the majority of him across my lap.

Clive and Cadmael slid into the front seats. Clive started the engine, and it purred to life. "I'd planned to take one of the SUVs, but this is a much better idea." He adjusted the rearview mirror and smiled back at me. "Sorry we don't have Champagne this time."

Clive and I had ridden in a car just like this on our honeymoon. The driver had left us two glasses of Champagne in the back. I smiled, remembering those magical days in Paris.

"Are they all here?" Cadmael asked, distracting me from memories of strolls along the Seine.

"Yes." Clive drove us out of the garage and onto the road. "Godfrey texted that the last has just arrived."

I turned in my seat, looking for a cat—or anyone, really—too fixated on the house or this car. Nothing. Where was the pooka, and what was he up to?

TWENTY-ONE

Everyone Has Their Suspicious Squinty Eyes on Us

It wasn't a long drive to the nocturne, but I spent it scanning for what might be the pooka before I remembered where we were going.

"So, who am I meeting tonight?" I asked from the back seat.

"Ahmed and Adaeze are the African Counselors," Clive explained. "Joao and Pablo are the South American Counselors. And Thi is the last remaining Asian Counselor. Each will, of course, arrive with an entourage of underlings. No one travels alone."

"For good reason," Vlad added.

"True," Clive agreed.

"And do we know all of these people?" I asked. "Are they cool?"

Vlad scoffed at that description but didn't respond.

"I've met all of them," Clive said. "Some I know better than others. Ahmed is Egyptian and I probably know him best. He is very old, has immensely strong mesmerizing abilities, and is—as much as any of us are—quite honorable."

Cadmael gave a grunt of agreement.

"Joao is Brazilian and innately charming. He uses that charm to disarm. Vampires who are older and should know better often fall into the trap of sharing more than they should with him. It may seem as though he's merely chatting to pass the time, but he is paying attention to every detail and storing it for future use.

"And Thi, I met in Vietnam perhaps two hundred years ago. She is quiet and easy to underestimate. One does so at their own peril. She is deadly and they never see her coming."

Cadmael nodded.

"The other two," Clive continued, "I've only met briefly." He looked in the rearview mirror and to his right. "What about either of you? Do you know Adaeze or Pablo?"

"Pablo, yes," Cadmael said. "Climber. Ruthless." He shrugged a shoulder. "Vampire."

My phone buzzed in my bag. I had a new text.

Godfrey: Visit me now.

Me: We're on our way...

I waited but there was no response.

Clive's gaze flicked to me in the rearview mirror. "Problem?"

"I don't know. Godfrey texted me to visit him right now." I looked around. "We're here."

The gates were just closing behind the car. Clive drove to the far side of the courtyard and parked. Voice low, he murmured, "He's not asking us to hurry up. Find him in your head. See what we're walking into."

I tipped my head back against the cushion, closed my eyes, and looked for the dead, or the undead, as the case may be. Three strong green blips with me and a concentration of far more close by. I zeroed in on the nocturne and found Godfrey quickly. He and Russell were almost as familiar to me as Clive.

I pushed on his blip. *You rang?*

Bloody hell! I'm waiting for it, and it still creeps me out when you do this. Yes. I rang. Audrey and I are picking up on some weird vibes with these Counselors. They're strangely suspicious of us. We're just hosting.

We've done this countless times for other groups over the centuries. Normally, the hosting nocturne is treated like a hotel. We're here to facilitate, but the meeting has nothing to do with us, so we go about our business.

What's different this time? I asked.

Audrey says Thi, the Asian Counselor, is hiding some very strong hostility. Thi is quiet and hasn't done anything unusual, but Audrey says she's seething. The Master thinks they're too interested in Clive and whether or not you're joining him. He told me to contact you, tell you not to come. It doesn't feel safe for you, missus.

Unfortunately, we're already here. I'll let the guys know. Thank you.

I relayed our conversation to the men in the car.

"I wondered at the time," Vlad began. "There were a lot of vampires in that training room in Budapest when Cadmael decided to expose you to everyone." The look he shot the back of Cadmael's head was dark. "A message could have gone out before we quieted them all. I meant to check phones, but—"

"It couldn't have been done," I told him. "How were you planning to unlock phones and check while we were dealing with a possessed vampire and bombs?"

"I'll take you home," Clive said, restarting the engine. "Maybe ask Dave to stay with you while I'm out." He was mostly talking to himself as he put the car in reverse.

"Clive, stop."

Guards appeared at the doors, trying to open them for us.

Clive slid down the window an inch. "A moment," he said, sounding aloof and far too important. The guards stepped back from the vehicle.

Voice so quiet it wouldn't be heard outside the confines of the vehicle, he caught my eyes in the mirror and said, "I'm not taking you into a possible ambush."

I held up a hand, trying to settle him. "First of all, we're already here. Everyone knows we're already here. Leaving now will just add fuel to the suspicion fire. Second, we need to know what they know and what—if anything—was passed on. I don't cherish looking over my shoulder for the rest of my life. Third, I want to meet these people. I can pick up a lot when I'm with them. Plus, once you guys meet me, you never think I'm actually dangerous."

"She has a point there," Vlad said.

I gave him a dirty look. He didn't have to agree so quickly. "And let's not forget, I can hold my own against vampires."

Cadmael gave a grunt of annoyance. "Vampires or pooka. Decide. We can't sit in this car all night."

"But if we did," I pointed out, "wouldn't it be super comfortable?" I looked at Vlad, whose mustache twitched. "Clive, this is silly. I'm the only one around with a heartbeat. They know I'm here. Let's just go. Besides, it's not like you lot couldn't kill them all."

"But then we'd have even more positions to fill," Cadmael groused.

"Stay where you are," Clive ordered. "You don't open your own door." He got out and opened my door, while the guards opened Cadmael and Vlad's.

Take no chances, love, and stick to my side. Clive wrapped his arm around me and the four of us made our way to the nocturne entry, Fergus on my other side.

Unlike most vampires, Audrey, Russell's second in command, didn't wear black. I loved that about her. My guess was she knew it was too harsh against her pale English complexion. Instead, tonight she wore a soft dusty rose blazer over a silver top and charcoal slacks. Her long blonde hair was coiled into a perfect chignon at the back of her head. Big blue eyes assessed our group as we approached where she stood by the open front door.

In life, Audrey had been a lady's maid. She'd been turned about two hundred and fifty years ago when the lady in question didn't want to lose a servant and so killed and turned her. Audrey had no idea she'd been working for a vampire, and one with the strong mental skills to keep Audrey mesmerized, chained to her and under her power. Audrey had only recently shaken off the shackles and was now living a more independent undeath, which included choosing her own clothes in colors and designs she enjoyed.

When Russell became the Master, he'd asked Audrey to be his second. Godfrey didn't want the job. He much preferred being a third. Less was expected of him, which suited him just fine. Russell had recognized in Audrey someone he could trust. Her integrity made her an easy choice for second. Though she was not new to being a vampire, she was new to exploring her own innate skills. Like others in her line, she too had strong mental gifts. In her case, she was able to sense the emotions of those around her.

Audrey inclined her head to our party. "You are welcome to the San Francisco nocturne. Our Master Russell is inside. Please join us and slake your thirsts." She smiled at me, touching my sleeve and whispering, "This dress is gorgeous on you." She fiddled with my hair. "It's lovely, ma'am, though I want to put it up for you. I think that would look better with the line of the dress."

We were whispering, but I knew all the vampires could hear us, so I said, "Maybe once they start their meetings, you can fix it for me. You know I can't do fancy things with my hair."

"I'd be right pleased, ma'am." She started to walk ahead and then paused, leaning into me again. "Oh, and Godfrey has a soda for you."

"Thank you."

One of the nocturne's vampires appeared with a tray holding goblets of blood for the vampires. Clive had been handed a poisoned cup of blood in Budapest, so this whole situation made me nervous. He sniffed the blood and then glanced at me, letting me know it was safe.

Godfrey appeared at my elbow. "Good evening, missus." After passing me a glass of soda, he leaned in, scratched behind Fergus' ears, and said, "I found a new one of those unexplained mystery shows for us to watch tonight."

"Oh, good. We can do that while Audrey fixes my hair." I took a sip and glanced around. Audrey and Godfrey had done what they could to make me seem harmless. It was my turn to try to discover if any of the many vampires surrounding us were plotting against me or mine.

"Good evening, my lady," Russell said, his deep voice settling my nerves. Russell, a tall and very handsome Black man, was now the Master of San Francisco. He had been Clive's second for at least a hundred years. Relatively speaking, he wasn't as old as many of the vampires present, not as old as his second or third, but he had a strength of character that made people want to follow him.

"Is it okay to hug the Master?" I asked.

His face broke into a heart-stopping smile. He opened his arms, and I walked into them. I'd missed him. It was a short hug. Vampires didn't really do displays of affection. The way Clive always kept his arm around me was unusual for vamps.

Speaking of which, Clive's arms wrapped around my waist. "Russell, it's good to see you. May I steal my wife? I'd like to introduce her to some people."

Russell inclined his head and moved back to confer with Audrey.

Clive walked us over to two people standing together. Gesturing to a rather severe-looking man with dark hair and almost black eyes, he said, "Ahmed, this is my wife Sam. Darling, this is my friend Ahmed."

I beamed. "Hello. It's lovely to meet you."

He smiled and his resting I'm-going-to-rip-your-heart-out expression transformed into an open, handsome face, complete with a dimple. "It's good to finally meet you. I think we have all heard about the little wolf who tamed the ancient vampire."

Laughing, I whispered, "Shh. He's very sensitive about the ancient part." I turned to the woman beside him. She was a stunning Black woman in a dark silvery gray dress that went to the floor with an elaborate gele head wrap in the same color.

She held out her hand to me. Vampires don't shake, but she knew I wasn't one and so was being polite. "I am Adaeze." She smiled and I felt warmth run through me. She had gifts I needed to think about and prepare for. "Even in Nigeria," she told me, "we have heard stories of the little wolf."

In these heels, I was close to Clive's height. "I think you mean the very tall wolf."

Chuckling, Clive kissed my temple. "They mean one who is young and new to our world."

"Oh," I said, tipping my head back and forth. "Fair."

"I hope your journey here wasn't problematic," Clive inquired.

Ahmed nodded. "Travel is always tricky, as you know. It is our winter, but your summer. A fifteen-hour flight is difficult to coordinate, though, at any time of the year when trying to avoid the sun. We ended up spending most of the day in a hangar until the sun went down." He glanced at Adaeze. "This is important, though. We have quite a mess to clean up."

"We had that problem flying to Budapest," I told them. Vampires are quiet talkers, but the room got even quieter when I mentioned Budapest. Godfrey and Audrey were right. All these vamps were on edge about Hungary. "We left at night, flew all day, and then landed right before sunrise. It was touch and go as to whether the driver could get us back and inside on time."

They're all thinking about it, I told Clive. *We might as well bring it up.*

I agree.

"And how did you enjoy Budapest?" Adaeze asked. Her expression read politely interested but it was a mask. I felt her intensity like a punch.

"Oh, well. The town itself was gorgeous. I went for lots of walks and had some amazing meals. The Guild house had been remodeled. It was scary and decrepit on the outside but beautifully opulent on the inside. My issue was that there were no windows—understandably so. It felt claustrophobic to me. And the only way out during the day was down a long, creepy tunnel." I gave a shudder. "Then we had that crazy fae guy messing with everyone." I shook my head. "The town? Ten out of ten. The rest? I do not recommend."

"Thankfully, Sam missed most of what went on. Her sleep schedule and jet lag meant she slept through the worst of it," Clive murmured.

"What did happen?" Ahmed asked, his brow furrowed and dimple gone.

Clive glanced around the crowded entry and said, "Let's discuss it in our meeting."

Ahmed nodded, though he didn't look happy.

TWENTY-TWO

It Would Be So Much Easier If We All Just Spoke the Same Language

Clive checked his watch. "Let me introduce Sam to the others and then she can chat with her friends while we meet. Oh, darling," Clive said just to me, "take the keys. You and Fergus don't need to stay all night. We can get home easily enough on our own."

I opened the top of my small bag, feeling the interest of those around me. A phone and lip gloss were obviously disappointing for some. Clive dropped the keys in and gave me a kiss. Personally, I thought we were killing this whole I'm-harmless-and-we-have-nothing-up-our-sleeves thing.

"Please excuse us," Clive said to Ahmed and Adaeze before walking me over to a group of three. "Good evening. Allow me to introduce my wife, Samantha. Sam, this is Joao and Pablo. They are the Counselors for South America. And this is Thi. She is the Counselor for Asia." Clive turned back to the three. "It's good to see you all, though I wish it was under better circumstances."

Joao was quick to smile, his dark eyes dancing as he reached out to shake my hand. I took it and only felt curiosity from him. The man was a heartbreaker. Pablo, less so. He wasn't ugly exactly, just severe to the point of discomfort. His gaze ran up and down my body once with a look of mild distaste before his focus was back on Clive.

I felt Clive's arm stiffen around me. He hadn't missed the slight.

Let it go, I told him.

I turned to Thi and felt her hate like a blast of hot air. She showed no outward emotion, but it was roiling under the surface. "Hello. Lovely to meet you," I said.

Her lips tipped up in the approximation of a smile, but her eyes were cold and empty. "And you," she responded.

"Darling." Clive squeezed me around the middle and let go. "I'm afraid we need to start our meeting now."

"Of course." I kissed him on the cheek and then glanced at the other three. "Have a nice meeting."

Joao grinned at this, but neither Pablo nor Thi bothered to look in my direction. Both turned to the underlings hovering behind them to speak in hushed tones too quiet for me to make out.

Russell walked back into the center of the entry. "We have a conference room downstairs, as well as gathering rooms for your people. If you'd prefer, though, we've set up a table in the library, which I thought you might find more pleasant. It's up to you, of course, where you'd like to meet."

Godfrey stepped up beside Russell. "While the Counselors decide, I'll show everyone else our facilities." Grinning, he gestured to the twenty or so underlings to follow him. "Come along. You'll be comfortable and entertained while we wait."

Godfrey had a way with people. He looked like the cover model of a historical romance, but it was the twinkle in his eye, the ready smile, that made him so effective. This is why he was third. No one would believe a second didn't have ulterior motives when he went to watch a football game with the other vamps. Godfrey had mastered an I'm-hiding-from-work-no-one-tell-the-Master façade. He was funny and irreverent, disarming people and discovering information people didn't even realize they'd uncovered.

He played up his reputation, but I would trust Godfrey with my life. When it came right down to it, he'd do anything for the people he cared about. Right now, though, what all the assistants saw was an activities director, not the warrior he was. And that was fine with him. "Come along, you lot. I have some crap TV to watch."

The assistants checked with their Counselors, who nodded, and then followed along in Godfrey's wake.

"The library is right down this hall, if you'd like to see it before you decide," Russell said.

"Bummer," I whispered to Audrey. "I wanted to hang out in there tonight."

Thi's eyes flicked to us before she inclined her head to Russell, an indication he should show them the way. The eight Counselors followed in Russell's wake, with Vlad taking up the rear. He glanced at me and rolled his eyes. I suppressed a grin in case anyone turned around.

"S'allright, ma'am," Audrey said. "You used to fancy the blue salon. We can go there."

Once the library door closed, I let out a breath. Audrey waved me into Russell's office, where she closed the doors and hit the button on the sound system, filling the room with low bluesy music.

She pointed to one of the visitor chairs and mouthed the word *sit*. When I did, she whispered in my ear, "You go ahead and do your thing. I'll work on your hair."

Nodding, I closed my eyes, found the green blips in my head, and checked first on the assistants downstairs. They wouldn't be as strong as the Counselors and might know sensitive information. There were a lot of them. On a sigh, I began.

The assistants or underlings or whatever they were called—I'd need to ask someone—didn't talk to each other. Godfrey was showing them around, but none of them seemed to care. They stayed in five distinct groups and peeled off from one another into different sections of the underground. Joao's people were in the music room. Pablo's were in the training room. Thi's were in the lounge. Ahmed's were in the kitchen. Adaeze's were in the TV room, ignoring the baseball game on the screen. A few of Russell's vamps were watching the replay of the game, but Adaeze's group stood in the corner, speaking another language.

Shit. Language again. This was just like the ghosts in Budapest. I didn't speak any of these languages. How was I supposed to know what they were thinking? I needed to start some intense language courses because this was pointless.

Before giving up, though, I checked on Thi's group. As she was the one who seemed to actively hate me, I decided to try something. I went to each of her four people and pushed an image of myself, dressed as I was tonight, into their minds. Two of them spoke quickly in low tones to the others. One of them pictured a furious Thi speaking on the phone before her eyes went vamp black and she crushed the phone in her hand.

The fourth one, though, pictured Thi at her desk. Her phone alerted and she read a short text. The fourth could see it from where she stood in the corner, but I couldn't interpret it. Thi didn't seem upset at that point, just mildly concerned. She closed the document she was working on and began to search for information on Sam Quinn.

I found Clive's blip in my head and pushed in.

Hello, darling.

Hey. Little problem with checking what the assistants know.

Is it that you don't speak their languages?

Yes. Yes, it is.

Sorry, love. Cadmael is currently explaining what happened in Budapest.

He was possessed most of the time. How is he explaining?

He's explaining the story we agreed upon. We decided he'd be the best believed of us.

I don't know if you could tell, but Thi hates my guts.

There was a thoughtful pause and then, *I couldn't.*

I felt it, so I checked with her assistants, forcing an image of myself on them. One of them had a memory of her receiving a text and then searching up info on me.

Bloody hell.

I need you to visit the memory with me so you can read the text.

When we get home, we can try. For now, you can stay with me and listen.

"But you three miraculously made it out without a scratch?" Pablo asked, an edge to his voice. "How fortuitous."

"Two of us," Vlad said.

Pablo's eyebrows went up. The others turned to Vlad as well.

"Cadmael and I were in the training room. Clive was late. Newlyweds and all that,"

Pablo sneered at Clive before returning his focus to Vlad. "I don't understand how you two survived. How were you immune to this possession you described?"

"Pablo," Clive began. "I realize that we don't know each other very well, but I would have thought that you'd have at least spoken to your historian about us." He tipped his head, as though studying a bug under a microscope. "For instance, I know that you were Alejandro's third before you betrayed him and took over his nocturne."

Pablo's eyes went vamp black. He leapt out of his seat and then froze, awkwardly falling onto the table.

"Just as I know," Clive continued, "that you never bothered to find out my gifts, or those of Cadmael or Vlad. If you had, you'd know that Cadmael and I are two of the oldest vampires in the world." Clive nodded to Ahmed. "Though my friend here may have me beat on age."

Ahmed tipped his head in acknowledgment. The way the others scowled not at Clive but at Pablo showed that they too were irritated by his lack of finesse, not to mention the shame of being snared by Clive and made to look a fool.

"Vlad's prowess in warfare is legendary, even amongst humans." Clive shook his head. "Asking how they survived a battle is like asking Joao how he gets so many women."

Joao laughed and nodded. "It is a gift." He gestured to his face and body. "How can any resist this?" He pointed at Clive. "You, though, are also known for your endless conquests."

Sorry, darling.

"Ancient history," Clive responded. "I'm a one-woman man now."

Joao shivered in mock horror. "Save me from a fate that is worse than final death."

Adaeze pointed at Pablo. "Will you release your hold on him?"

"Oh," Clive said. "Of course."

Pablo flew back from the table, eyes locked on Clive, fangs locked and loaded. "I will kill you," he hissed.

"Sit down," Cadmael growled. "You embarrass yourself." He looked around the table. "We have positions to fill. I suggest we get to work."

"Yes," Ahmed agreed. "We have two Australian Counselors to choose, two Asian, and one European. Though I think we should first choose a Guild leader." He paused, looking around the table. "Cadmael, I know this isn't something you enjoy, but I think we could use you right now."

Clive and Vlad nodded. Joao shrugged one shoulder, not seeming to care, though I felt his disgruntlement. He would have liked to have at least been asked if he wanted it.

Clive turned to Cadmael. "Will you take it?"

Cadmael, looking put out, finally nodded.

"Good," Clive said. "That's decided." He turned to Thi. "Do you have recommendations for the Asian Counselors?"

What followed was a long discussion about people I didn't know. It was endless. And then if certain people were chosen as Counselors, who would take over as nocturne Masters? I checked out and started listening in on the thoughts of the other Counselors.

Pablo was still fuming. He didn't know anyone who was being discussed and was instead envisioning killing Clive. Joao knew them but didn't care. He thought Thi should have the final decision. She was the one who was going to have to work with them. Ahmed and Adaeze wanted the strongest candidates, not only for the Asian nocturnes and Masters, but for the Guild.

When they got around to discussing a European Counselor, Bram was suggested, but Clive didn't think he'd want to give up his nocturne. Clive said he'd call and talk to him about it, though. I'd met Bram when we were in the UK. I thought he'd make a wonderful Counselor, though he did seem well suited to his nocturne.

I was starting to nod off on my bench against the wall of Russell's office when I heard Pablo say, "Even here, in your precious city, vampires are coming out and making themselves known, taking the blood they require, and leaving it to others to clean up. How can you go on about oversight and control when even the vampires in your former nocturne are part of the revolution?"

Pablo was pleased that everyone had stopped to listen to him. He'd spent most of the meeting being ignored and he was furious. It was time to make the English scum squirm.

Ahmed said, "We saw those reports as well. Can you tell us what you know?"

"Of course," Clive responded. "I know the human press has labeled the killer a vampire, but he is not."

That got people's attention. They were expecting what they'd heard in previous investigations: vague beliefs and possible conclusions, not outright denial.

"What are you talking about?" Pablo sneered. "The humans were drained of blood and had bite marks on their necks."

Clive nodded. "True, but it wasn't a vampire." He gestured to Cadmael and Vlad. "The three of us investigated after the first killing and the second. There was no vampire present. The bodies were killed in a way that made it look as though they were our victims, but they're not."

"There's video of the second killing," Vlad put in. "None of us could drain a body that fast."

"Show us," Pablo demanded.

The others were still irritated with him, that was obvious, but they too directed their laser-sharp focus on Clive. They all wanted to see the video.

Clive nodded. "Of course. First, though, we'd like to explain what we actually believe is going on."

TWENTY-THREE

Emerging Patterns

C live first told them what a pooka was, how it had posed as Clive in order to attack me, how it had been a cat outside our house before shifting to the likeness of our friend. Vlad cut in to explain that he'd conducted the investigation in Bucharest and had never found a vampire trail at any of those killings either.

Clive pulled his phone out of his pocket and pulled up the video. "Before we begin, remember that the killer, who I believe was the cat I saw on the roof, had seen all three of us investigating the first murder. Notice all the details he gets wrong with Vlad's appearance." Clive hit play.

I knew it had ended when all eyes swung to Vlad.

Ahmed gestured to the side of Vlad's face. "The scars are missing."

Vlad nodded.

"The height is wrong," Clive added, "and the hair is a couple of inches too long. The killer saw Vlad from a rooftop while Vlad was turned to the side, talking with Cadmael."

"This fae thing," Adaeze began, "can look like anyone?"

"Why are you believing this ridiculous story?" Pablo spat.

Joao's beautiful face darkened in a momentary display of disgust before it cleared again. I had no idea how these two worked together. "Because this makes sense," he said. "Far more than a phantom uprising of vampires wanting to return to the days of vampire hunters sneaking into our daytime resting places to stake us while seizing our fortunes. I, too, was involved in the investigation in Rio. Other than the way in which the humans were killed, there was no evidence that a vampire was involved."

Joao pointed at Clive's now dark screen. "We cannot drain a victim that quickly and no one vampire, even in the throes of blood lust, would entirely drain a victim. We simply can't hold that much blood. It's ludicrous and why previous investigations assumed it had to be a group of vampires working together."

"But why does it pretend to be one of us?" Adaeze asked, looking at Ahmed and then Cadmael. "Is this retaliation for Budapest? You said the fae prince possessing our people was killed. Were these things in league with him?"

Ahmed shook his head and then looked at the others, who wore equally confused expressions. "The killings started before the Budapest meeting."

"Have any of us encroached on fae land?" Joao asked. "I know Sebastian isn't here to ask anymore," he said, looking at Vlad, "but had you heard about Underhill being compromised by any of us?"

Sebastian had been the other European Counselor and one of those killed in Budapest. As an English vampire, he oversaw the UK, which was where many fae strongholds were. The fae could be and were anywhere in our realm, but historically there was a larger number in the British Isles.

Maybe that's not it at all, I said to Clive. *You guys only care about vampires, but is the same thing happening in cities where a different supernatural being is in leadership? In werewolf-run cities, are victims being found mauled to death? We need to ask Bracken.*

Do you mind if I do it now? I think it would be better if they were involved.

No. Go ahead.

"In the interest of transparency," Clive said to the room, "my wife's great-uncle is a supernatural historian. If you'd be amenable, I can call and ask some of these questions. It occurs to me that this may be happening to other groups, not just us, but since we aren't paying attention, we haven't noticed."

Vlad raised his eyebrows in response. I was pretty sure the little shit knew I was in Clive's mind, chatting with him.

The other vampires glanced at one another. Finally, Adaeze said, "Yes. See what he might know."

Clive scrolled through his contacts and tapped on Bracken.

How do you even have that?

I thought it would come in handy, and look, it did.

Smartass.

It rang once and then we heard, "Hello?"

Clive didn't bother tapping on the speakerphone. Everyone could hear perfectly well without that. "Good evening. This is Clive, Sam's husband. I remembered you saying you worked at night, so I hope I haven't woken you."

"No. Not at all," Bracken said, his voice brightening with interest.

"Good. I think it only right to tell you that I'm meeting with others of my kind right now and that they can all hear you."

Pablo looked pissed that Clive was telling someone they were there. Adaeze and Ahmed were staring at the phone, but both gave a slight nod, clearly agreeing it was right to inform him.

"Are you agreeable to this discussion?" Clive asked. "Or would you prefer not to speak with us?"

"How interesting. Am I allowed to know who's with you?"

Pablo threw an arm out in a slashing gesture. Vlad rolled his eyes at the display.

"I'm sorry," Clive responded, "but I'm afraid that's impossible. Would you mind explaining to those assembled about the pooka? I'm not sure my description was complete."

"Of course, though the information on them is limited."

Meri says they're like the boogeyman to the fae.

"I can see how that would be," Clive responded smoothly.

"One of our fae friends told us that even amongst the fae, pookas are seen as a type of boogeyman."

"Yes," Bracken said. "Oh my goodness, that is exactly right, so trying to get concrete facts has been quite difficult. I spoke with a relative's selkie guard. He was willing to shift and give me what info he had. He confirmed that at one point there were three pookas loose in this realm. Members of the queen's guard were sent to return them to Faerie."

Not to kill them?

"They weren't asked to hunt them, merely to return them?" Clive asked for me.

"Oh, heavens no," Bracken said. "The queen loves and protects all her people. She would never punish them for their nature. They love nothing so much as chaos. Sometimes it's good chaos and sometimes it's bad."

Ask about the feeding on emotions thing Meri said.

"Is it true that pookas feed on the strong emotions their chaos creates?"

We heard scribbling over the phone. "That has always been my theory, but I have yet to find someone to confirm it. There has to be a reason, don't you see?" More scribbling. "This is very exciting. You know a member of the fae who confirmed this idea?"

"Yes," Clive said.

"Marvelous," Bracken murmured while he continued to write a note.

"This person is the daughter of a merman," Clive said, causing Joao's eyebrows to raise. "She said a lot of what they think they know about pookas is mixed up with cautionary tales about behaving or the pooka will get you."

"Yes. It's fascinating, isn't it?" Bracken asked, his words coming fast in his excitement. "You used the term boogeyman and it's a good one. Even the fae are frightened of the pooka. Chaos lacks reason, logic, empathy. One can't prepare for a pooka. One must only deal with the aftermath."

"We have a question," Clive told him. "We've been focusing on killings in cities around the world that appear to be the work of our people, but we're wondering if there have been similarly unexplained killings in cities led by other supernatural groups."

"Yes, yes, yes," he mumbled, with the sound of pages flipping in the background. "We've had the same thought. I've only just started, but I've found a few. Lake Okeechobee in Florida is panther country. About twelve years ago, there was a series of hiker maulings. The local claw investigated and found nothing. They said that not only was there no scent of a panther, there was no scent of anything other than the victim."

Vlad nodded.

"Yes," Clive said. "The same is true of our current killings. We didn't pick up on any scent other than the victim."

Vlad tapped Clive's arm.

"Oh, and a very faint smell of cat, which we believe is one of the pooka's default forms. There are also many feral cats around the wharf because of the fishing boats and fish mongers."

"Interesting," Bracken mumbled, scribbling. "There are cats all over the world. I wonder if it has become his custom to wear that form, as it makes him easy to overlook. Hmm." He turned a page. "Here's another. Newfoundland is run by the wolves. The local pack investigated a string of hunters being killed by wolves thirty years ago. For a while, they assumed it had to be the natural wolves, but the violence of the killings was out of character for natural wolves. The point seemed to be the killing. Wolves, either natural or shifter, would eat the choicest pieces of the victims. They wouldn't slash and bite just to inflict pain and bloodshed, leaving the good meat to rot. It made no sense and again, they didn't find any strong scents that led them anywhere.

"Much like your cat scent, they caught the trail of a natural wolf pack, but it was an old one. They hadn't traveled the area where the hunters were found for weeks. The killings went on for less than a week and then they stopped."

Bracken flipped anther page. "I'm not sure if this next one fits. They aren't the ruling supernatural in a city, but I believe it's connected. In the Amazonian Rainforest, there is a shadow of black jaguar shifters. They've ruled the area for generations."

Joao nodded, though he looked uncomfortable.

"There were some workmen surveying the rainforest for a logging company. Three of them were lost and later found mauled to death. It caused quite a scene. There was a lot of money involved in the deal and a great many protestors demonstrating against the deforestation when the bodies were finally brought out. There was an investigation, but it was hushed up. The government didn't want other companies to stop their negotiations."

Again, Joao nodded.

"The odd thing," Bracken continued, "is that the daughter of the—well, they don't use terms like Alpha for Jaguars. He was sometimes referred to as the Rei—the little daughter of the Rei disappeared. They never found her body. There was some talk about it being vampires—there had been increased tensions between the groups, mostly to do with the vampires making money off the loss of the jaguars' habitat. Anyway, the vampires denied any involvement, but the jaguars never believed them. I could be wrong, but the strange chaos amongst humans, vampires, and shifters feels very much like the work of a pooka."

Joao's brow was furrowed as he scratched his cheek.

Ask about the stolen black jaguar! Russell and Audrey found a female who had been imprisoned by a vampire. George, Owen, and Alec are taking care of her, hoping she'll eventually shift and tell them who she is and where she belongs.

Bracken flipped another page. "In 1902, in Sowa, Botswana, there was a string of villagers being dragged from their huts in the early hours of the morning. Their bodies were later found a little way away from the village. Their bodies were covered in huge bites and claw marks. Everyone assumed the lions were hunting men."

Adaeze nodded, her eyes narrowed.

"That area, though, is ruled by lion shifters. The Pride Male swore it wasn't them. They couldn't find a scent trail and had no idea who was doing the killings. He ended up moving the pride a few kilometers away to avoid the human hunters who were encroaching on their territory.

"As I said, I've only begun the research. I'm still scanning the indices to my journals for similar events. I'm sure there will be more. And these are just the cases I had notes on. I think it's safe to say that there are plenty of other incidents I haven't yet heard of or researched."

"Unfortunately," Clive said, "I believe you're correct. Can I ask, though, about the daughter of the Rei that they believe was stolen?"

Bracken flipped a few pages. "Yes, of course. What's your question?"

"When did this happen?"

"Oh, let's see. It was twenty-two years ago. The little one was three or four years old at the time. There were some conflicting reports."

Do jaguars start shifting that young?

"Excuse my ignorance," Clive said, "but when do jaguar shifters begin shifting? Was she a child or a cub when she disappeared?"

Bracken paused. "That's an excellent question and one I'm sorry to say I didn't ask. Different shifting breeds begin at different times. Some shift for the first time in the cradle. Some wait until adolescence of the human side. As I recall, jungle cats begin shifting quite early. I can ask people who know to get specifics on jaguars."

He gave a soft chuckle. "I have an excellent memory, but I'm afraid there are a fair few facts rattling around up there. My gut response is that they begin shifting as toddlers, so around the time the little girl disappeared. As I said, though, I can find an answer that's better than my gut."

What's her name?

"One more thing," Clive began. "Do you by any chance have her name?"

There was a pause. "I do. It's Rafaela. I must ask, though, because these questions lead me to believe you know something about her. Her family is still desperate to find her. They haven't given up hope and regularly scour the rainforest, looking for a clue as to what happened to her."

I can feel your heart racing, darling, but this is a tricky situation. She was found with a vampire. We could inadvertently start a war if we tell them we know where their stolen daughter is.

Clive.

I know. Let me do this diplomatically.

TWENTY-FOUR

Could This Have Been an Email?

"I've heard some things," Clive told Bracken, causing Joao to still. "I have no answers for you right now but would appreciate the time and space to do a little research of my own. I assume, if I do find something, that you'd be able to get a message to her family?"

"I could," Bracken responded. "Yes, indeed. I met with the family myself, you see. They're heartbroken. Still. I understand that you can't tell me anything right now, but please share with me what you know when you can. They've been mourning her loss for twenty-two years."

"I understand, and I'll get back to you," Clive said. "Thank you again for your time and knowledge. We are grateful." He disconnected the call.

"Why didn't our own historians find this?" Pablo shook his head, staring away from the group.

"Other than that jaguar story," Ahmed said, "where we were painted as the villains, none of those killings involved us." He leaned forward over the table. "All this time we've been told that our own people wanted to out us to the world. We've been scrambling, the older ones trying to teach the younger ones how difficult it was before we became fiction, before vampire hunting fell out of fashion."

"Yes, and why was that?" Pablo sneered. "Members of the Guild were involved in those investigations. How did you miss all of this?"

"We didn't." Vlad looked like he was one shitty comment away from handing Pablo his final death. "My report said that although it appeared to be a vampire killing, there was no evidence of one being involved."

Joao stood and began to pace around the library. "Mine was similar. We could find no trace of the killer. That was in the report. Sebastian said he'd heard rumblings of vampires wanting to be out to the world and so saw this as connected."

He was also the one flaunting the rules of secrecy to feed on innocents.

I know, darling, but we have no idea if any of these Counselors knew what was going on in Budapest.

"Sebastian remained Guild Master longer than was customary," Cadmael explained. "He stationed himself in the Guild House, which put him in close proximity to the twisted old fae living in the condemned upper floor. We must assume he was compromised. I suggest we go back over the decisions the Guild has made in the last decade to see if we still support them. Leadership throughout the vampire world is changing. We will need to change as well."

Joao paused his pacing in front of the fireplace. "Why did you keep asking about the missing shifter?"

"Because Russell and Audrey rescued a black jaguar shifter who was being held by a vampire," Clive told him.

Joao's eyes turned vamp black. "No. They swore to me they had nothing to do with the little girl's disappearance. I spoke to the shifter family myself. I assured them it wasn't a vampire." He was nothing like the carefree playboy now. Like a bowstring, he was vibrating, barely holding himself back from mass murder. "Who?"

"Russell said he was a vampire who identified himself as John. We can ask Russell to join us and explain," Clive said.

Joao nodded stiffly. Clive glanced around the table. No one protested, so Clive went to the door and said, "Russell," knowing Russell would hear.

The Master's office door opened and Russell walked down the hall. "Yes? May I assist in some way?"

Clive waved him in and closed the door. "I was explaining to the Guild about the jaguar you and Audrey rescued. The group would like to know more about the vampire who was holding her."

Russell nodded solemnly. "I see. He told us his name was John and that he was a newborn from Texas when he applied for membership to the noctur—"

"When was this?" Joao interrupted.

"Just a little over a month ago."

The Guild members glanced at each other, looks of consternation on their faces.

"It was a lie, though," Russell continued. "I first met him in— I'm not sure which state. It might have been Texas. It was in the mid-1800s in the antebellum South. He was a paddyroller who had—"

Adaeze gestured to catch Russell's attention. "I'm not familiar with this term."

Russell thought a minute, clearly running back what he'd just said to find the unfamiliar term. He nodded. "Paddyrollers or patrollers were armed white men who acted as a kind of militia, chasing down escaped slaves, punishing us for defiance, and making money by selling us back to plantations in need."

"I see," Adaeze responded, her eyes turning black.

"They were ignorant and violent men. When I first came into contact with this John, he was one of a group of patrollers who had been made vampires and I was one of the escaped. So, when he walked into my office almost two hundred years later, pretending to be a newborn, I knew he was lying. I've only recently become the Master. I had no idea why he was here, but I assumed it was because a Black man in authority—especially this Black man, who'd made him look a fool all those years ago—bothered him. I'm afraid my temper got the best of me, and I handed him his final death before I could question him more thoroughly."

Adaeze nodded. "Good."

"Was he the one who stole her?" Joao demanded.

Russell looked at Clive for context.

"He's asking whether you know if this John was the one who originally stole the jaguar cub in the Amazon or if she had been trafficked."

Russell shook his head. "I don't know. We weren't aware there was an imprisoned shifter at the time. We found her later, her pelt covered in burns and vampire bites, reeking of his scent."

"What did you do with her?" Joao demanded.

Vampires were masters of subtlety, so when Clive leaned ever so slightly toward Russell, it was tantamount to a declaration that he had Russell's back and that Joao needed to calm the fuck down.

Russell kept his focus on the Guild members around the table. "One of our dragons is a veterinarian."

"*One* of your dragons?" Pablo's look of boredom didn't match the tension in his voice.

Ahmed glanced over at Pablo, shaking his head. "How have you not heard about the Battle of Alcatraz?"

Russell nodded. "We didn't feel we were the right ones to look after an abused shifter, one who had been abused by one of our own kind, so we took her to our veterinary friend."

"What has she said?" Joao took a step forward. "Was it a vampire who originally stole her?"

She hasn't shifted and spoken, I told Clive. *She's traumatized, but Alec says she's getting stronger.*

Russell didn't respond, so Clive said, "She's been traumatized by her captivity and abuse. She hasn't yet shifted to her other form, so no one has spoken to her yet."

Joao shook his head. "We have to make this go away before

that happens. It can't get out that she was taken and tortured by vampires." He threw his hands in the air and began to pace again. "We'd end up at war with shifters."

Pablo raised his eyebrows. "Did you miss the part about her being protected by dragons?"

"What?" Joao stopped and looked between Pablo and Clive. "She's a jaguar. Will they care?"

It's a good thing I'm not in that room. My fingertips are tingling. I want to separate his head from his body.

I know, but stay where you are and let me handle it.

"They will care very much. If anyone tried to get close to her, they'd die a fiery death. We have five dragons living in this town who are very protective of this shifter. What you have to understand about dragons is that they are an ancient force and though there are different clans in different parts of the world, they are all dragons and would drop everything, sacrifice anything, to come to the aid of another dragon. The clans are very tight-knit families, and this jaguar is now under the protection of the Drake clan."

Clive gestured to Ahmed. "A very large part of the reason we won the Battle of Alcatraz against a far greater number of Master vampires is because we had dragons working with us, flying over the island and the ocean, burning any of Garyn's people that they found." Clive glanced at the others. "So, no, we can't just silence the shifter to hide our own culpability."

"We need to tell her family," Adaeze said.

"Now, wait—" Joao began.

"Enough," Cadmael grumbled. "Have your people investigate," he said to Joao. "I would think an American, and a Texan no less, would stand out in the rainforest. If he wasn't the one who stole her—and given what Russell has told us about him, I'd assume he acquired her later—then we need to trace the trafficking. We need to know where and when our people were involved in the supernatural trade."

"Yes," Vlad agreed. "We also need to look into other missing shifters. I doubt this was an isolated incident."

Thi cleared her throat. "Why would any of our people be involved in this? It seems more likely to be warfare between shifters." She gestured to Joao. "I understand this happened in your territory, but so has a great many other things that have nothing to do with us. I don't think it falls to us to spend our time and effort on shifter concerns."

"It was a vampire imprisoning the jaguar," Adaeze reminded her. "We *are* involved in it. And if we had been paying more attention to what was happening around us, we would have figured out what this pooka was doing long before now."

Thi inclined her head. "Assuming there is a pooka and it's killing to mimic us. There seem to be a great many unknowns and assumptions being made."

"Yes, exactly," Pablo said, tapping the table near Thi's elbow. "They're presenting conjecture as though it's fact."

Vlad slumped back in his chair. "Now I remember why I hate this job." He checked his watch. "I think we've reached the end of our productive time. If we've moved into the bickering phase of the meeting, I have a book to read."

Cadmael closed his eyes a moment. "Unhelpful. Agreed, but unhelpful." He looked up at the clock on the wall. "It's after three. We have phone calls to make for the Counselor candidates we've discussed. Let's break now, contact who we need to contact, and regroup tomorrow to continue the discussion. We have a monumental amount of work to do to rebuild the Guild. I don't want us getting bogged down in unnecessary arguments."

Adaeze and Ahmed nodded and stood. Pablo looked ready to continue fighting, but when Thi nodded and stood, he knew he'd lost his ally and so stood as well. Joao was still looking harassed, standing by the fireplace.

"You all know where your rooms are," Russell said. "Your people are downstairs, though I assume you can call them to you, if you'd like them up here. The nocturne's facilities are at your disposal. If there's anything that you need, please feel free to ask one of my people." He inclined his head and left the library.

"I'm going to go find my wife and wake her up." Turning to Cadmael and Vlad, Clive added, "We'll be out at the car in a few minutes, if you two would like a ride."

I'm in Russell's office.

I know, darling. On my way.

I blinked my eyes open and realized that Audrey had stayed with me. Pushing myself up to a seated position, I said, "Thank you. That was kind of you to stay with me."

She waved away my thanks and came over to fix my hair. After she'd gone to the trouble to put it up for me, I'd proceeded to lie down on the bench for a few hours. "I wasn't going to leave you vulnerable, missus. Has the meeting broken up, then?"

I nodded as Clive walked in. "There's my little sleepyhead." *Play it up. You've been asleep for a few hours, remember?* "Come, Fergus."

Right. Sorry. I yawned loudly and Clive grinned before picking me up and carrying me to the door, my head tucked into his neck.

Russell and Godfrey were standing in the entry as Clive walked by with me in his arms. My head was down, but I felt the interest of a few vampires as Clive walked us past the stairs.

"Tell her we said good night," Godfrey murmured. "And tell her to come back tomorrow so we can finish the docuseries. We were at a good part when she fell asleep."

"I will. Thank you," Clive said, walking out the front door and to our car.

"Allow me," Vlad said, opening the back door.

Clive deposited me in the plush back seat. Fergus jumped in and then Cadmael and Vlad took their seats.

Once we were out on the road, I opened my eyes. "Gee, that was fun."

Vlad huffed a laugh.

I scratched under Fergus' chin. "Will they think it's hinkey that you two are staying with us instead of at the nocturne with everyone else?"

"You couldn't pay me enough to stay with that lot," Vlad

grumbled. "I've got better things to do than worry about who's listening at keyholes."

"At least there are fewer of them right now," Cadmael said.

"Not for long," Vlad reminded him.

When Clive pulled up to the house, I scanned the streets for a cat but didn't find him. What was he up to?

TWENTY-FIVE

If at First You Don't Succeed...

A pair of vampires move like shadows around the piers. The hunter watches, wondering why they haven't returned to their crypt yet. His nose twitches. The coppery stench of old blood nauseates him. He keeps to the deepest shadows, far from the weak streetlights, prowling the water's edge on silent cat feet.

He sees movement, a flash of light, and then a human is carrying boxes down a gangplank toward a small fishing boat. The fisherman begins the process of readying to set sail as the hunter ghosts down the pier toward him.

The hunter is patient. He knows how to wait for his moment. When the fisherman finally notices the still cat watching him, he waves his hand and stomps a foot.

"Shoo!" he whisper-shouts. "I don't have any fish yet and I don't like cats."

The hunter doesn't move. The man looks annoyed for a moment and then shakes his head and continues his work.

More headlights flash in the parking lot. The hunter knows his time has come. Bunching his muscles, he prepares to jump onto the boat, but then catches that grimy, coppery stench again. When he turns, he sees two black blurs racing toward him.

Quick as a thought, he transforms into a seagull, skimming the water.

He bats the air, his wings pounding, as he flies high over the wharf, leaving the bloodsuckers far behind, lost in the gloom.

Another small boat is already heading out to sea, so the gull keeps pace before landing on top of the cabin. The fisherman is at the wheel, checking his digital map and talking to himself.

The hunter understands how to adjust in the moment. This one will do just as well. In fact, the hunter decides he can stage this kill even more dramatically. Yes. This change of plans worked out just fine for him.

He drops to the deck wearing a new guise. Looming over the fisherman, he anticipates what will soon come. The hunter spins the captain's chair. The fisherman grunts in surprise, his hand trailing off the wheel, inadvertently sending the boat in circles.

The man's shock transforms almost immediately into anger. It's too late, though. The hunter has sprung forward and latched onto the fisherman's neck.

The hunter almost smiles as he feeds. The new mustache tickles his lip. He decides he rather likes it.

He drinks down the blood, along with the fisherman's rage and fear. It's a heady concoction.

When he's drained the fisherman dry, he lets the body fall at an unnatural angle. It will make more of an impact for whoever finds him. The sheer volume of blood makes the hunter queasy, so he shifts back into a seagull and the discomfort disappears.

At the risk of getting dizzy, he waits until other boats arrive and then the shock-horror-fear feast will begin in earnest. His laughing caws cut through the sound of the engine as he waits.

TWENTY-SIX

I Can Never Unsee It

My alarm went off, jolting me out of sleep. I smacked the nightstand, turning it off, and turned back into Clive, who tightened his arms around me. Keeping vampire hours was going to be the death of me.

Later, I was woken again by the bed shaking. It took me a minute for my brain to engage and realize that Fergus had his front paws on the side of the bed and was bouncing it.

"Yes. Fine. I'm getting up." I checked my phone on the nightstand. It was already past noon. Shit. "Sorry, buddy." I stumbled through the dark house and down the stairs to the first floor to fill up his food bowl. After I threw open the back door for him, I went back to refill his water and then just flopped the top half of my body on the counter for a quick rest.

"You're late."

I just about jumped out of my skin. "Well, that got the old heart going." I turned to find Vlad's dark eyes shining from the depths of the den. "Quit being a dick."

"Is that any way to greet a guest?" he asked, sounding quite put out.

"You're not a guest. You're an intruder." I went to the refrigerator and started pulling out ingredients for an omelette. I was starving. "Did Clive get a hold of Bram last night?"

"He left a message. The timing was off."

I was making a four-egg omelette with cheese and the last of some leftover spicy ground beef. I poured a little salsa over the top, grabbed a fork and a glass of water, and then went out to the patio to eat.

"Nothing personal," I called in. "It's lovely out here and dark in there."

I thought I heard him chuckle, but I wasn't sure; the wind in the trees was loud today. Zipping up my hoodie, I dug into breakfast as Fergus flopped onto my feet.

After sending a quick text to Owen to explain my tardiness, I finished my food. When he sent one back letting me know it was all under control, I relaxed. I could have raced to get ready, but if The Slaughtered Lamb was covered, I could move at my own pace.

When I brought my empty plate in and closed the back door, Vlad said, "I need to tell you what happened last night."

Shoulders slumped, I rinsed off my plate. "Damn it. What did he do?" I went to the den and sat on the couch opposite Vlad's darker corner.

He flicked on the lamp beside him. "Russell called Clive after you went to bed. Two of his scouts located the pooka-cat and almost caught him, but he shifted into a seagull and flew off over the water."

I blew out a breath. How were we ever going to catch this thing?

"Today, though, there are reports of a fisherman being attacked on his boat, which was found floating in circles. The fisherman was drained of blood and left on the deck of his boat."

Fergus dropped his head in my lap and I leaned over to kiss it. "That poor man."

"There's more," Vlad said. "This hasn't been released to the media yet, but the nocturne's human liaison sent me a video.

Apparently, the fisherman was recording himself. He has an account where he posts sunrise videos. There is a brief image of the killer."

My phone buzzed. I pulled up the incoming text and clicked on the link. The man was talking about the early morning on the bay and then there was a flash behind him. It was brief. The man was spun in the chair, causing the phone recording him to tip on its side, but for a half a moment Clive, with Vlad's huge mustache, was standing behind the fisherman. *Shit.*

"You and I know what this is," Vlad said, "but I don't know that the authorities will."

Shitshitshitshitshit. I dropped my head into my hands. "So even if we luck out and he moves on to his next chaotic mess, we get to look forward to security footage around the world showing you, Clive, or a combination of the two of you killing people from now on?"

"After five hundred and seventy years, I might have to shave my mustache off." He ran his fingertips over it. "No. I'll take my chances."

I studied the video again, freezing on the pooka wearing a Clive costume. If I didn't know, would I think that was Clive? As the Master of the City, Clive attended quite a few big charity events over the years. He's known. "It appears to be Clive wearing a big, fake mustache in, like, the world's lamest attempt at disguising himself. It would be hilarious if it weren't so horrific. And if someone on the force recognizes his face and wants to question him, what do we do during daylight hours?"

"Call the liaison and let her know what's happening. She'll get the nocturne's lawyer. He can negotiate an evening interrogation." His fingers drummed on the arm of the chair. "This isn't the first time we've had to deal with the authorities. What about you, though? Has Clive provided you with an ID and records?"

Vlad knew that up until quite recently, I'd lived much of my life off the grid.

I nodded. "We had to do that so I could get a driver's license. Actually, he started the process before that so we could get a proper marriage certificate. He's weirdly concerned with making sure every bank account, investment, and property has my name on it, so I had to exist to the government and banking organizations."

"Nothing weird about it," Vlad said. "Being a vampire is a dangerous business, and he has a wife, one who is herself long-lived. He's making sure you're provided for in the only way he can after he's gone."

My heart gave a squeeze and my throat tightened. I needed a minute. "It's important to him that I'm surrounded by strong friends too."

"And that you can defend yourself. In Budapest, when you were challenged, I thought he'd insist on fighting in your stead. When he didn't, I was shocked—on the inside, of course. I pride myself on my lack of emotional displays. But when he finished with his opponent, he held himself in check and watched you. I could see what it was costing him to let you do it yourself."

He shook his head, a smirk under his great mustache. "And then you held Dakila up by his hair and sliced through his neck with those claws of yours in the showiest *fuck you* to all the vampires discounting you. I thought Clive would burst with pride. I realized then that you were right when you told me my assessment of him was all wrong. I saw what I thought I'd see and never looked past the pretty face, the charm." Vlad scratched the side of his nose. "I kind of hate him."

I huffed out a laugh, breaking the fear paralysis holding me in place. I didn't want to talk about or even think about trying to live without Clive. "By the way, you guys do know I'll be telling George and Alec about Jade's family, right?"

"If Jade is Rafaela, then yes, I assumed so. As your husband knows you better than I do, my guess is he does as well."

Fergus climbed up on the couch and creeped onto my lap, like I wouldn't notice him. "Alec named her Jade because of her beautiful green eyes. Like Clive told you all, she hasn't shifted yet, so they didn't know her name."

Vlad stretched out his legs and crossed them at the ankles. "Chances are, she doesn't know her name either. She was taken as a toddler and has been imprisoned and abused ever since. I know her family has been looking for her, but she may not remember them at all. Poor thing."

"At least she's with Alec, who understands what she's been through." I thought a moment. "A lot of horrific things happen in the supernatural world."

Vlad nodded. "In fairness, they happen in the human one as well. The issue is we're stronger and can take more abuse. If she were human, they likely would have found her little body in the jungle twenty-two years ago. We're strong enough to survive torture, which can be both a blessing and a curse, depending on how you look at it."

I considered what I had experienced, Alec and Fyr's imprisonment, and Jade. Then I thought about all those poor women in the Budapest asylum and what had been done to them, how they'd died. My mind jumped straight to one of the first real conversations I'd ever had with Clive when he told me about his sister, who'd been raped and killed. Her death spurred him to go in search of the men who'd done it. He'd accepted the dark kiss, becoming a vampire, to better exact his revenge on them. Alec, Fyr, Jade and I were all still here, healing, creating happier lives for ourselves. Clive's sister Elswyth had been gone for a thousand years, and her final moments were terror and pain.

"It's a blessing." I stood, dislodging Fergus with no small amount of effort. "I need to get cleaned up and go to work. I'll see you tonight."

"I'll wait and walk through the folly with you," he said, as though appointing himself my vampire guard was completely normal.

"Okey-dokey." I went through the house with Fergus on my

heels, realizing that Vlad had waited until I'd eaten to tell me about the pooka's killing. The man was obsessed with my food consumption. Which, given our last conversation…was really sweet, and I needed to stop being annoyed with him for foisting food on me.

When I got to the bedroom, I closed the door after us and jumped onto the bed to give Clive a kiss on the cheek. "Promise me you'll never grow a great big mustache. I can't unsee it. It'll haunt my dreams."

After I was showered, dried, and dressed, I sat on the side of the bed to put on my shoes and socks, and to give Clive another kiss. "Have a good day, love. Rest up. More vampire shenanigans tonight."

Vlad was waiting for Fergus and me at the bottom of the stairs. "You didn't get a chance to exercise this morning, so we can run through the folly, if you'd like."

"Thanks. We'd appreciate that." I didn't mention that jogging in jeans wasn't the most comfortable because, again, I didn't want to reject kindness from a vampire.

Once we'd entered the folly, we hit a fast pace and kept going. We were just entering the Shire when I felt my phone buzz in my pocket. I checked the screen and saw it was Bram, so I stopped. Vlad looked around my shoulder to see who was calling.

"Hello, Bram. How are you?" I held the phone between Vlad and me so he could hear clearly.

"Good day, Sam. It's good to hear your voice. I hope I'm not bothering you." Bram's voice had a lovely Irish lilt.

"Not at all. It's good to hear from you too. How was soccer season?" Bram's nocturne was filled with huge soccer fans. Godfrey had lived there for many years before coming to America to rejoin Clive.

He chuckled. "First of all, it's football—"

"Oh, I should tell you that Vlad is with me and so is listening," I told him.

"Yes, of course," Bram responded. "I'd heard that Vlad and

Cadmael had traveled to the States. Hello, Vlad. It's been a very long time. I hope you're well."

"I'm good," Vlad said.

Rolling my eyes, I added, "And he hopes you're doing well too." I elbowed Vlad and whispered, "Jeez, dude, learn some manners."

TWENTY-SEVEN

At Least There Are Cookies

B ram laughed. "I'm calling you because your husband and I are doomed to missing each other's calls in the summer. I could email him, but I wasn't sure if the content of the conversation was too sensitive for that."

"Oh, right." I looked at Vlad. "Can I ask him or should you do it?"

"As you're not a member of the Guild, why don't you allow me. Bram, as you've probably heard, we lost a number of our Counselors recently. We need a new European Counselor, and you were recommended. Are you open to making that change?"

"And just so you know," I added, "when your name came up, everyone nodded and agreed you'd be a perfect choice."

Vlad shook his head but didn't seem upset.

"I mean, you should do whatever's right for you," I added. "I just think it's nice when people know their hard work is recognized and appreciated."

"Thank you, Sam. That's very kind of you to share that with me." He paused. "A Counselor? I hadn't considered that." He paused. "I'll need to think about that, won't I? I'll try to reach Clive before sunrise here and hope it's close enough to sunset there so we can connect and discuss this."

"He can wake up early," I told him.

"I know he can, thankfully, or we wouldn't be able to talk with one another for a few months. My best to you and Jane," he said.

Jane was the Irish Wolfhound I'd found on the moors. "Actually, Jane was traveling under an assumed name. She dragged me through a fae rip in the realms near your nocturne and we ended up in the Cotswolds, where her owner informed me I had inadvertently stolen his dog Alice."

"I hope you told him that you kept her safe from a pack of werewolves hunting her," Bram said.

"Hmm. I don't think I ever did. *But*, he let Clive and me adopt his wolfhound puppy, so it's all good. Here. Wait. I'll send you his pic." I took a quick photo and texted it to him. "This is my son Fergus."

Bram huffed out a laugh. "Very handsome and an excellent name."

"Thanks. I know you're busy, so I'll let you go. Hopefully, you're able to connect with Clive later."

"I hope so too. Have a good day," Bram said before he disconnected.

I stowed the phone and began jogging again. "For you guys, I hope he decides to do it. For his nocturne, I hope he doesn't. They love him."

"Unfortunately, we sometimes end up advancing the problematic ones because we can't afford to lose the effective ones from their critical positions," Vlad said.

"Is Pablo evidence of that?" We slowed to a walk as we rounded the small pond that marked the entrance to my old apartment.

"I have no idea how he ended up in the Guild. Back when there was a full complement of us, I avoided meetings. Sebastian was there to represent Europe. They didn't need both of us, so I stayed home, ostensibly to advise my people if needed. Really, I was just avoiding the headaches."

"Understandable. I'd imagine it's hard to hold yourselves back when people are begging for a whooping. It's a good thing I wasn't in the room last night when Joao was talking about killing Jade so he wouldn't have to deal with the fallout of her being found with a vampire."

When we reached the living room of the small apartment, Vlad sat down and grabbed a book off the end table. "That one is weak. He uses his good looks and charm to get what he wants and then secrets away information to manipulate those around him, ensuring he always gets whatever he wants. He's not used to being told no. He's what I thought your husband was."

At my dirty look, he grinned. "It'll be interesting to see what happens tonight. Cadmael, a far older and more powerful vampire, and the new head of the Guild, gave him a direct order to look into Rafaela's abduction. We'll see if he does it. Joao's not used to being ordered to do something he doesn't want to do."

Fergus got up on the sofa and flopped down so he was leaning against Vlad's hip like they did this every day, and maybe they did. Vlad crossed his feet on the coffee table and opened his book.

"Okay. You guys have a good one," I called, moving into the kitchen, where Dave was already at the stove. I checked my phone. How late was I? "What are you doing here so early?"

"What does it look like?" he grumbled, stirring something in a pot. As it smelled delicious, I leaned in for a better look.

"You and your long hair need to back away from my food."

I moved away and watched him for a minute. "What bug crawled up your ass today? My hair is tied up and I was just looking."

Flames went up his arms. He turned to me, expression thunderous, and I wished I had my demon sword at my side. Wait a minute. I grabbed my axe, which wouldn't hurt him the way it would the fae, but it could still fuck him up real good.

"Who's your dad?" I demanded.

His face went blank for a moment and then he shook his head, going back to stirring the pot. "You know who my dad is. You met him and lost your scars—you're welcome. I'm not a pooka. I'm just in a shitty mood, okay? Maggie went back to Ireland to visit her family." He shooed me away from him, pointing me toward a plate of bonus peanut butter chocolate chip cookies on the counter.

Dave had started cooking years ago to help with bouts of uncontrollable anger—half demon and all that. Cooking relaxes him. He picked up baking more recently and has been making baked goods for Stheno to sell at The Viper's Nest. We tried putting a cake stand filled with brownies, cookies, and whatever on the bar to sell here, but Fyr and I kept eating them. Okay, fine. It was mostly me. Now, when Dave bakes, he puts aside the rejects for me. They may have looked wonky, but they tasted great.

Maggie was Dave's banshee girlfriend. She should be his banshee wife, but unless they'd married in secret, it hadn't happened yet. I didn't know why he was dragging his feet. Oh. Unless maybe she was the one dragging feet.

"Why haven't you locked her down yet?" I asked.

"I'm working on it," he growled.

"Not hard enough. We both know you can be anywhere in the world any time you want. Why not just go visit her?"

Flames spouted from the backs of his hands again. "They don't like me. They don't want her seeing a demon, even one who's only half."

"That's why you've got to go, be on your best behavior, and bring gifts to try to buy their affection. Come on, do I have to explain everything around here?" I took a big bite. "*Mmm,* and bring cookies with you. Treat Maggie like the queen she is and you'll win them over."

The personal flames disappeared and his shoulders lost some of their tension. "I'll think about it. Go away now."

"Message received," I said, grabbing another cookie before heading out to the bar.

Owen was brewing a pot of tea, and I could see Meri in the bookstore helping one of the wicches find a book. I walked through the tables, picking up empties with my free hand, while I used the other to hold my cookie.

Owen stared at said cookie, his brow furrowed. "Where did you find that?"

I pointed at the kitchen with my elbow. "They're peanut butter chocolate chip and they are excellent. Here, take the empties in and grab yourself one. They're on the counter on the right." When I finished loading a tray with cups and glasses, Owen took it in to load the dishwasher and grab a snack.

I filled Grim's tankard of mead, delivered the pot of tea to the wicches by the window, and wiped down the bar while I waited for Owen. He came back a few minutes later, biting into a big cookie but looking back over his shoulder.

He sidled up beside me and whispered, "What's going on with Dave? He's more ragey than normal."

"He's okay," I told him. "He's just got personal junk going on. Speaking of personal junk, can you give me Alec's phone number?" I pulled out my phone and scrolled through contacts. "Yeah. I don't have it."

Owen pulled out his own phone and sent me the contact info. "What's up? What do you need Alec for?"

I glanced around, not wanting to share this with the bar in general. I waved Owen to come along with me, and we went to the stairs and climbed a few before sitting on them. We were in that weird in-between space. We weren't in the bar, but we also weren't above ground. Sounds were muffled here.

"I have some news to share with him." I handed Owen my phone. "Call him and keep the phone to your ear. That way we can all hear."

He did. It rang twice and then, "Hey, Sam."

"Hi, Alec. Can you hear me okay?"

"Sure. You sound a little distant, but I can hear you," he said.

"Okay, cool. Owen is holding my phone so he can hear too. I haven't been given permission to tell you this, but whatever. I found out information last night that might relate to Jade."

Owen sat up straight, staring at me while he kept the phone at his ear.

"Apparently, there is a family of black jaguars in the Amazon rainforest. They are the ruling shifters in that area. The daughter of the leader, or Rei, was stolen twenty-two years ago. She was only three or four years old, and her name was Rafaela. The family is grief-stricken and has been looking for her ever since she disappeared.

"The local vampires were questioned, but they swore they had nothing to do with it. It's possible they didn't. If she was stolen and trafficked, they may have found her later. We don't know. The vampires are going back to check the stories they've been told."

Owen let out a deep breath.

"Now, if Jade is Rafaela and she really was stolen that young, she may not recognize that name or even remember how to shift. I thought I remembered one of you telling me she'd been caged and chained with silver. If they kept her from shifting for so long, she might not remember how or even that she has another form."

"And what's the language acquisition of a three-year-old?" Owen asked. "She may not be fluent in any language."

"She understands me," Alec protested. "I know she does."

"Twenty-two years," Owen whispered, his eyes closing. "Poor Jade."

"If it's her," I said. "We don't know for sure if our Jade is connected to this stolen Rafaela, but my gut says she is."

Owen nodded.

"Hang on," Alec said. "She's out on the patio, watching the waves."

We heard him moving and then the sound of the ocean got louder. "Hey," he said. "I'm on the phone with Owen and Sam. She told me a story." He paused and then asked, "Do you know the name Rafaela?"

She made a series of low roars that sounded like a chainsaw.

"No. Wait. It's okay," he said to her. "I'll call you back," he said to us before the line went dead.

Owen handed me my phone. "Twenty-two years." He ran his

hand over his face. "I need to call George. I'll be down in a minute."

I patted his knee and then trotted back down the stairs. Meri was waiting for me at the bottom.

"I thought I heard you." She glanced up the stairs, her brow furrowed but didn't ask. "I have some news."

"Oh, good." I pointed to the bookstore. "We should—" but then I stopped myself. Why was I keeping this a secret? I turned back to the wicches and Grim in the bar. "Have you all heard about the vampire killer in town?"

They looked at each other and then nodded.

"First thing you need to know is it's not a real vampire," I told them.

That piece of information seemed to shock them.

One of the wicches raised her hand. "But they were drained of blood and had bite marks on their necks."

"Yes. And the vampires thought he was one too and were trying to find him. They couldn't because he's not a vampire. He's a pooka, which is a fae—I don't know—malevolent spirit, a chaos agent. He can shift to look like anyone. Or any animal, for that matter. My great-uncle, who's a Corey wicche, is also a supernatural historian. He's been looking into this for us, and it seems like this pooka moves around the world, taking on the likeness of whichever supernatural being is in a place of power, and then terrorizing people and causing messes."

Grim had slid off his stool, the only one to look enraged. "We have a pooka?"

I nodded and his axe came off his back. "You should have been stopping us at the door to make sure we are who we seem to be. Have you altered your ward to keep him out?"

Uh, shit. "Not yet."

TWENTY-EIGHT

Revelations Right, Left, and Center

"D o you have the axe the queen spelled for you?" he demanded.

Dave swung out of the kitchen to stare at Grim's back.

"Yes." I pulled it out of its sheath.

"Well, that's good, at least. Press it up against everyone's skin. See if anyone reacts."

I held the axe tight against my chest. "It would hurt you and Meri."

Liam and his friend Dermot were sitting at a table by the ocean entrance. I hadn't seen them arrive. They must have come in when I was on the stairs with Owen. Liam and Dermot were selkies. Liam used to be a regular until my vicious sorcerer aunt possessed him and forced him to try to kill me. I survived, though we were both hurt. Liam was horrified by what had happened, so he was avoiding The Slaughtered Lamb and me these days.

Dermot waved. "Us too."

"The blade won't kill us if we touch it," Grim explained, his brows slammed down low. "Don't be daft. The queen wouldn't give you a weapon that would kill us willy nilly. If we have ill intent against you and try to hurt you, you can fight back with an artifact that has the power to destroy us. She did it to give you a fighting chance against the king's assassins."

"How do you know so much about Sam's axe?" Dave growled.

"Stand down, demon." Grim didn't bother to turn around. "You aren't the only one here to protect her."

Dave and I shared a look.

"Wait. What? Grim, you were sent to this realm to protect me?"

He shrugged one of his beefy shoulders. "'Twasn't sent. I was here. Algar said our lady would like eyes on you. I'm just here to observe and help if needed."

I took an involuntary step back. "You've been spying on me?"

"Not spying." He was clearly annoyed with our questions. "I had started coming here anyway. Algar said that as long as I was here, I should keep them informed."

"Sounds like a fucking spy to me," Dave sneered.

Grim finally looked over his shoulder at Dave. "'Tweren't like that." He turned back to me. "No one's checking up on you. I'm more like a phone, but slower. If you wanted to get a message to the queen, you could go through me. The same is true in reverse. If she wants you to know something, you can get the information through me. That's all. No one's asking me to pass on secrets. It's more that I'm ready if you need me."

"That was why you went with me when I had to travel into Faerie last year?" I ventured.

"Aye. Liam, Maggie, and me. Though in Liam and Maggie's cases, they were just doing it to look after you. I'm the only one who agreed to take on the role." Hands on his hips, he scowled at me. "None of this is here nor there. Algar needs to know we have a pooka."

"My dad already passed it on," Meri told him.

Grim turned his attention to her and then flicked his gaze out the window, where Meri's dad was watching us. "Who did he tell?"

She glanced at her dad and gave him a big, fake smile and a wave. "Everybody smile at my dad," she hissed, and we did. "He was already worried about me before I started asking about pookas."

"If he's here, how did he let Algar know?" Grim wore a pained grimace, which seemed to be as close to a smile as he could get.

"There's a spot nearby, at the bottom of the bay, that's a doorway into Faerie," she said.

Dave, Grim, and I all looked at each other with mirroring expressions of *what the fuck*?

"Wait. Has that always been there?" I asked. Maybe that was where the kelpies that hated me kept coming from. I turned to Liam and Dermot. "Did you two know that?"

They nodded. "There are a lot of water fae here because of it," Liam explained.

"I thought the Wicche Glass Tavern was the closest doorway. You're telling me I built my bookstore and bar over a doorway?" I started to rub my hands over my face and then remembered the axe. I swung it over my shoulder and replaced it in its sheath.

"Don't put it away," Grim scolded. "We need to check for the pooka."

"Who are we checking?" I countered. "All the fae in the room have proven who they are and my touching my axe to a wicche isn't going to do anything to them."

"I already checked," Dave said. "Everybody is who they seem to be."

"Okay. First thing's first," I said, walking behind the bar and placing my hand on the wall. "Let me fix the ward."

I closed my eyes, unspooling my magic like a long gold thread in my chest. I mentally wrapped it around the hand touching the wall and thought, *I, Sam Quinn, key to the ward on The Slaughtered Lamb, ask that pookas, no matter what or who they look like, be barred from entering. Whether by the stairs, the water, or the air, no pooka shall pass my ward and enter.* I felt a pull on my arm as my magic traveled through the walls, floors, ceilings, and windows, locking us away and keeping us safe.

When I opened my eyes, I found Dave watching me. "I'd already put a demon ward on the place when I heard we had one."

"Thank you." Our voices were both quiet. Regardless of our standing in a room of a dozen people, we were only talking to one another. I'd once thought of Dave as my most trusted and beloved grumpy uncle. Some hard truths had been learned recently, and we were now uncomfortably cautious with one another. It wasn't that I didn't trust him. I'd trust him with my life. It was more that I was struggling with grief and disillusionment. I knew he was trying, and he knew I was too. Forgiveness over my mother's dead body was proving difficult for me.

"I know," he said softly.

"Well, why the devil didn't you tell us from the start you'd already warded against them?" Grim grumbled, climbing back up on his stool and taking a gulp of mead.

"Okay, but, Sam, I still have something to tell you," Meri said.

I turned to her. "Right. I'm sorry."

"Dad did some investigating." Her voice was low. Dave and the fae could still hear her, but the wicches, who didn't have sensitive hearing, went back to their own conversations. "He said that the merfolk at the wharf have been feeling something off. They hadn't seen the pooka, but when my dad asked about one, it made them realize that must have been what they were feeling. They're pretty nervous. Pookas don't care for water fae.

"My aunt Nerissa started closing the club early the last couple of days because all my cousins were feeling super creeped out at work. When they leave at the end of the night—if they're not returning to the ocean—they walk together in a group to their cars."

"Do you know," I asked, "is there a doorway to Faerie at The Bubble Lounge?"

Meri glanced at Grim and then lowered her voice even more. "There's not supposed to be one there, but a couple of my cousins said they felt a pull into the other realm more strongly in the last few months."

"Do they know where it is?" Maybe someone could close it.

"Um." She coiled her long blonde hair around her nervous fingers. "They think it's the glass ceiling that your cousin Arwyn made. They said they sometimes hear the high-pitched buzzing voices of the flower fairies and smell the blooms that grow along the riverbanks in Faerie when they are in a back corner of the club. No one has tried to jump up, touch the glass ceiling, and test the theory, though. When they have to clean in that corner, they do it quickly and go. Auntie Nerissa even moved the tables so no one has to serve in that area."

I rubbed my forehead. This was crazy. "There's no way Arwyn did that on purpose."

"Oh, no," Meri said, shaking her head. "No one thinks she made the doorway. Maybe more like her spelled glass focused the fae-ness, like a magnifying glass in the sun." She grimaced. "When a lot of us are all in the same area, the veil between realms becomes thin."

"That seems dangerous," I said. "I'm surprised the queen lets the fae stay in this realm if their presence here destabilizes Faerie."

Meri nodded sadly. "It's true, but I don't want my dad to leave. The queen wants them back in Faerie—not us halflings, of course, but the true fae." She glanced out the window. "But the queen loves her people and wants them to be happy. A lot of fae have lived in this realm for so long, this is home. They don't want to go back. They have lives and loved ones here."

"Like your dad." I reached out and rubbed her arm.

"Yeah." She looked down a moment and then shook her head. "I haven't told you the important part yet. Dad was told that the only way to kill a pooka was to attack when they were in their in-between state. He said they never go directly from one form to another instantaneously. There's a state in between when they are vulnerable, and completing the shift won't heal them."

"Okay," I said. "Thank you and please thank your father for us. I'll pass it on. Hopefully we can figure out a way to stop it."

Owen walked down the stairs. "Hey."

"I'll go back to shelving now," Meri said before ducking back into the bookstore.

Owen watched her go. "Everything okay?"

I nodded. "She was passing on some information about pookas."

"Oh, good." He stared down at the phone in his hand, clearly not paying attention to my response.

"Owen, is everything with *you* okay?"

"George wants to fly to Brazil," he said, "and look for Jade's family now. Alec overruled him, saying she wasn't ready." He ran his hand through his hair. "The thing is, George isn't sure if that's really what's best for Jade, or if it's Alec who isn't ready to let her go."

"Nothing needs to be decided now," I told him. "My great-uncle knows the family. You guys wandering around the Amazon looking for them makes no sense. When everyone is ready, he'll call, and they'll likely come here to get her or maybe tell you where to meet. Either way, there's no rush. I think Alec is right."

"Yeah." Owen dropped onto the stool beside me. "George wants to go now because he remembers how torn up he felt when they were in the same position as Jade's family is now, not even knowing if Alec was alive or dead all those years. It's killing him to knowingly do this to other people."

"I get it. Maybe if he understands that my uncle can contact her family at any time, that he doesn't have to go find them, it'll ease the anxiety a bit."

"I'll tell him," he said, pulling out his phone again.

I stopped him with a hand on his shoulder. "Just go. We're fine. Go to the zoo and meet him at the merry-go-round to talk it out."

He nodded, pocketing his phone and grabbing his backpack from behind the bar. "Thanks, boss. I will." And he was up the stairs and out.

Thankfully, after all the hubbub, the afternoon was blissfully quiet and uneventful. Liam and Dermot donned their seal skins and went back to the ocean. The wicches who'd joined us for lunch had gone. It was too early for the after-work crowd, so Grim was on his stool with his mead. Meri was pretending to shelve while reading in the stacks, Dave was baking, Rose, one of my regular wicches, was drinking tea and reading a paranormal romance, and I was sitting on my stool behind the bar, wondering if my dog wished he was Vlad's.

I was feeling sorry for myself and my lack of pooch to keep me company when there was a loud thump at the water entrance. What in the world? I rounded the bar to check as Grim looked over his shoulder.

When I got close, I could see it was Liam. He was pushing at the ward, but it didn't give. Shit. Did I adjust the ward wrong?

"Why isn't he in his seal skin?" Grim growled from beside me. "His eyes are wrong."

I yanked out my axe and plunged it into the water. It hit the Liam-looking pooka in the face, causing a large red welt to form on his cheek.

He bared his teeth, his eyes now glowing red, as he punched the magical water membrane. There was another loud thump, but the ward didn't give.

He began shifting and I pulled the axe back to throw it through the patch of water, but Grim grabbed the axe handle, stopping me.

"That axe is too valuable. We can't lose it. Only use it when you're sure you can kill him; otherwise he could destroy it and we'll have no weapon against him."

Liam shifted into a large orca. He eyed us, looped around to swim away, and then torpedoed through the water to smash into the window, the asshole.

Rose stood, her fingers twitching as she built a spell. Dave pushed out of the kitchen and fire engulfed the orca. He smashed his fiery body against the glass again and again. My eyes flew to the edges, looking for cracks or leaks. This was just like that horrible vision my sadistic aunt had trapped me in last year, the one where the Kraken squeezed and broke the glass, causing tons of seawater to wash out my bookstore and bar. My stomach dropped.

TWENTY-NINE

Closing It Down

I didn't know if it was Dave's new ward or my pooka upgrade, but the glass held tight. The pooka shifted to an octopus and started toward the ocean entrance again, but Dave sent another volley of fire. The pooka then shifted to an eel and disappeared into the seaweed.

Meri went to the window and stared into the ocean. "Do you see my dad?"

The fear in her voice had all of us moving closer to the window to search for him.

"If the pooka was wearing Liam's face," Grim said, "then he was watching us earlier. Your dad swam away after you moved back to the bookstore to work."

Meri looked between Grim and the ocean. "But how would you know that? You always sit with your back to the window."

"Mirror," Grim grunted.

I turned to look, and sure enough, there was a mirror directly across from where Grim always sat. It was unnoticeable unless you were bent down, just a rectangular mirror under a shelf of liquor bottles. I realized now that the mirror was the perfect height for a dwarf to see what was going on behind him.

I felt like an idiot. All these years, I'd thought Grim was

staring into space when he was really watching the ocean and patrons behind him. In my defense, dwarfs are incredibly warlike beings, so I'd thought he was working through some battle trauma.

"There he is!" Meri cried, waving to her father as he swam toward the ocean entrance.

He popped through the hole a moment later and she threw her arms around his neck. A flood of Mermish was going back and forth between the two, as each seemed to be assuring the other that they were okay.

Grim went back to his stool while I walked Dave back into the kitchen. "Is it dangerous to remain open with this thing trying so hard to get in?"

He leaned back against the counter, his muscular arms over his chest. "Yeah. I've been wondering the same. The wards will keep him out, but what about your customers who pass through those wards?" He shook his head. "I don't know."

I didn't want to do it, but I also knew I couldn't live with one of my friends getting hurt or killed by the pooka because I decided to stay open. I wasn't curing cancer here. People could take a few days off.

"I'm closing it down," I said as I went back out to the bar. Meri was still talking with her dad. Rose was back at her table, but she wasn't reading. She was looking nervously out the window.

"Okay, everyone." They turned to look at me. "I don't feel like staying open is safe for you. I'm going to close down until the pooka is caught. Your safety is too important to risk."

Rose nodded and stood. "I think you're right, dear." She glanced up the stairs. "You don't think he's up there waiting, do you?"

"I'll walk you to your car," Dave said, swinging open the kitchen door.

Meri translated for her dad, who nodded in my direction.

"Meri, you go up with Dave. He can make sure you and Rose both get out of here safely."

"You two, go ahead," Grim said. "I'll take Meri up when she's ready."

Dave turned to me. "Everything is stored in the kitchen. I think maybe I'll do what you suggested and visit Ireland for a couple of days. If they let me stay."

"Good." I grinned. "Tell Maggie I said hi and remember to be on your best behavior."

"Yeah, yeah," he grumbled, going up the stairs with Rose.

I closed the stair and air entrances for anyone trying to enter and then waited for Meri and her dad to finish talking before I sealed that one too.

"Thanks for looking out for Meri," I murmured to Grim.

He nodded. After a moment of silence, he said, "'Tweren't spying." He glanced at me quickly before staring straight out the window again. "I wouldn't betray you like that."

I rested my hand on his shoulder and felt the tension ease. "Thank you for caring and keeping watch."

He gave one decisive nod and then went back to waiting. Meri's dad dropped back into the ocean and I sealed the ward while she ran to the bookstore to grab her backpack.

I waved them out and then started cleaning up and closing down. On the way through the kitchen, I found a plate of cookies and brownies, so I picked it up and carried them with me.

I expected to find Fergus and Vlad where I left them, but the apartment was empty. I missed my pup, but at least I had a big fat meringue, filled with chocolate. As I munched, I walked home through the folly.

I whistled for Fergus, but he didn't come. Maybe he was visiting Cadmael on the island. I wasn't in any rush. If anything, I'd just cleared my schedule for the foreseeable future, so I enjoyed my stroll through the folly. What the dragons had created for us was pure magic.

As I wandered through the Shire, I considered sleeping in our hobbit hole tonight, a staycation of sorts. Of course, Clive had his vampy convention to deal with, so I guess sleepaway camp would need to wait. We really needed to throw a party in the folly for our friends as soon as the dragon builders were done.

When the path meandered into Middle Ages Canterbury and I passed Clive's family farm, I couldn't help but remember how he looked plowing shirtless in the sun. They may have originally been Leticia's memories, but they were all mine now.

At the entrance to the island, I whistled again, but Fergus did not come running. Where was he? I almost turned around and went back to The Slaughtered Lamb in case he'd fallen asleep in the bookstore and I hadn't noticed when I was closing. Residual fear from the pooka and not seeing Fergus in hours had me jogging the rest of the way home.

I zigzagged through the cars and hit the elevator, which wasn't waiting on this level. That gave me hope that for some reason Vlad had taken Fergus home. When the elevator opened into the den, I found Vlad sitting in his corner, lamp on and book open. The back door was open as well.

"Shouldn't you be working?" he asked, looking annoyed at the interruption.

"What the heck are you doing here and how did you open the door and not die?" Seriously, what the hell did he get up to during the day while I was busy?

At the sound of my voice, Fergus raced in and launched himself at me. We both fell back onto the couch, as he did his best to lick my face and I tried to save myself.

"Fergus. Door," Vlad said.

Fergus hopped up, ran to the back door, and nudged it closed before returning to the couch.

"He needed to go out," Vlad stated simply, as though that was obvious. "He enjoys lounging in the garden. There's a squirrel that's been driving him to distraction. And Fergus opened the door himself. He's quite clever."

I hugged my horse of a dog and then scratched his belly. "Is that true? Are you an extra special clever boy? Yes, you are." He kicked his giant feet in the air—almost punching me—as I rubbed his tummy.

"The question remains," Vlad said. "Why are you home during the day?"

"Oh, that." I explained our pooka encounter to him and my decision to close it down until the pooka was dealt with.

He'd leaned forward as I spoke but finally relaxed when I said I'd sent everyone home and that our two vulnerable people had been escorted out by warriors.

"So," I said, standing up, "as we've got hours before we have to go to your vampy tea party tonight, I'm going to join my husband and take a nap."

"You should eat first." His gaze dropped to the plate of cookies on the coffee table. "And something more substantial than sweets."

I almost argued but bit it back. "I could eat."

Fergus joined me in the kitchen, hoping for snacks, so I gave him a bully stick. He went back to the den to enjoy it while I made myself a sandwich. I ate it at the counter and then put my plate in the dishwasher.

"I'm going up now," I called, heading for the stairs.

"You should learn to chew more quietly," was his response, which made me laugh.

I closed the bedroom door, stripped to my undies, and then slipped back into bed with Clive. When I rested my head on his chest, his arms wrapped tightly around me. Releasing a sigh of contentment, I let the exhaustion pull me under.

I woke to kisses up my throat and along my jaw.

"Such a lovely surprise to find you in bed with me," Clive rumbled, his voice deep with sleep.

My fingers plunged into his thick hair, and I pulled his mouth to mine. When I finally came up for air, I confessed, "I was walking through the folly earlier and thinking about young, hot, human Clive plowing the field, sweaty, straining muscles on display…"

Clive grinned. "Were you now?"

I nodded, my hands creeping down his body. Suddenly, my panties were gone. He nibbled under my ear, driving me crazy. Holding himself over me on one elbow, he dragged his other hand down my side and then slipped it between my legs. When he found me ready and my hips lifting toward him, his eyes went vamp black.

He kissed me again, hooking his arm under my leg, opening me to him, and then he was sliding in. He held himself still as we shared one breathless moment, and then the chain broke. Fanning the flames, he created an inferno that burned us both. Toes curling, I wrapped around him, meeting him thrust for thrust, thinking I would burst, that I couldn't possibly hold him tighter or love him more.

Groaning, I fell off the edge—or I suppose was pushed—but Clive was right behind me, his fangs deep in my neck.

My brain was so scrambled, it took me a minute to realize I was hearing a persistent buzzing. I smacked Clive's shoulder. "That's probably Bram. Talk to him while I shower and get ready."

He rolled to his back and reached for his phone. Grinning at me, he swiped it open. "Bram. It's good to hear from you." He paused. "You did? She hadn't mentioned, but we haven't had much time to talk."

Blushing, I grimaced and scampered off to the bathroom. When I was almost done blow-drying my hair, Clive walked past me and stepped into the shower.

"He's taking the position."

I turned off the hair dryer. "Really? I thought he loved what he was doing."

He ducked under the water. "He does, but his second has been ready to be a Master for a long time and Bram is ready to try something new. Like me, he's been doing the Counselor's job—in his case, Sebastian's—for quite a while. The Masters call him if they're having a dispute and need advice. Sebastian was apparently too busy to take these calls, so they stopped calling him and started contacting Bram."

I had to tear my eyes away from Clive soaping himself. My brain was going to short out.

"Nonsense." He crooked his finger. "Come here. I think you could use a little more cleaning."

I turned the hair dryer back on and pretended I couldn't hear him, though I did hear the laughing.

As he stepped out and grabbed a towel, he said, "We're going to meet at The Bubble Lounge before going to the nocturne. The visiting Counselors want to see it and investigate for themselves."

"Oh, I forgot. Meri gave me some pooka info." I told him about our pooka visit and her father's tip for killing one.

Clive wrapped his arms around me, his front to my back. "I know you didn't make the decision lightly, but I think you were right. It's too dangerous to stay open when he seems to be fixated on you."

I gripped his arms. "I'd never forgive myself if he grabbed Meri or Owen—or anyone, for that matter. It's not worth it."

He kissed the side of my neck. "Perhaps I'll be lucky again tomorrow and find my wife in our bed when I wake." He gave me a quick squeeze and then headed off to his closet to dress.

THIRTY

Passing Notes

I left my hair long, put on some eyeliner, mascara, and lip tint, and then went to my own closet. "So, we're thinking a cocktail dress, is that it?" I called over.

He stepped into the doorway of my closet, already wearing a crisp white dress shirt and charcoal slacks. "You can wear whatever you'd like. I don't know that The Bubble Lounge has a specific dress code."

I nervously pulled the silk robe belt tight. "I know, but I want to look appropriate. I don't want to embarrass you in front of your friends."

Chuckling, he pulled me into his arms and kissed me. "You could never embarrass me, and *friends* may be overstating the relationship." He pulled back. "I'd forgotten. Does Thi still want me dead? Do we know what that was about?"

"I forgot too," I told him. "I fell asleep last night. Once I get dressed, we can try to visit her thoughts together, and you can tell me what she's thinking or what she saw."

He checked his watch and nodded. "We should have time." Scanning my clothes, he said, "Personally, I'm still voting for leather pants. If I can't have those, though, I'd say a little black dress or trousers and a turtleneck, whichever you feel more comfortable in."

"Okay." I pushed him out. "You finish getting dressed and I'll figure it out." Once he was gone, I went to the far end, where the cocktail dresses were hanging. I pulled down a black dress made of a thin, whisper-soft wool. It was form-fitting on top, though it flared a bit at the hip. Shoulderless, it had a narrow halter tie around the neck.

I couldn't reach the zipper in the back, but that was okay because I wasn't sure I could leave the house like this. Yes, my scars were gone now, but I still felt them. I wondered if they'd always be there in my mind.

I was so lost in thought, I hadn't realized that Clive was back until he was zipping me up. He rested his hands on my exposed shoulders and watched me struggle. "It's chilly out. You might be more comfortable with a jacket or a cardigan."

I turned in his arms and rested my head on his chest. Once the tightness in my throat loosened, I said, "Good call." I had a black cashmere cardigan with brushed silver buttons. I slipped it on and then put on a pair of closed-toe strappy stilettos. I turned to Clive. "Okay?"

"Perfect, though I think you could use some color in your accessories." He went to the jewelry drawers and pulled out a stunning collar of interlocking platinum swirls with emeralds and blue diamonds nestled in the swoops and dips. I stared and then blinked a few times.

"Where did that come from?" I glanced up at him. "Tell me those aren't real. What if I lose it?"

"I have faith in you." He lifted it over my head and secured it in back. It fit perfectly and hid the straps of the dress, so it looked as though the dress itself had an emerald and diamond collar.

"And these." He handed me emerald earrings and a wide bracelet that matched the necklace. All of which, of course, matched my blue diamond wedding ring.

"I'm going to need armed guards to follow me around." My hands shook holding the treasure.

"You don't need guards. You have me." He attached the bracelet around my wrist and waited for me to put on the earrings.

At least they had screw backs, which made them feel more secure. Short of someone ripping them out of my ear—

"Stop. Darling, you yourself could fight off any ne'er-do-wells. If you require backup, though, I imagine eight vampires would be enough."

"Okay. I'm being stupid." I looked in the mirror. "Are we sure this isn't too much?"

"We're sure." He took my hand and led me back into the bedroom. "Let's take a look into Thi's head and see why she wants one of us dead, shall we?"

Clive took off his suit coat and we sat on the sofa. I closed my eyes, still holding his hand in both of mine, and I sought out the little green blips that meant vampire. Other than the three near me, the rest were clustered together in the nocturne.

Linking with Clive was second nature now. *When we've tried this before, Godfrey couldn't hear you, but we don't know if Thi has any special gifts, so I don't want you to say anything once we get started, okay?*

Of course.

When you're in her mind with me, squeeze my hand, so I know you're hearing and seeing what I am.

I will.

Here we go.

Sorting through the nocturne vamps, I found Russell, Godfrey, and Audrey right away. I had to mentally touch on each of the others to find the one I was looking for. I'd visited Thi and her assistant yesterday, which helped me recognize their mental signatures today.

I wrapped the coil of my magic around Clive and pulled him into my candy-coated brain. Did that description sound stupid? Yes, but it's how I visualized it, and it worked for me, so back off.

Once I had Thi's blip located, I let my consciousness spread out, engulfing her blip, and then quietly seeped in. I was much better at this than when I first tried to do it last year. I used to stab my way in, but the older, more powerful vamps felt the intrusion. Now? Not so much.

I heard her voice but had no idea what she was saying to the assistant I had listened to last night. Clive squeezed my hand. Okay, good. I let him listen for a bit and then pushed an image of myself from last night into her mind. The tone of the conversation changed. Clive held my hand firmly throughout. Eventually, he tapped my hand twice and I pulled us out.

When I opened my eyes and turned to him, Clive was already watching me.

"You're truly remarkable." He kissed me and I lost my train of thought. He finally pulled back and said, "At first, it was nothing. A conversation very like our own—what are you wearing? When you pushed your image at them—and you are far more beautiful than you think you are—the conversation changed. Thi asked if Mai noticed anything special or dangerous about you after Thi had gone into the library. Mai said that after Godfrey had deposited them in the lower level, she'd come back up looking for you. She knew you were in the study and that you were getting your hair done, but she didn't hear anything being said."

"Did she mention that text I saw in her memories?"

"Of sorts," he replied. "Mai said she didn't understand why Chaaya had texted that you weren't what you seemed to be."

"Anything else?"

He shook his head. "That doesn't mean there wasn't more to the text, but they didn't mention it."

"I could try to find the memory again," I volunteered.

He checked his watch. "We don't have time. When you go into memories, you're often in there for hours. But there is one more thing I'd like you to do, if you're feeling up to it."

"What's that?"

"I want to go into Joao's thoughts like you did Thi's. There's something off there. It could be nothing, but I want to make sure that he, too, didn't get a message from someone in Budapest. I can't put my finger on it, but I'd feel better if we knew if he was plotting against us."

"I don't like spying on people if I don't have to. It feels creepy. If you think he's a threat, though, I can do it."

He pulled my hand to his lips and kissed it. "Thank you, darling. I wouldn't ask if I didn't think it was important."

I went through the process again, pulling Clive along with me. Joao wasn't talking with anyone. He was texting someone, though. Clive squeezed my hand, so he was on the job. I zoned out while Joao continued to text in what I assumed was Portuguese and then finished getting dressed.

When it seemed like he wasn't doing much, I pushed an image of myself into his brain. He slammed the closet door closed and then started texting again. When Joao finally left his room and started down the nocturne stairs, Clive tapped my hand and I pulled us out.

He stood, pulling me up with him. "We should get started too. I want to arrive first. I contacted Nerissa to let her know we were coming. I'd like to go inside and see if you feel anything in the corner of the room Meri was talking about."

I brushed my hands down my dress, hoping I didn't wrinkle it. "But what was Joao thinking?"

"I'll explain in the car."

I strapped on my axe and grabbed a small black handbag. When we started down the stairs, Fergus came running toward us from the den. Clive gave him a full-body scratch and then picked up a note on the counter. He barely glanced at it before stuffing it in his pocket. He turned to me with a bright smile. "Ready, darling?'

I held out my hand. "Nice try. Hand it over."

He *so* did not want to. It was written all over his face. "It's nothing. Shall we give Fergus a treat before we go? I believe Vlad already fed him dinner."

I left my hand out and waited.

Finally, he took the crumpled paper out of his pocket and handed it to me.

In Vlad's perfect penmanship, I read,

I'm finding it too noisy to read here. Let me know when you two are done and I'll come back.
P.S. Fergus has been given his dinner. Have you fallen on hard times? Is there a reason the poor dog gets dry kibble?

I felt my cheeks flame, remembering my telling Clive about my hot farm boy fantasy and then what happened afterward, remembering what we had done the day before and then finding Vlad down here. The things we'd said to one another, the sounds—dear God, the sounds… I needed a hole I could drop into and stay in until old age and dementia helped me forget this moment.

Clive grabbed it from my hand again and shoved it back in his pocket as he pulled me into a hug. "I'm sorry, love. The man is a menace. Perhaps we should start leaving notes around the Viper's Nest when he visits Stheno."

I pulled back and stared at him. "Vlad and Stheno? That already happened?"

He nodded. "But do you see me trying to embarrass him?"

"That's actually kind of a scary combination," I whispered.

Clive shrugged. "It's none of my business. I wish he felt the same about our love life." He kissed my temple and held me tightly against him. "I can ban him from the house, if you'd like. We gave him a perfectly acceptable apartment to stay in. Just because he can walk around during the day doesn't mean he has to walk over here."

I patted his chest. "It's okay." I shook my head, like I did in my other form when I was trying to shake off unease. "I'm sure it was intended as a joke." I pushed away and checked my bag for my phone.

"Let it go," I told him, petting Fergus' head, as he was leaning heavily into me. "It's no big deal." I got a stick of chicken jerky for my pup and then checked the back door. Why? I don't know. No one could break in that way, but it kept me busy and moved me farther away from that note and the knowledge that someone— nope. Not going there. I needed to suck it up and brazen this out.

It was just a joke. I knew that. After everything I'd been through, though, intimacy was hard for me. Someone else listening made me feel like I'd been displayed naked on a billboard in Times Square. Whatever. I couldn't think about it now. Later, after everyone had gone home, I could curl up in bed and deal with the humiliation. Right now, we had vamp shit to do.

"Oh. You were in a hurry," I said, straightening my dress again and brushing off Fergus' hair. "Sorry." I went to the elevator and pushed the button.

Clive was beside me, taking my hand. I knew he'd feel me trembling, but he didn't say a word.

"Be a good boy," I called over my shoulder. "We'll be back in a few hours." As the elevator door slid shut, I saw Fergus climbing up on the couch and I smiled. I needed to keep my mind on my pup and not the men waiting in the garage.

The elevator door opened and Clive squeezed my hand, leading me toward the men standing by the car.

"Cadmael, can you sit in back tonight?" Clive asked. He walked me to the front passenger seat, opened the door, and then closed it for me once I was in my seat.

In the rearview mirror, I saw Clive toss the crumpled note to Vlad as he circled around the back of the car. All three vamps got in at the same time.

"Sam, I—" Vlad began.

"No," Clive said, shutting him up.

The drive to the wharf was silent. Clive kept one of his hands wrapped around mine the whole way there.

When we pulled into the parking lot, there was a valet waiting to take our car. Clive rolled down the window. The attendant was fae. He looked in and recognized us.

"I'll take it back myself," Clive said. The valet nodded, getting out of Clive's way.

He circled around the nightclub and parked beside a shiny black limo. One of the nocturne's vampires sat behind the wheel and nodded to Clive when our car came to a stop. "The others are here."

THIRTY-ONE

My Clothing Doesn't Require Ventilation, Thank You Very Much

C live patted my hand, which I knew meant he wanted me to wait for him. Cadmael and Vlad got out and went to the site of the second murder, checking the area around the dumpster. Clive opened my door and held out his hand to me.

"I'm sorry I made us late."

He kissed the hand he was holding and then tucked it in the crook of his elbow. "You didn't. We can check out the area Meri told you about after the others leave." He placed his hand over mine and I nodded, letting out a shaky breath.

"Right. Okay."

Clive didn't bother with the dumpster. He walked us to the front door of the club. The other two must have caught up because Vlad opened the oversized door for us. I didn't realize my head was down until I heard Clive's voice in my head, *Chin up, darling.*

When I looked up, I saw Nerissa, the mermaid owner of the nightclub, heading toward us. "Good evening. I'm so glad you were able to join us." She moved in to kiss my cheek, which was super weird as we weren't on cheek-kissing terms, but she whispered, "Two at the bar. Don't know them. Be careful."

Clive turned at that and then I could see him cataloguing everyone sitting at the bar. "Nerissa, thank you for making room for us." He slid me to his other side so he could kiss Nerissa on the cheek. He did it so effortlessly, so charmingly, you'd never clock it unless you were me and knew he was putting himself between me and the bar.

Nerissa gestured us forward. "The rest of your party is straight ahead."

"Thank you," he said, wrapping his arm around me. *Middle of the bar. Two men. They smell of elven steel.*

Shit. Did we just walk into two of the king's assassins having a cocktail?

No. See the way their eyes are darting around. One of them is watching the vampire table, the other just saw us and elbowed the partner. They were waiting for us.

How did they know we were coming?

Excellent question for later. In the meantime—he gave me a fast, hard kiss—*don't die.*

If anything happens to me, save the jewelry.

You're not funny.

We'd been walking toward the bar, our bodies loose, not projecting our awareness of them.

The two men slid off their stools. The room was quiet. I spared a glance at the rest of the nightclub and saw patrons frozen, some in speech, some with forks on their lips, some mid-twirl on the dance floor.

Okay. We were doing this. Clive and I spread out to give ourselves room. I snatched the axe off my back.

One of the fae men flicked his eyes at Clive and then at Nerissa, hissing, "The king will hear of this."

"Not if you don't survive," she replied, stepping back into the shadows.

Oh. It wasn't just the humans who were frozen. The vamps and the fae servers were as well. Nerissa had left Clive and me free so I'd have a fighting chance.

Nerissa told them we were coming, Clive said.

I got that. I tossed my little handbag to the side at Vlad's feet. *But she's also the one trying to help.*

"That's not yours," the one on the right sneered at me, staring at the axe.

They were both tall, broad-shouldered warrior elves. They'd made an attempt to blend in, wearing black dress shirts and black pants. One had light brown hair and the other's was white-blond. That was really the only difference between them. Both were inhumanly beautiful and both looked pretty excited about handing me over to the king, or short of that, killing me on the spot.

"I beg to differ," I said, spinning the handle. "I won this from the dwarf who tried to kill me. The axe stayed with me when his dead body returned to Faerie. It changed alliances. I have an elf's sword at home too. Are you sure you want to do this?"

We need you in god-mode, Clive said in my head, referring to the hyper fast gear I can sometimes shift into. I focused on needing to protect Clive from harm, which usually helped me access it.

I'll try.

Try hard.

The one closest to me lunged and Clive dove, taking the elf down before he could get his hand on me to abduct me to Faerie or swing his sword to decapitate me. While they fought, the other one leered and flipped his sword in his hand.

"Alone at last," he smirked.

Razor-sharp claws slid from the fingertips of the hand not holding an axe. Heart racing, desperately hoping that Clive had it, I let my eyes go wolf gold and my jaw elongate to hold my wolf's teeth.

The elf took in my altered appearance and displayed a moment of fear. It was instantaneous, but it was there. I wasn't running away. I wasn't following his script.

"Your boss is obsessed with me," I told him, my voice still clear, though my jaw had reshaped itself. "It's embarrassing."

His sword was slicing through the air toward my head and the world slowed down. God-mode engaged. I blocked his sword with my axe, knocking it back while I leaned forward, my claws digging into his face.

He leapt back, shocked, his face in ribbons, and then he charged. We went at it, back and forth. He jabbed under my arm and I felt a breeze. My cardigan was catching strays.

"This is Chanel, you asshole. You're paying for that."

Nonplussed, he sidestepped and aimed for my heart. I did a disarming move that would have made sense if I too was wielding a sword. It worked with the axe, mostly, though I felt the sting on my wrist that meant I'd been cut. Thank goodness I was wearing black. It forgave so much.

I didn't feel Clive's fight behind me. I wouldn't look, couldn't take my eyes off my opponent, but it felt like that fight was over. I didn't feel crushing grief or irreparable pain, so I hoped Clive was fine.

The elf I was fighting looked over my shoulder with an expression of shock, but I wasn't born yesterday. He wasn't distracting me.

When he leapt forward again, I spun out of the way, grabbed his arm, yanking him forward, and then swung my axe at his back while he was off balance. Thankfully, it hadn't been a ploy on his part. He really was off balance, so when I swung, my axe connected with his flesh and he popped out of existence.

Spinning, I braced for what I would find with Clive and his elf. Clive was watching me, his hand around the elf's neck, choking him out just enough to make him pass out but not to kill him.

"If I finished the job, he'd reappear in Faerie. The only way to truly get rid of him is for you to kill him with the axe."

I didn't want to give the elf a chance to heal and extricate himself from the chokehold, so I swung for his chest and he popped out as well.

Clive was in front of me, raising my wrist so he could check the wound.

"I'm okay," I said. "I barely noticed it."

"That's the adrenaline talking," he said before his tongue traced the cut.

My body went up in flames as my skin knit together. His eyes were vamp black. He stepped into me, gathered me in his arms, and kissed me senseless. I was vaguely aware of people talking around us and music playing.

My axe was replaced in my sheath and my clutch was slapped into my hand. Vlad was behind me, hiding my axe and sheath until they disappeared.

"I smell Sam's blood. What happened?" Vlad asked.

"Not right now," Clive murmured, walking us to the table.

All the vamps were on high alert, looking in every direction. They'd been frozen for the action, but they knew they'd missed something.

"I had no choice," Nerissa said behind us.

Clive pulled me closer and looked over my shoulder at our hostess "There's always a choice. You chose incorrectly. Sam came here, at your request, to investigate for you and in return you told the king's assassins she was coming."

Nerissa stood tall, staring Clive down. "I've worked hard to maintain and grow my business. If I hadn't told them, they would have destroyed it. I risked myself and my business to warn you. It was the best I could do."

I patted Clive's tense chest. "It's okay," I told him. "She shouldn't lose everything because the king has it out for me." I turned in his arms, though he made it difficult. "Thank you for the warning."

Nerissa's gaze bounced between Clive and me before she finally nodded, her stance deflating a bit. "Thank you for understanding. I'll send Champagne to your table."

"Don't bother," Clive bit out. When I rubbed his wrist, he added, "Sam prefers soda or juice."

I hadn't realized that Vlad and Cadmael were still flanking us until we started toward the table holding the Guild members. There were only three empty chairs, but rather than getting a fourth, Clive pulled me into his lap and wrapped an arm around me. Resting his free hand on my thigh, he spoke mind-to-mind.

When he cut you and I smelled your blood, it took everything in me not to snap my elf's neck and jump into your fight.

Look at it this way, I responded, *at least he cut the wrist that wasn't wearing the expensive bracelet.* I reached up to touch my necklace and earrings. *All good, right?*

You're perfect.

"What did we miss?" Cadmael murmured, knowing everyone at the table would hear but the humans wouldn't.

I didn't know what we wanted the other vampires to know, so I kept quiet.

"The fae king sent two assassins to abduct or kill Sam," Clive said. "We killed them instead."

"I don't understand," Ahmed said. "What was done to us that we didn't see any of that?"

"Everyone in the club, other than Sam and me, was frozen," Clive replied.

Nerissa brought over a glass of cranberry juice and placed it on the table in front of me.

"Thanks." I smiled, hoping she knew I didn't blame her for the king having it out for me.

She nodded and disappeared back into the depths of the nightclub.

"The fae can do this to us?" Pablo demanded, outraged. "Why were we not told?"

The other vampires ignored him.

"The fae are made of magic," I responded. "There's not much they can't do. Like all of you, though, they have different gifts. As for why you weren't told, perhaps you don't have a lot of fae in South America? I don't know why you wouldn't know about them. You were a Master before you became Counselor, right?"

I felt Clive's humor coming through our link. *I love you.*

A few of the vampires seemed to be fighting a smile while I drank my juice.

Vlad tapped my arm. When I looked over, he opened the flap of his jacket, flashing me the elf's sword. "You forgot something. You're quite careless with your weapons. I won't always be around to pick them up for you."

"Nice," I said, noting the glove he was wearing to hold it.

Pablo stared at it with a strange combination of anger and hunger. "I thought you said you killed two."

I glanced back where we'd fought and then remembered whose lap I was sitting on. "The fae hate vampires. You're death. They're life. There was no way an elven sword would switch its allegiance to a vampire, so the second one disappeared with its owner."

Pablo's eyes went vamp black, his expression darkening.

"Nothing personal, dude," I said. "I thought you already knew how the whole vampire thing worked." I turned to Vlad. "Is he a trainee?"

When he moved to fly over the table at me, he instead fell back in his seat, paralyzed, his eyes brown again and filled with fear.

"Don't ever threaten to harm my mate," Clive ground out. "She asked a valid question. *Why weren't you told?* How very passive of you. Being Master means looking over all the supernatural beings in your territory. Yes, there are fae in South America. They go by different names than European fae, but you have them, which you should know. Being angry with my wife won't hide your ignorance."

I thought it quite telling that none of the other vampires said or did anything to stop Clive.

Glaring at Pablo, Clive ran his hand up and down my arm. "Do you have yourself in control now? Can I release you?" He leaned forward. "Know this: If you ever threaten my wife again, I will hand you your final death in the most drawn out and painful way possible. Do you understand what *I'm* telling you?"

THIRTY-TWO

Dancing (Almost) in Faerie

P ablo nodded through the pain and then relaxed back into his
chair on a gasp.

"Why is she even here?" He muttered.

Cadmael opened his mouth to respond but Vlad interrupted,
looking at me. "Did you know you have a hole in your sweater?"

Clive was still glaring at Pablo, but I ignored them and
responded to Vlad. "Yeah. That sword you're holding made it." I
looked across the table at Adaeze and then down at my cardigan.
"Is it noticeable?"

She tipped her head to the side, weighing her words.

"Yes," Thi responded.

It was on the tip of my tongue to say *I wasn't asking you*, but I
held it in.

Adaeze finally nodded, though she looked sorry to do it.

I took the sweater off and folded it, laying it on the table in
front of me. "Maybe I can get it repaired."

Clive kissed the side of my head. "I'll get you a new one."

"It's that stupid elf who should be buying me a new one.
Jackass."

Adaeze grinned. "I like your jewelry very much."

"Thank you." I reached up and touched the necklace. "I was so worried I'd lose something tonight—they're new—but I hadn't counted on some damn elf trying to hack it off me." I held up my wrists. "At least he cut the one not wearing a new bracelet."

The vampires stared at my red, healing wound with an intensity that was off-putting, so I dropped my hands below the table.

Clive slid the chair back and stood, his arm still around me. "I'm going to dance with my wife. We'll meet you back at the nocturne afterward."

Cadmael nodded, standing as well. "Yes. They were able to investigate both of the killing spots before you arrived. I think they've seen what they wanted to. We'll go now." He glanced to his side. "Vlad, take that sword out the back."

Clive walked me through the tables to the dance floor before spinning me into him. Our slow dancing was at odds with the upbeat music, but I wasn't complaining.

This is like the first time we danced in that South of Market vampire club. Everyone around us was bouncing and grinding but we were slow dancing in our own little bubble.

I remember.

You were so angry that night.

One of the benefits of no longer being the nocturne Master is that I don't have to listen to outraged complaints about my spending time with a werewolf. I'm blissfully content only having the voice of my mate up here with me.

I nuzzled into his neck.

It scared me when I smelled your blood, he told me.

I'm okay now. I tucked my arm into his jacket and felt safe and protected.

Clive slid his jacket off and draped it over my bare shoulders. *Better?*

I slid my arms through and felt more secure. Nodding, I wrapped my arms around him again. *Oh, I forgot. What was Joao texting about?*

You.

I reared back to look him in the eyes. *What? Why me? I barely said hello to him last night.*

It was an incomplete text thread, but he was asking what the other person had learned and if they knew why they should be—it doesn't translate exactly but—wary of you. Then he made a string of vulgar comments about seducing you in order to learn your secrets.

He must have felt me tense up because he began to rub my back.

"Creep," I muttered.

"He is," Clive agreed. *Now, what do we notice about this corner?*

I glanced around this section of the dance floor and saw no tables nearby. A large potted plant sat here instead. As it was the only plant in the nightclub, it seemed odd. *Is this the corner?*

Clive nodded. *I've been watching. The servers avoid this area. There's a storage room back there.* He tipped his head past the potted plant to a discreet door in the far wall. *The staff are walking behind the stage to get over here, instead of just walking where we're standing.*

I closed my eyes, swaying with Clive but concentrating on what was around us. *Are there cameras over here?*

Clive looked up around the ceiling. *Yes. Far side of the band but pointed in this direction. Nerissa is probably trying to determine if the pooka is sneaking in through her club.*

Block me from the camera and any of the humans around here.

He swayed, moving me a few degrees away from the front of the club. *That's as hidden as I can make you.*

I shifted my nose into a long wolf's snout and tilted my head up to sniff. A chill ran down my spine. I'd recognize that scent anywhere. In my mind's eye, I could picture the overblown blowsy flowers bobbing in the wind along the river running through Faerie. The sun sparkling on the water, long grass in dappled light beneath huge, sheltering trees, rich loamy earth, I could see it all and I felt the pull to visit.

Shifting my nose back, I said, "It's a doorway. We should go."

Clive nodded, taking my hand and weaving through the tables

toward the bar. Nerissa stood in the back, watching us. Clive went toward the kitchen exit, but I pulled him to a stop beside Nerissa.

"Is there a way to close it?" I asked quietly.

Chin up, eyes scanning the club, she didn't seem to have heard me. Finally, though, she shook her head.

"Have you seen anything on the camera?" I asked. "Is that how the pooka ended up here?"

She gave a reluctant nod. "I think so. The cameras are new. Inside and out. I didn't see it arrive, but it only makes sense. I saw the two I warned you about drop through, though," she murmured before walking away from us.

Clive pulled me along. The kitchen staff gave us dirty looks but then went back to work, ignoring us. Clive's phone buzzed. As he read his text and began to text back, I looked through the back door. The nocturne's limo was heading around the club to pick up the vampires in front. Once it had passed, I saw Vlad leaning against our car.

I kept walking, wanting to clear the air. "Listen," I said as I approached him, "I know it was a joke intended for Clive, and my reaction probably seemed way too much. It hit me wrong, and I had a hard time finding my balance again."

"Look who I found." He crouched behind the car parked next to ours and Fergus bolted out from between the cars.

Vlad's voice had sounded weird, but I was so distracted by my little buddy being here that the loss of his Romanian accent didn't hit me until later.

"What happened? How did you get here?" As he galloped across the small parking area, I registered his size. He was larger than he was an hour ago. When he lifted his head to look at me, my knees weakened and I tore the axe from under Clive's jacket, inadvertently shredding his collar.

Knuckles white, I crushed the axe handle as the dog slowed, head low, stalking me, muscles bunching, readying for attack. "This isn't chaos. This is cruelty and you know it."

The pooka dog growled, showing teeth far bigger and sharper

than a normal wolfhound, even an unusually large one. His long, sharp claws made a horrible scraping sound on the gravel, like nails on a chalkboard.

A moment later, I felt my husband's presence beside me.

Eyes still on the Fergus-wearing pooka, I said to Clive, "I wrecked your jacket."

"It wasn't a good night for our clothing."

Someone landed on my other side. Vlad, still holding my sword in his gloved hand. "Sorry I'm late. I was on the roof."

The pooka stared at us, at my axe and Vlad's sword, deciding Clive must be the weakest of us. The Fergus-looking monster charged and Clive flew at him, wrapping his arms around him and crushing him. The sound of bones breaking was loud in the quiet night.

And then Clive's arms were empty. The pooka had disappeared, except they couldn't disappear.

"No slats to drop under here." I rushed forward, scanning the gravel at our feet. "He shifted to something too small to see easily." I started slamming the blunt head of my axe on the ground, hoping I'd get him.

Nerissa appeared behind Clive, her hands around his neck yanking his head. Clive did a backflip over the top of her, breaking the hold. Knees on her shoulders, he wrenched her neck and she disappeared, leaving him crouched on the ground.

I pounded the ground beside him again and then we heard a grunt. Vlad went flying by us, but he flipped himself over and landed already running back, sword up, to fight the huge grizzly bear that had appeared in the parking lot.

Clive pushed me behind him. Vlad was mesmerizing with a sword. He was so damn fast, it was like a threshing machine was attacking the bear and then he, too, was standing alone in the parking lot.

A gray-haired man walked down the darkened alley between the nightclub and the property fence. "Oh, dear," he said. "Terribly sorry to interrupt. That nice valet said my car had been parked back here. I'm in an awful hurry I'm afraid." He tapped his pockets, like he was checking he had his keys and his wallet.

Vlad moved forward, sword raised, but I held up my hand for him to wait.

"Sam, don't," Clive said as I moved closer.

The harried man looked up and I saw kind, green eyes. "Oh my," he said. "Your face is perfectly symmetrical." He patted his chest, his fingers trembling. "That helps."

Meri appeared around the corner, brow furrowed. Her gaze jumped from my axe to Vlad's sword to the strange older man.

"Meri, go in. You can't be out here." I rushed forward to move her along, but the older man grabbed my arm.

Clive and Vlad moved as one.

The old man pushed me behind him, unaware of his imminent death. "That's the pooka, my dear," he said, fingers twitching at his side.

Shocked, I studied Meri and realized he was right. Her eyes were wrong. Who was this guy? I pulled him back with me, right into a vampire wall. Clive and Vlad separated and then stepped around us to put themselves on the front line.

The older man tried to move up beside Clive, but I held him back.

"Stay here," I whispered.

He turned to me and paused a moment, just staring. "So very lovely," he murmured, "just like my grand-niece."

The Meri thing started crying. "I need help," it said in an un-Meri-like way.

The old man tapped Clive on the shoulder. "I know what I'm doing. If you'll allow me…"

Clive took a step to the side just as the Meri-thing grew huge, sharp teeth and leapt. The man dropped into a crouch, the fingers on his empty right hand flicking in the pooka's direction. The pooka howled in pain, trying to shift.

The old man waved me forward. "Hurry. Hit him with your axe now."

I raced toward not-Meri and swung the axe, but the pooka disappeared as the axe hit the gravel.

"Damn it!" I checked the blade to make sure I hadn't bent or dulled it. It was perfect. Fae bladesmiths were just that good.

The old man stood, brushing himself off. "We were hoping that spell would have slowed his shift longer. Disappointing."

THIRTY-THREE

In Which Mustaches Are Discussed

Clive, Vlad, and I shared a confused look.

"We?" I asked.

"Yes. Oh." He patted his pockets again. "Sorry. How rude of me." He moved forward holding out his hand. "I'm your great-uncle Bracken."

I shook his hand and felt steadier. "I'm so glad to finally meet you in person."

"And you," he said. He looked between Clive and Vlad before holding his hand out to Clive. "And you must be Clive. It's good to meet you."

Clive shook Bracken's hand, his expression amused. "How did you determine which, if either of us, was her husband?"

Bracken waved away the question. "That was easy. I knew you were English. I heard your voice on our phone calls. Aside from the fact that you look English, you were the one to reach for Sam's arm when she stepped forward to shake my hand. You didn't stop her, but you worried about the safety of the doddering old fool who'd just thrown a spell at the pooka, which seemed like a supportive, loving husband sort of thing to do."

He turned to Vlad. "And, I must admit, you look very much

like your portrait. As I knew Sam was not married to the Voivode of Wallachia, I assumed I could rule you out as Clive."

Vlad mustache twitched. "I haven't heard that title in an age."

"What does it mean?" I asked.

"Warlord of Wallachia, my home," Vlad said.

"He was a great general of enormous forces, my dear," Bracken told me. "In fact, if there's time, I'd love to interview you."

Vlad's eyebrows went up. "I'll think about it."

"Fair enough," Bracken said, turning back to me. "Perhaps we should go somewhere else to talk. The pooka could be listening and taking notes." He patted his pockets again. "Before I forget." He pulled a delicate chain out of his pocket. "This is for your fae friend. Arwyn made a talisman for her to ward off unwanted obsessive attention."

He held the necklace up in the moonlight. Hanging from a thin silver chain was a tiny, but beautifully detailed, starfish. "She said this should help repel the stalkers. Can you give this to the young woman for her?"

I held out my hand. "Absolutely. Please tell Arwyn we said thank you. This will be life-altering for her."

He nodded, placing it in my palm. "Good."

I looked at Clive. *Can we invite him to the nocturne?*

"We were on our way to the local nocturne," Clive told him. "You're welcome to join us, but you will be entering a house filled with my kind."

Bracken looked between the three of us, excitement glowing in his eyes. "Thank you for the invitation. I'd love that."

"Perfect," I said. "I'll drive with Bracken and show him the way. Clive, can you call and let them know we're coming?"

"I can take him," Vlad said.

Both Clive and Vlad were tense, watching us.

"He's my great-uncle. Relax."

Bracken patted my arm. "They're just worried. I'm an unknown and you don't reach their advanced ages by trusting the unknown. You can just give me the address, or the Voivode can drive with me."

Vlad's mustache went up on one side. "You may call me Vlad."

"Thank you, and I am Bracken Corey."

"Perhaps we should hold the rest of the conversation until we're behind warded doors," Clive reminded us. "Sam, will you drive with me?"

I blew out a breath. "Okay, but he can clearly hold his own with the pooka." I smiled at Bracken. "I'll see you at the nocturne."

When we turned, Bracken said, "Wait. Which car is yours?"

I pointed to the silver and green Mercedes-Maybach.

Bracken glanced at Clive. "I've never seen one in person."

"Clive has quite a collection," I told him.

"Little boys and their toys," Vlad mumbled, making Clive shake his head.

Bracken went to the back of the car and held out his hands, his fingers twitching. He turned around a moment later. "No pooka stowaways. Drive safely, my dear." He walked past Clive to where Vlad was standing. "If you'll come with me, I'm parked out in front."

Clive opened my door, and I got in. A moment later, he was sliding behind the wheel.

"You're not really worried about him, are you?" I asked.

He started the engine and pulled out. "He's right. If we're not wary and suspicious, we don't last long."

"You weren't suspicious of me." I paused, studying his profile. "Wait. Were you suspicious of me?"

He reached for my hand. "Darling, you were so clearly... hurt—"

"You can say broken," I interrupted.

"Never broken." He lifted my hand to his lips. "Bruised and battered, perhaps. And, no, I was never suspicious of you." He turned out onto the main road. "Remember in New Orleans when Owen talked about your aura being a bright and shiny gold? He'd said that was the reason so many wicches flocked to The Slaughtered Lamb. They could see your innate goodness and so trusted you. Vampires can't see auras, but your kind, pure heart is visible a mile away, even to our undead eyes. I don't know anyone else who could have befriended so many supernatural beings. We were a veritable United Nations of Supernaturals fighting Garyn's forces on Alcatraz. That happened because of you, darling."

"I don't think that's—"

"Hush. I need to call Russell." He tapped the phone app on the dashboard screen and hit Russell's name.

"Good evening." Russell's deep voice filled the car.

"Hello, my friend," Clive responded. "Sam and I are on our way to the nocturne. We have an unexpected guest on his way as well. Will you allow Sam's great-uncle Bracken, who is a wicche, to enter the nocturne? He's currently driving with Vlad to you."

"He has no reservations about entering a nocturne?" Russell asked.

Clive grinned. "He's an interesting one. I didn't get fear from him, only excitement. And don't be surprised if he asks to interview you."

I laughed. "Hi, Russell. Maybe tell the rest of the vampires, so they don't have to meet him if they don't want to. A bunch of them seemed reticent to even let him hear their voices last night."

"My lady, how would you know that? You were in my office all night." I could hear the humor in his voice.

"Just a lucky guess," I said.

"Hmm, well, I'll talk with the Counselors, and I'll have Godfrey alert the guards."

"Thank you," Clive responded before disconnecting the call.

"Do you mind if I invite Bracken to stay with us tonight?" I asked. "I don't like the idea of him driving all the way back to Monterey so late at night."

"You've been taken in by his old appearance." Clive glanced over, the corner of his mouth ticking up. "Did you see how smoothly he crouched and spun before throwing that spell? How easily he stood from that crouch? I wouldn't be surprised if the gray hair and wrinkles were a glamour. He's looking the age he is, as your great-uncle. Never forget he is a Corey and a powerful wicche. As to your original question, of course you can invite him to stay with us. It's your home too and he is your relative."

When we pulled up to the nocturne's gates, they were open, and the guards bowed their heads to Clive. He might not have been their Master anymore, but he was still greatly respected.

We parked next to a new green Bronco. "It's a green car party," I said, making Clive laugh.

He came around to open my door. Apparently, the guards had learned their lesson the last time and didn't try to open our doors this time. So many unspoken vamp rules.

Clive took my hand and tucked it into his elbow. "I think it makes sense for you to join us while we're talking with your uncle."

The guards at the front doors inclined their heads to Clive as we passed.

"Good. I want to hear what he has to say."

Audrey was waiting for us in the foyer. "Welcome to the nocturne. Can we slake your thirsts?"

Clive smiled. "I'm fine, Audrey, but perhaps…" He raised his eyebrows at me.

"I'm good too. Thank you."

Audrey nodded. "If you'll come with me, I'll escort you to the library. Your guest has already arrived."

We followed her down the hall. Her formality told me that we were being observed. She opened the library door, and we walked past her. She closed the door behind us, no doubt returning to Russell's study.

Inside the library, Bracken was at the shelves, studying the books. Cadmael, Vlad, Ahmed, and Adaeze sat at the table. It looked as though Joao, Pablo, and Thi had decided to sit this discussion out. Russell stood near the door. I gave him a quick hug as I walked in.

Bracken turned to Clive, his eyes shining. "Russell tells me you had this library built."

Clive nodded. "The ballroom was rarely ever used. It seemed a waste of space."

Ahmed and Adaeze smiled. Even Vlad's mustache twitched.

Clive glanced around. "Why is that humorous?"

Bracken grinned as he took the empty chair beside Vlad. "He also told us that your choice of a library might have had something to do with your desire to woo a bookish werewolf."

Clive scratched his cheek, his gaze on me. "Perhaps it was." He pulled out a chair for me. "Bracken, have you introduced yourself to everyone?"

"We were waiting for you two to arrive," Russell said.

"Why don't you sit with us," I asked Russell.

His face softened. "I haven't been asked."

"I'm asking you," I told him. "And, officially, this is your table, your nocturne. You can sit wherever you want."

He took the chair beside me and gave a solemn nod. "I'll try to remember that."

All eyes turned to my great-uncle. "Good evening. My name is Bracken Corey. I'm a member of the Corey wicche coven. I'm a historian of both supernatural and human history."

"I looked it up," I told them. "He has lots of human history books on the bestsellers' list."

He nodded. "I'm grateful for my success. Writing those books allows me to research the supernatural stories, which don't pay. No one needs to share their name with me, but I'd love to know who each of you are, if you're willing."

Cadmael, looking as stern as ever, began the introductions. "I am Cadmael." He nodded in Bracken's direction and then looked across the table, waiting to see what the others would do.

"We don't mind. I am Adaeze," she told him, inclining her head in greeting before looking to her side.

"And I am Ahmed." He reached out a hand and shook Bracken's.

"We met Bracken at The Bubble Lounge right after you left." I explained to the others what had happened with the pooka.

"Impersonating Vlad again?" Cadmael mused. "Why you?"

Vlad stared back. "Good taste?"

"I think it's the mustache," I told Cadmael. "He once pretended to be Clive with Vlad's mustache." I shivered. "Do not recommend."

Russell chuckled beside me. "Now I can't unsee it," he murmured, tapping the side of his head.

"Right? And you weren't even there for the real thing." I leaned forward, catching Vlad's eye. "No offense intended. You have the bone structure and attitude to pull it off handsomely. On anyone else, it looks like a bad disguise."

He rolled his eyes at me. "Nice save."

Bracken was watching the conversation like he was at a tennis match. Sitting forward, gaze intent, he enjoyed the byplay and seemed to be taking mental notes.

"He keeps returning to Vlad's appearance because he enjoys his mustache?" Cadmael asked, doubt clear in his voice. "That doesn't seem like a compelling enough reason."

I shrugged. "It's got to be boring, don't you think? He's been at this for a long time." I looked at Bracken, who nodded. "I'd imagine that when anything catches his fancy, he focuses on it."

The vampires nodded. They knew what it was to be very old, to have done it all, and to cling to those things that made them even slightly interested. It was like Clive and his cars.

More like Clive and his wife, he said in my head.

Quit eavesdropping. What if I was thinking about how hot Ahmed was looking?

I'd be forced to rip his head off, darling. I'd imagine it would be difficult for you to find a pile of dust hot.

I gave him a dirty look, and he kissed my temple.

I don't do it intentionally, he told me. *Part of my brain is always focused on you and sometimes your thoughts drift in. Just to be clear, though, if you found another man attractive, I would not kill him. I might go into a dark room to mourn for a few years, but that would be the extent of it.*

I grinned at him. *An emo vampire. A teenaged girl's dream.*

His lips twitched.

And just to be clear on my side, I don't think of other people the way I do you. I mean, Joao is objectively attractive, but he gives me the creeps. I wouldn't want him anywhere near me. You, I always want near me. You're the one who makes my heart race and butterflies flutter in my stomach. Only you make me feel comfortable, confident, and maybe even a little bit sexy. The world is filled with potential friends and enemies, but you're my only love.

He lifted my hand to his lips. *I have some work to do if I'm only making you feel a little bit sexy. You are a great deal more than that. And there's nowhere I'd rather be than by your side, loving you in any way you'll let me.*

"It's fascinating," Bracken said. "They haven't said a word and yet seemed to have had a complete and very affecting conversation."

"You'll get used to it," Russell replied.

THIRTY-FOUR

Bracken Tries To Interview Everyone

"Oh," I said, remembering. "I meant to ask. How did you know where to find us tonight?"

"Arwyn, of course." Bracken glanced at the other vampires. "I have another great-niece who is a very powerful wicche. We worked together to create that spell to slow down the pooka's transition. Unfortunately, it wasn't slow enough for us to kill him tonight."

"When you spoke with us last night," Adaeze began, "you mentioned other events, not related to vampires, that you believed the pooka to be responsible for. I realize it's only been a day, but do you have any other information for us?"

Bracken brought out a journal he had in his interior breast pocket. "Now, I can't be sure, of course. A pooka hadn't been identified as a possibility, but I do have other incidents that follow the pattern we've seen here and so make me believe they are the work of our current killer. I've actually been wondering if reports of a chupacabra in Puerto Rico in the nineties was really a pooka.

"Also interesting is a string of killings in the Pacific Northwest in the seventies. No one was ever arrested, but the prime suspect was a local sheriff. Multiple witnesses reported seeing a man who looked like him. They all identified his photo within an array of suspects, but his alibis were solid. A church congregation all swore he was at services. His wife submitted an affidavit that he was with her on one night in question. On another night, the dispatcher vouched for him, saying the two of them had been the only ones on duty all night. He took a lie detector test, and it came back as truthful."

He flipped through his notes. "He doesn't fit any of the attributes of a serial killer. Psych tests said he was a hard-working, honest man who was struggling under the weight of others' suspicions. He was a man who prided himself on doing right and was being accused of killing innocents.

"As individual alibis," he continued, "perhaps they could be doubted. Maybe he disappeared when no one noticed. Taken together, though, they don't make sense—unless he has a twin."

"Did he have a twin?" Ahmed asked.

Bracken shook his head. "Not according to the medical records from his mother's hospital stay and her labor and delivery report."

"So the pooka isn't only targeting supernaturals," Cadmael said.

"I don't believe so," Bracken responded. "But to Sam's point earlier, the sheriff was a very good-looking man. He was tall, and muscular, part Native American, with light green eyes. He wore his hair in a long braid down his back. It was part of what made him so easy for witnesses to recognize. I think, though, like Vlad, the pooka found the Sheriff interesting and so wore his likeness for a while, killing innocents and destroying this poor man's life."

"How do we kill it?" Ahmed wondered.

"It seems interested in Sam—" Cadmael began.

"No." Clive shut him down.

I put my hand on Clive's thigh and felt his tense muscles. "We'll do what we need to do to stop it."

Clive placed his hand on top of mine and squeezed.

"We can table that for now," Bracken said. "As to the other topic last night, may I contact the Silva family about their abducted daughter?"

"Silv—oh, Jade?" I asked.

"Rafaela," Clive murmured.

"We don't know yet," Cadmael said. "One of our people is investigating. We don't want to set this in motion if we don't have their daughter."

Bracken looked annoyed. "I see." He'd been very forthcoming with information for us, and we were stonewalling him. "But you do have someone's abducted loved one. I'd like to help her find her home."

"Understood. We'll tell you what we can, when we can. For now, though, we need to meet with our colleagues. Perhaps we will have an update on the situation," Cadmael continued. "I would suggest you and Sam come up with a plan for the pooka while my people meet."

I leaned forward to catch my great-uncle's eye. "Bracken, would you like to stay with Clive and me? Then you wouldn't have to drive home so late and we could talk."

He nodded. "Thank you. I'd like that very much."

I kissed Clive on the cheek. "I'll drive home with Uncle Bracken, so don't worry about looking for me later."

"I enjoy worrying about you," he said.

I'll be fine, I assured him.

See that you are.

Bracken replaced his journal in his pocket and stood. "Thank you for your hospitality. I'd love to speak with anyone who'd be willing to sit for an interview. I'm able to provide information, like I have for you in this case, because others have spoken with me." He took a card out of his pocket and placed it on the table. "My contact information."

He walked around the table and held out his arm for me. "Come, my dear. We'll get out of their way."

Russell rose as well. "I'll walk you out."

Once we were in the hall, I told Bracken, "You know, Russell has had a very interesting life."

Russell raised an eyebrow at me. "My lady, why would you throw me under the bus?"

Grinning, I tipped my head onto his shoulder. "Because there's a lot more to the human experience and the vampire one than some pasty white guy with a strange accent crooning, 'I vant to drink your blood.' Your story is America's story."

"For some," he allowed.

"For many who passed before their stories could be told to someone like my great-uncle. who would honor and preserve it."

Russell nodded, walking us out to Bracken's SUV. "I'll think on it."

"I can't ask for more than that," Bracken said, offering another card with his contact information. "If you choose to, I can come to you."

Russell slid the card into his pocket and escorted me to the passenger side of the vehicle. He opened the door and waited until both Bracken and I were in. He bent down and speared Bracken with a look that felt very much like a threat.

"You will make sure nothing happens to her," he warned.

Bracken nodded. "I will see to it that no harm comes to her in my care."

I tapped Russell's arm.

His expression softened. "Yes, my lady?"

"I'm a big, scary werewolf, you know?"

"Of course you are," he said, though I didn't miss the twinkle in his eye.

"You're asking for it, buster." I made a fist with my right hand.

He patted it. "Remember, thumb on the outside." Laughing, he closed my door.

Chuckling, Bracken backed out and drove through the opening gates.

"Jerk," I muttered.

"You have such an interesting relationship with the vampires," he said. "They are a very formal lot with a love of hierarchy, but you they allow to break norms and behave as you wish."

"Clive says since I'm not a vampire, I don't have to follow their rules."

Bracken shook his head as I directed him where to go. "I've known other humans in contact with vampires. They were treated lower than the lowest vampires. They treat you like a beloved little sister. It's quite fascinating."

"Okay, first of all, I'm not human. And there are *plenty* of vampires who hate my guts. Granted, most of them are dead now, but still. I'm a werewolf-wicche mix, and the wicche is a necromancer. Do you know what vampires are?"

Bracken glanced at me and then back on the road. "Undead humanoids who survive on blood?"

"The *undead* part being the most important in this case." I had him turn again.

He looked at me twice in quick succession. "Do you have power over vampires?" He was having a hard time tamping down his excitement.

"No. And you can never write that in your notes or put it in a book. If that were known, even suspected, I'd be hunted by just about every vampire out there."

He nodded. "I understand."

We drove in silence for a while, with me only telling him which turns to take. Eventually, when we were close to home, he said, "I think it only fair, given what you have hinted at, to share a secret of mine with you." He glanced over to check my response.

I nodded.

"I, too, am not just a wicche. I'm a bit of a black sheep in the Corey family, though most have no idea why. Only my mother was a Corey, you see. My father is fae. Like your cousin Arwyn, the fae blood makes our magic much stronger than other pureblood wicches."

"Ah, the pureblood thing," I groused. "My Aunt Abigail hunted my mother and me most of my life because my werewolf blood was sullying the Corey bloodline. I'm an abomination, apparently."

He patted my knee. "She was a bad egg."

"It's up here on the right." I pointed. "That one." Our house was a gorgeous modern Tudor design. Clive had purchased the apartment house that stood here and had it torn down to the studs and rebuilt into a house for us. He chose this location because it was across the green from the steps to The Slaughtered Lamb. My morning commute was about a minute and a half, and we had amazing views of the ocean.

"The garage door is on the side, so turn here. I'll jump out and alter the ward so you can enter."

Bracken was staring up at the house and when he turned the corner, one side of his SUV lifted like he'd driven over the curb. "Sorry," he said. "I hadn't realized I was cutting that so close."

He pulled into the driveway and I stepped out, glancing around for any animals too interested in us. Seeing nothing, I went to the garage door, pulled on my magic, and placed my hand on the doorframe.

Allow Bracken and his vehicle to enter our home. I typed in the long security code and the door slid up. If I hadn't altered the ward, he wouldn't have been able to enter, even if the door was up.

As he started down the drive, I jogged ahead so I could show him where to park. At the bottom of the hill, the garage opened to the right into a huge showroom of luxury cars. I pointed to the left, so he could get out easily.

"My goodness," he said, grabbing an overnight case from his back seat. "You weren't kidding. This collection is extraordinary." He started to follow me to the elevator but then stopped in his tracks. "Is that the 1965 Aston Martin DB5?"

He dropped his bag and went to the little silver roadster, staring at it in wonder. He glanced back at me, eyes glowing. "This is James Bond's car."

I laughed. "That sounds about right. Clive is terribly posh."

"My word. Do you think he'd ever let me drive it?" His expression was so bright, I'd never have guessed he was in his late sixties. Which then made me realize that Clive might be right about the glamour.

"We can ask," I told him. "He's very generous, but also pretty careful with his cars." I picked up his bag for him. "Little secret, though: If I ask him, he'll say yes." I hit the elevator button.

Bracken took the bag from me. "Because he's hopelessly in love with you."

I grinned. "Yeah. There's that."

The doors opened and we stepped in. They re-opened a moment later into the den. Fergus stretched his long body on the couch and rose above us. Bracken stopped, his fingers twitching at his side.

Fergus stepped off the cushions and leaned into me. His head was between my waist and my arm, so he could nuzzle me while checking out our visitor.

I did my best to block Fergus. "Please don't curse my pup."

THIRTY-FIVE

Everyone Is Dealing with Something

"Wait. Let me get Daddy's jacket off or it'll be covered in dog hair." I draped Clive's jacket over the chair Vlad liked to use in the corner. "I think that collar can be repaired." I turned back to my giant little guy. "Buddy, this is my great-uncle Bracken. He's going to stay with us tonight." I flicked on a lamp so they could see each other.

Bracken dropped his bag again and offered his hands to Fergus to sniff. "A Wolfhound? Does he hunt you?"

"He would never. He loves his mommy." I went to the back door and opened it for the pup, following him out.

"How lovely," Bracken said. "You've created a perfect English garden here, haven't you?" He wandered down the path, through the flowers and trees.

"Would you like me to turn on a light?" I asked.

"Not necessary," he responded. "I can see perfectly fine by moonlight. Which reminds me." He came back into view around a tall flowering bush. Pointing up at the full moon, he asked, "Do you feel a push to shift?"

I nodded. "I feel it, but I can resist if I need to. It's not like old horror films where as soon as I see a full moon, the transition begins."

He nodded. "Declan takes his pack out for a run at the full moon. He said the pull is quite strong for most werewolves, but he can resist it, if need be. I assume it's because you are both Quinns."

"Maybe. I do go for full moon runs because they feel good and I want to, but if I can't, like tonight, I just feel kind of prickly and uncomfortable. I'll run tomorrow night." I checked the time on my phone. "Or maybe a quick one tonight."

"Do you run in wolf form in the city?" he asked.

I tipped my head back and forth. "Not through the city streets. I have tunnels to the Presidio and to the North Bay from The Slaughtered Lamb. More often than not, I choose the North Bay because there are forests to run through."

"With no pack, do you run alone, or does Fergus accompany you?"

"Are you interviewing me?" I gave him my squinty, suspicious look.

He tapped his pockets again. "Sorry. I—I have difficulty with new places and situations. I've found that if I assume the persona of an outgoing researcher, I can short-circuit the anxiety and interact with others." He shook his head. "I'm sure that sounds ridiculous." He rubbed his forehead, clearly embarrassed. "It's hard to explain, but adopting this persona helps me seem more normal and helps me get out of my RV. My curiosity and interest are stronger than my other issues."

My throat felt tight and my eyes went suddenly wet. I nodded. "After my attack, I hid. A wicche friend of my mother's knew I loved books and reading, so she suggested working in a bookstore. I knew I could never go out in the world and hold a job like that, so I daydreamed about opening a bookstore. It had to be a hidden bookstore that only other supernaturals—not werewolves—could enter. Helena, Mom's friend, said she'd speak with Clive about it."

I sat on a patio chair and Fergus put his head in my lap. "Eventually, I met with him. It was one of the scariest moments of my life. Not because he was a vampire, but because he was a strange man. He was so gentle with me, though, guiding me through my ideas, helping me picture exactly what I wanted. He hired the architect and the builders. I thought it was my uncle who'd loaned me the money to start The Slaughtered Lamb. I found out seven years later that it was Clive who'd paid for everything. He felt sorry for a poor scarred and brutalized wolf and so stepped in to help her make a life for herself."

He got a funny look on his face. "You were a teenager?"

I nodded. "Seventeen."

"And you started dating him then?"

I held up a hand. "Oh, no. My goodness. I was doing what you said. I was trying my hardest to pretend to be brave, greeting the people that came to The Slaughtered Lamb, serving them tea and beer, trying to learn how to make cocktails, researching and buying books—I've added all of yours to the collection, by the way—and recommending titles when I was feeling very brave, though I had to practice what I was going to say multiple times in my head before I built up the courage to say it out loud.

"Almost immediately, Clive told me he had someone who wanted to work as a part-time cook, so I could offer food. That was Dave."

"Ah, yes," Bracken said. "I've met Dave. You weren't frightened to have a half-demon work there?"

I shook my head. "No more so than anyone else. I was afraid of everything, and he was just grumbly and cranky enough to knock through some of those walls I'd built around myself. I used to work opening to closing every day, manning both the bookstore and bar, but Dave would sometimes come out to help at the bar if I was busy. He's horrible with customers, but he had two extra hands and knew how to make any cocktail requested.

"I was lucky to have Owen, wicche extraordinaire and all-around awesome person, offer to work here during my third or fourth week open. He came in for a book, saw me use a tea bag to brew tea, and told me I needed to hire him because he couldn't watch me do that."

Bracken laughed. "Wicches and our teas."

"Exactly. So, no, Clive and I weren't dating. I'd contented myself to always be alone. I assumed I was too broken to ever be romantic material. It wasn't until last year, when Abigail found me and renewed her campaign to kill me, that Clive and I started spending time together, trying to figure out how I kept getting locked into horrendous visions and if whoever was doing that was the same person leaving dead, scarred wolves in the water outside my window."

I waved my hand. "It's a long story."

"Clearly, somewhere along the way, his feelings changed," Bracken said. "He built a library to woo you, after all."

I shrugged. "That's a him story, not a me story. In answer to your question from way back, though, I used to do full moon runs alone, thinking no one saw or knew about me. It turned out the whole supernatural community knew I was a werewolf but never mentioned it, as I didn't seem to want to discuss it. Last year, I started getting chaperones because Abigail was back. Lately, though, Fergus goes with me and usually Clive, if he's free."

"Fascinating." He looked in the back door. "The den we walked through is a very handsome room. May I see the rest of your home?"

"You betcha." I slapped my thigh. "Come on, Fergus. Let's give Uncle Bracken the tour." Our house was gorgeous, and I enjoyed showing it off.

When we got to the second floor, I ducked into my bedroom to change into slippers. In the hall opposite the bedroom door, I found Bracken studying an old painting.

"That's one of Clive's. It's how San Francisco used to look two hundred years ago when he'd first arrived."

Bracken held up his phone. "May I take a picture?"

"I don't see why not."

When he finished, I waved him toward the door at the end of the hall. He glanced in, turned to me, and grinned. "And then he built you a second library."

The library took up what had been two apartments. It had

vaulted ceilings, with mahogany bookshelves lining three of the walls. Like in the nocturne, there were small, engraved brass plates identifying the different sections of the library. Each wall had a brass ladder on rails, making higher shelves more accessible. The floors were the same dark wood, though they were topped with rugs in deep oceanic tones.

A large desk stood at the far end. This room could serve as my office, if I wanted one, but I didn't. I just wanted a library. The desk had a beautiful periwinkle leather chair behind it, but I chose soft fabric couches and chairs in watery blues for the rest of the furniture. I wanted a cozy refuge, a place where reading could give way to napping.

"It was only fair. I had to give up the nocturne library. It had a window seat with curtains and everything."

Bracken nodded, understanding the seriousness of the situation. "Like Jane Eyre."

I reached out and squeezed his forearm. "That is exactly right. The nocturne's window seat had a view of the back garden, the city, and the bay beyond. Sometimes, I'd just hole up in there and stare out the window to think and daydream. Clive always knew where to find me."

Bracken scanned the room and then pointed at the closed curtains in the corner.

I turned off the lights and nodded for him to go ahead. "As a vampire lives here, all the windows on the second floor have metals shields that drop to block the sun. All except this window, which is why it has such heavy curtains."

He pulled them back and took in the cushions, pillows, and blankets. "This is quite the cozy reading fort you've created." He sat and looked out the window at the green across the street, the huge trees, the ocean in one direction and the bay and Golden Gate Bridge in the other. "Perfect," he said wistfully.

"Why no sun shields on the first floor?" he asked. "You have guest rooms down there. No vampire guests?"

"We have a guest room up here, too, if we need it. Most visiting vampires prefer staying at the nocturne. It has everything they could possibly need. It's also safer for us—meaning me—if we don't have vamps hanging out here. Now that Clive has given up the nocturne, he enjoys the privacy and solitude."

"Especially now that he has a wife?" he suggested.

I nodded. "We actually do have Vlad and Cadmael staying with us, rather than at the nocturne, right now, but they're not in this house. Well, Vlad often pops in, but we gave him my old apartment behind The Slaughtered Lamb to stay in, and Cadmael prefers the folly."

"The folly?" he asked.

"Oh, my goodness." I stood abruptly. "You'll love it. Do you know about dragon follies?"

"I've heard of them," he said, "but I've never seen one. Have you?" He took out his journal.

I waved him forward. Fergus bolted up from his library bed to follow us. "When we were in Wales, we stayed in the Drake family keep. A couple of the dragons were not happy about playing host to vampires, so they gave us the most disgusting storerooms in the basement."

We went down the stairs to the first floor. "Clive sent Russell and Godfrey to find any place safe for them and vaguely comfortable for me. They came back having found the folly. We sneaked out and moved to the folly in the woods. As it's a dragon's folly, it was underground, so sun-safe for the vamps. We didn't get to explore the whole thing, but the first huge cave was intended for the littlest dragons, so they could play pirate. It was absolutely incredible. Godfrey wanted to move in and stay."

I took Bracken and Fergus back into the den and opened the elevator panel, tapping the button. As we were the last to use it, it opened right away. "The next room, though, was the one that made all the vampires lose their minds. It was a medieval castle with a neighboring village. The dragons liked to attack the castle. Anyway, what was so amazing about it is that the dragon builders created what looked like an infinite sky. There are hidden controls where you can set the time of day you want, and this medieval world was set to midday. The vamps, for the first time in many hundreds of years, were able to stand in the sun."

"That's extraordinary," Bracken breathed, his journal twitching in his hand. He so wanted to start taking notes.

We walked across the garage. "We helped the Drakes rescue a long-lost loved one, and as a thank you, Benvair herself asked the builders to let us hire them for a folly. We had to pay a mind-numbing fee, but the fact that the dragons built a folly for a vampire and a werewolf was unprecedented. They were none too happy, but it was a lot of money, so they sucked it up and did it."

I walked us to the big metal door. "It's basically done, but they're working on making sure all the details are working properly. Once they leave, we're on our own. No dragon repairman is responding to a service call."

I opened it and gestured for him to go ahead. "What's important to keep in mind is that the folly exists in its own magical space. The folly is far bigger than the distance from our house to The Slaughtered Lamb and yet here it is."

When we walked into the cave tunnel entrance, Bracken turned to me. "Is that the ocean I hear?"

Grinning, I pointed ahead to the light seeping into the dark tunnel. Fergus ran ahead; he loved the island. When we arrived at the open doorway, sand scattered across the rock-hewn ground, Bracken stared in shock. He took a tentative step into the sand and marveled at it all. Bending down, he sifted the grains through his fingers.

"Remarkable," he murmured. He looked up at the clear blue skies, the puffy clouds in the distance, and the ocean. "I understand why the vampires feel as though they are actually under the sun." He shook his head. "I can't wrap my mind around it."

"I know. And the ocean contains fish and sharks, even sea monsters, in case we want to wage wars."

"I could spend years just exploring this island." He glanced back at me. "Is it as big as it looks, or is that mountain and the rest of the island an optical illusion?"

"This is where Cadmael stays. He says it's truly the size of an island. He's explored it."

Bracken moved forward, to follow Fergus, but I grabbed his arm. "You can explore later. We're not done. There are other rooms."

The shock on his face was almost comical. "You have more than an island and an ocean between your house and the bookstore?"

"Indeed, we do. Come on, Fergus!"

THIRTY-SIX

Bloody Hell

B racken scribbled in his journal as we made our way through the tunnel.

"That's the only separate, contained room, probably because of the ocean. Do you see the light up ahead?"

Bracken glanced up and nodded.

"That's Canterbury in the Middle Ages, when Clive was alive."

Bracken's step faltered with that news, and then he pocketed his journal again. The tunnel opened and we were walking through green fields, the spires of the cathedral rising impossibly high off to our right. We crossed a wooden bridge spanning the Great Stour river.

Bracken stopped halfway over and stared down into the water. "Fish?"

I shook my head. "They're like the sea monsters in the ocean. They're there and they respond like the real thing, but they're not alive. They're pieces of dragon magic."

Bracken stared around us in wonder. "The grass, the trees, the birds I'm hearing, the butterflies fluttering over the flowers...none of it is real?"

I shook my head again. "No real sun, remember? We're underground. Do you feel that, though? It's still warm on our faces.

There's a breeze, carrying the scent of freshly tilled earth and wood smoke. Don't let the real–artificial thing weigh you down. Just enjoy your visit to the Canterbury of a thousand years ago."

We walked in silence for a while, Bracken absorbing everything he could. "Can we enter the cathedral? Are there interiors to these cottages, the church, or are they facades?"

"They're complete, inside and out."

"Amazing," he murmured. "They can recreate any time period? How in the world can they accomplish that?"

"No idea." I smiled, tipping my face back to the sort-of sun. "Dragons are ageless. Maybe they were here for it." I pointed to the thatch-roofed homes. "The cottages are very simple, which Clive says is accurate, but they all have the basics needed to live in this time period. Up ahead, do you see the fields and the plow?"

Bracken nodded.

"That's Clive's family farm."

Bracken turned sharply. "He was a farmer in life?"

I nodded, remembering how he looked plowing that field in Leticia's memory.

"I never would have guessed that. I thought maybe a member of the aristocracy."

I laughed. "He'll enjoy that. No. He's been a lot of things, farmer and warrior foremost among them. If you want to learn how to handle a sword, any size or shape, Clive's your guy."

I looked around for Fergus. He loved to explore, but he always made a point of checking in before running off again. I thought I saw his head pop through a bush for a moment. "Fergus!" I called, but he didn't reappear.

Bracken looked behind us. "Is he still on the island?"

Uneasy, I said, "I don't think so. I just saw him a minute ago. Maybe he caught a new scent. He usually shadows me, though."

We walked on, but I couldn't shake the feeling that something was off.

"Wait," Bracken said. "The folly changed."

I nodded vaguely, noticing a tail whip behind a tree. "We've left

Canterbury and have entered Middle-earth." I pointed out areas in the shire taken directly from Tolkien's stories.

"A horse?" Bracken asked as the tall chestnut mare cantered down the narrow dirt road.

"Yeah. Clive doesn't like it. He says it's close enough to the real thing to be deeply disturbing. He grew up with horses and has a way with them. Unfortunately for him, horses don't like vampires."

Bracken glanced at me before returning his gaze to the horse. "That's probably another reason to favor cars. They don't shy away from him."

I hadn't thought of it that way, but he was right. I continued scanning for my little buddy, getting more uneasy. He wouldn't stay away from me for this long.

When the horse got close, it stamped and shook its head, tossing its mane. Odd. I'd never seen it behave like that. When I finally turned to study the horse, my insides froze. Bracken held out a hand to scratch its muzzle and I threw out my arm, knocking my great-uncle off his stride, as I yanked my axe out again.

Bracken's hand flicked under my raised arm, casting his spell, and the horse screamed, rearing back, its huge hooves waving in the air before my face. *Shitshitshit.* I sidestepped the hooves and swung, but it disappeared. I almost landed on my butt from swinging so hard with no target. Luckily Bracken had ducked out of the way.

"Did you see where it went?" I searched the area frantically, looking for any movement, my axe at the ready.

"I'm not sure," he said. "I think the grass on that side of the path moved, but it could have been the wind." His fingers twitched at his side.

Fergus yelped and I flinched, spinning toward the sound. In the distance, on the hill with the hobbit holes, a massive tree stood, its branches spreading wide, sheltering the hill. With another high-pitched yelp, Fergus raced beneath the tree, coming over the top of the hill and sprinting down the path between hobbit holes. A moment later, he disappeared through a door left ajar.

I took off at a sprint, Bracken right behind me. I looked right and left as I ran, searching for the pooka. "Do you see it?"

"No," Bracken called, falling behind.

I ran through the meadow and around the pond at the base of the hobbit hole hill before racing up the path. There were seven colorful round doors in total, four on the first level, near the pond, and three on the second, below the tree. Outside each door was a wildish garden of vines and flowers. I slid to a stop in the doorway of the last one on the upper level.

"Fergus?" I barely paused in the front room, as he obviously wasn't in there.

I heard a whine down the hall and ran, shoving open doors and scanning rooms as I went. "Baby, where are you? Are you okay?" I got to the last room, the bedroom, and heard that quiet whine again. I went to the other side of the bed, but still no Fergus. Where was he?

The bedroom door slammed shut. I brought my axe up and spun, finding Clive leaning against the door. The tension in my body relaxed.

"Help me find Fergus. He's hurt." I rushed around the bed and skidded to a stop.

Clive's eyes were wrong. They were more blue than gray. The way he looked at me was wrong. There was no love. Clive, looking at me like I was a stranger, hurt me in ways I didn't have the strength to consider.

Clive?

We're coming, darling.

I stared into the pooka's dead eyes. *He's already here.*

The pooka dove at me as the bedroom door flew open, knocking him off balance. Bracken stood in the doorway, his fingers twitching. I swung, wanting to destroy this counterfeit Clive. He disappeared and I came dangerously close to eviscerating my great-uncle, who, despite his age, nimbly avoided the axe.

I'd barely begun searching the floor for a shape-shifting rodent when I was thrown backward and catapulted through the bedroom window, my stomach landing on the window sill. Bracken lunged and grabbed me, but I'd already been cut to shit. In a folly filling with vampires. *Bloody hell.*

Clutching the axe like the lifeline it was, I held tight while Bracken lifted me off the glass impaling me, using far more strength than he should have possessed. A crash sounded from the front room.

Was I in pain? Probably, but adrenaline was numbing everything at present. Was I bleeding freely? Also yes. Bracken's fingers were moving, so maybe he was trying to deal with the horror show I was fast becoming.

"Sam!"

Bracken and I exchanged a glance and then moved. Clive was silhouetted in the front doorway. He raced toward me and then got body slammed by someone coming out of the kitchen. They grappled a moment and then Clive had Clive by the neck, trying to separate his head from his body.

Bracken threw a spell. One of them screamed but they both crumpled to the ground, continuing the high-speed brawl and barreling into the front room. The sounds of wood splintering and glass breaking followed.

Bracken and I ran, both tense and ready. I felt the other vamps closing in on this hobbit hole. They sent a buzz through my blood.

Envisioning my magic uncoiling in my chest and then dancing down my arms to my fingertips, I readied one of the few spells I had in my arsenal, one I'd stolen from my aunt when she tried to kill me. I didn't know if it'd work on the fae, but it was worth a try; Bracken's spell barely slowed the pooka down. I wanted to disorient him, hoping that might give me another moment to swing my axe.

I slid into the front room, axe poised at the ready, and found

Clive with his arm around Clive's neck, crushing it, though he seemed frozen in the act.

"Sam, help me." The Clive in front tore at the immovable arm around his neck. He had Clive's British accent and his gray eyes.

Too many things happened at once: The vampires burst through the door, Bracken threw his spell, both Clives convulsed, Vlad sprung forward to pull the Clives apart, and Thi shouted to kill them both.

Blood dripped into my eye. I knew my blood called to the vampires assembled, but I couldn't deal with them right now. The pooka was wearing my husband as a disguise, taunting me to kill my love. I'd give it to him. He was a quick study. This new Clive glamour was much better than his previous attempts.

"I'll do it," Pablo grumbled, trying to take Vlad's place.

I shoved both men out of the way. Pablo went flying into the desk under the front window. Vlad caught himself and stepped out of my way. When I felt Thi and Joao readying to attack me, I held up my free hand. Over my shoulder, I growled, "If either of you makes one move to stop me, I will kill you. Do not doubt my ability to do it." I was past caring.

I stepped closer. The Clives were identical, but I knew my husband. I threw the spell I'd been holding, the one that felt as though your brain turned to glass and shattered. It was hopefully raining glass in his mind right now.

"Samantha, don't!" Cadmael shouted.

Clutching his head, the gray-eyed Clive gasped, "Sam, no. Darling, it's me." He even had Clive's accent down.

My Clive, eyes black, stared back at me, unmoving. I threw Abigail's death spell at the pooka, hoping to force a shift to stop the pain and heal.

"She's killing him," Joao hissed. "Cadmael, stop her."

I saw more movement by the door and then heard Vlad tell the others to shut up.

I wiped my hand on my dress. I didn't want the blood running down my arm to make the axe slip. "Bracken, the one in front. Spell him again."

"My dear, are you sure?" Bracken thought I had the wrong Clive too.

"I know my husband. Spell him."

Bracken flicked his fingers and the gray-eyed Clive's back bowed in agony. Finally, there was a flicker. Please, God, please. Don't let me be wrong.

The gray-eyed Clive flickered, barely keeping his form, and then he began to shift. I surged forward, swinging with all my might. There was a loud, percussive pop, and then he was gone. For good this time.

I dropped the axe and flew to Clive. His arms came around me.

"Everyone out," Vlad said. "You, too, old man. Give them a minute." He ushered them out and away from the door.

I held Clive as tightly as I could. "Are you okay?"

"Darling." He brushed away my tears with his thumbs. "You're the one ripped to shreds, not me. When you killed him, the spell he'd put on me lifted."

I looked down all the trails of blood running down my body. I was bleeding badly, but I didn't really feel it. It was more like I was watching a movie. "Can you close them up? The others are far too interested in my blood."

THIRTY-SEVEN

Well, Shit

C live got to work, lapping up the blood and closing the cuts. It was over. We got him. It was a huge relief, but I felt numb and stared into space. "We'll have to ask my great-uncle to get all the blood off the floor and desk. This is Russell's hobbit hole. We don't want to leave him with a scent that drives him nuts."

Clive put his hand on the side of my face and turned me so I was staring into his eyes. "Your pupils are so big, darling. You're shaking. You're in shock."

"I'm okay," I said, though my voice sounded strange.

"You're not."

I licked my lips, trying to say the words that were strangling me. "I knew it was you. I knew it. I knew." I choked on a sob, holding myself in check. "But what if I'd been wrong?" I whispered, my hand flying up and covering my lips. "What if I'd killed you?"

"Darling," he crooned, pulling me into his arms again and rocking me. "You knew exactly which one I was. I never doubted it for a moment." His hand rubbed my back. "There could be a room crowded with a hundred Sams, and I'd pick you out every time."

He leaned back, his hand warming the side of my face. "You're so cold, love. Can I ask Bracken to come back? I'm worried about these gouges in your stomach. They're deep."

I nodded and then there was a knock on the door.

"Come," Clive called.

The door opened and Bracken was there. He waved a hand and all the blood on the floor disappeared. Clive had me lie down and then Bracken crouched beside me, holding his hands over my stomach, his fingers twitching.

"I'm not a healer," he murmured, his voice soft and calming, "but I've picked up a few things over the years." He was quiet for a moment. "Ah. She has a shard of glass embedded in her abdomen," he said to Clive. "It hasn't nicked any vital organs that I can tell, but we have to get it out."

"Lie still, love," Clive said, placing my head in his lap.

I grabbed Clive's hand. "I think it hurt Fergus."

Clive squeezed my fingers. "He'll be fine. He was sleeping in the tunnel. When the spell on me lifted, the one on him probably did too."

Bracken looked uncomfortable and then met my gaze. "I don't want to lift the bottom of your dress, but I need to get to your stomach."

Clive leaned forward and ripped the tear in my dress wider, so my skirt could stay down and Bracken could work. He held his hand over my stomach again. I heard myself whimpering. It was cutting me again on the way out. Clive intervened, pulling away my pain while he brushed my hair from my face.

"Sorry, my dear," Bracken said, "but we have to get it out of you before it does more damage."

"I know. I'm okay now," I rasped out. Closing my eyes, I turned my head in to Clive's stomach, his scent soothing something that had splintered in me.

There was one more dull yank and slice before the glass was out. I didn't know what Bracken was doing, but there was an internal tug and then heat filled my belly.

"What I can do is done," Bracken said. "I'll step out now."

The door closed and Clive moved, lifting my dress and running his tongue along the line of cuts and gashes. He took another moment to check my head, my shoulders, looking for other cuts.

"Thank you. I just got rid of my scars. I don't want to start a new collection."

He gave me a kiss and helped me up. "I've told you before, darling. Scars are sexy."

I looked down at myself. "How problematic is this dress?"

He shook his head and said, "Very," before unbuttoning his dress shirt. "This feels familiar," he murmured, referring to that time almost a year ago when I'd killed my rapist and was standing in a bloody t-shirt that was too short to cover important bits. He'd given me the shirt off his back then too.

He was right. It wasn't just the gaping hole in the center. It was also soaked with blood, which wasn't handy when we were about to go out where vampires were waiting for us. I peeled off the dress; Clive licked a few red smudges off my skin and then helped me into his shirt.

Grinning, he tucked my hair behind my ear. "The jewelry, the shirt." He pulled me into his arms. "It's putting ideas in my head."

"Pff't. Like those ideas weren't already there." He was right, though. This was a serious after-sex-putting-on-my-lover's-shirt look. "Am I decent?"

He took my hand. "Absolutely. Let's go."

When we stepped out, the vampires were ranged around the Shire, intensely interested in the folly. Bracken was outside the door, waiting.

"Oh, good," he said. "I was going to suggest getting rid of the bloody dress, given the circumstances."

I gestured into the hobbit hole. "It's on the floor. Can you burn it up or something to get rid of it?"

He nodded. "Good idea." He twitched his fingers, there was a pop of flames, and then a smudge of ashes on the wooden floor. With a wave of his hand, the ashes disappeared and, other than a small dark spot on the wood, the dress and blood were gone.

Clive held out his hand to shake. Bracken took it.

"Thank you very much," Clive said. "I'd hate to think of how much more damage could have been done while we waited for a healer."

Bracken tipped his head. "Not at all. I'm glad I was here. I think, perhaps, I was meant to be here."

The vampires all went on alert and turned as one toward the back entrance to my apartment. A moment later, a tall elven warrior jogged toward us. Her long silver-white hair was braided down her back. A heavy sword hung at the hip of her long tunic and breeches. Her leather boots were silent as she made her way down the path.

I lifted my hand. "Galadriel." I wanted the vampires to understand that she was known to us.

Why in the world she was here, though, was anyone's guess. Last I'd heard, she hated my guts. She blamed me for my great-aunt Martha's death. She'd said she'd kept her wife alive and happy for fifty years. I showed up and a week later Martha had been tortured to death by Abigail. In her defense, that was all true.

Clive and I went down the steep path, Bracken on our heels.

"Where is it?" Galadriel demanded, her sword in her hand.

"We already got it," I said.

She shook her head. "He shifts and regenerates. Where did you last see him?"

"We know. My great-uncle here, Martha's younger brother Bracken, used a spell to slow the pooka's shift so I could strike him down with my axe."

Galadriel's shoulders relaxed and she sheathed her sword. "I will let my lady know that he has been dispatched. She will grieve his loss, but she understands that he needed to be stopped. It was why I was sent."

"We rather hoped someone would have come sooner," Clive said. His tone was mild, but the reproof was clear. "Before more innocents had died."

Galadriel gave Clive a look that would have had me backing up. He didn't flinch.

To distract the rising tension, I said to Bracken, "This is your sister's widow. Galadriel, Bracken. Bracken, Galadriel."

The warrior finally tore her glare from Clive and took in Bracken with a nod. "Martha didn't like to talk about her childhood, but she said if anyone had had it harder in that cursed family than her, it was you." She held out her hand and they gripped forearms.

"I was very sorry to hear of my sister's passing," he said. "She was my favorite. I was so very glad to learn, though, that she had been happy, that she'd found love and acceptance. Thank you. She deserved all the happiness."

"Yes," Galadriel agreed, her body held taut. She turned back to me. "My mistress, and therefore Algar and the guard, have been quite busy. She wasn't able to spare anyone until now. I will tell her you have removed the threat from this realm. She will be pleased to hear it."

"Is she okay?" I asked.

Galadriel took a moment and then said, "My lady is, unfortunately, always under threat by those who would presume to usurp her." She stared at Bracken a moment. "She will be interested to know that you're here, that you've already made this connection. My lady sees far and sees true." She nodded, considering. "I must get back. I am needed." She turned and sprinted back toward my apartment.

I looked at Clive. "What the heck did that mean, and how did she get in?"

He shook his head. "I'll do you one better. How did the pooka get in?"

Bracken held up a finger. "I believe I know the answer to that one. When we turned the corner outside your house, it felt as though I'd driven over the curb. I'm a very good driver and according to the mirrors, I was not next to the curb. I think that was when the pooka became a stowaway."

I rubbed my forehead. "And then I altered the ward to let you and your car in through the garage. I invited it in."

Clive kissed my temple. "What matters is that the two of you destroyed it before more were killed."

"And vampires blamed for it," Vlad added.

"Fergus!" I shouted, worried I didn't see him yet.

Clive smiled. "He's coming. I hear his paws thumping on the ground."

The vampires were eyeing me warily.

"So," Thi said, "not just a werewolf, but relative of wicches and friend of the fae?"

"That *my lady* and *mistress* talk," Adaeze began. "Was she referring to the queen of the fae?"

I glanced at Clive and Bracken before nodding.

"The queen of the fae sent one of her warriors to protect you and hunt the pooka?" she clarified.

I nodded again.

Her eyebrows went up on a sly smile. She was standing closest to the pond, so the rest of the vamps behind her couldn't see the smile.

That should make them stop and wonder before any of them tries to move against you. The voice in my head, though, wasn't Clive. It was Adaeze. Interesting.

"If this is done, can we get back to Guild business now?" Pablo asked, sounding bored and annoyed.

Bracken raised his hand. "Before you begin, might I inquire if the one investigating Rafaela's abduction has learned anything more? I'd very much like to contact her grieving family. I would, of course, tell them that as soon as the vampires knew she had been rescued, they did what they could to find and verify her family."

The vampires were silent, no one making a move to indicate which was Joao. Cadmael himself waited, rather than covering for Joao.

Finally, Joao said, "My people haven't finished investigating, but early indications are that it probably is her. They have found no other reports of a black jaguar—male or female—being abducted. They're a rarity in the shifter world, so…" He trailed off, looking as if he'd rather be anywhere other than right here, having to answer this question.

"Marvelous," Bracken said. "I'll call Cipriano and let him know we may have located his daughter."

Ahmed gestured around the folly. Turning to Clive, he asked, "How do you have this?"

"That's a bit of a long story," Clive told him. "The short version is that we helped rescue a dragon who had been abducted by Aldith Atwood. You no doubt heard about her menagerie of supernaturals that she imprisoned to feed on."

There were multiple heads nodding. Not Pablo's, though. That must have been something else no one had told him.

"One of her captives," Clive continued, "was the brother of one of Sam's good friends. We helped her friend and the matriarch of the Drake clan rescue their loved one, as well as the rest who were suffering under Aldith's hand. The Drakes knew that Sam loved the folly we'd visited in Wales and so negotiated with the dragon builders to create one for us."

Adaeze grinned again, while Ahmed shook his head and said, "Your wife is little sister to the dragons as well? You seem to have married up, my friend."

"I have, indeed," Clive said, pulling my hand to his lips.

It felt like a bit of theater with these three trying to drive home the point that I had very powerful people in my corner, and the others should think twice before starting any shit.

"Well," Ahmed said. "I vote we conduct our Guild meetings here." He looked up at the faux sky. "I know it isn't real, but that doesn't change the fact that it feels as though we're walking in the sun for the first time in hundreds of years."

"That's interesting," Clive mused. "I don't recall offering my home."

Ahmed waved away his response. "Nonsense. You already have two of us staying here. What's a few more?" He looked back toward Canterbury. "I might build myself a treehouse on that island."

"The island is mine," Cadmael said.

"I beg to differ," Clive interrupted.

"There's plenty of room. I can stay on the far side of the island." Ahmed looked quite pleased with his plan.

"Whereas I'd like to stay in this little village," Adaeze volunteered.

At what was probably my look of panic, realizing far too many vampires wanted to move in, she said, "It would only be for perhaps one week a year. We have our own communities to look after. We usually only meet in person once a year."

Clive glanced at me and then back at the others. "Sam and I will discuss it later. In the meantime, perhaps we should return to the nocturne."

"There's a tavern in Canterbury," Cadmael volunteered, "that might serve for our meeting place tonight."

Clive gave him a long look but eventually nodded. "For tonight, as we are all here." He raised his eyebrows at me and I squeezed his hand.

"My dear," Bracken said. "May I see your bookstore while they continue their meeting?"

"Of course." I gave Clive a kiss on the cheek as he pulled his phone from his pocket. Before I could leave, he pulled me back and showed me his phone screen.

The text had been sent to both Clive and me.

Meg: It's your turn to help me. Cape Taenarum.

"Cape Taenarum?" I looked at Clive. "Where the heck is that?"

"Greece," Bracken replied. "It's reputed to be the entrance to the Underworld, Hades' realm."

Clive scratched his cheek. "She is a Fury, so that tracks."

"You know the Furies?" Bracken asked, his eyes alight.

"Just one of them," I replied. "Meg." I blew out a breath. Well, shit.

Acknowledgments

The Mermaid's Bubble Lounge is my twelfth published novel (there are also four short stories). I'm someone who is wary of good fortune, someone waiting for the other shoe to drop. *Quick! Knock wood if you acknowledged something good happening.* Perhaps because of that, I haven't risked considering the broad view of this career I have. I keep my eyes focused on the current project and then the next and then the next… So, twelve books later, 3600-ish pages written, it hits me that I'm doing it. My childhood dream of one day being able to make up stories for a living is my new reality. I can't think about it too much, though. That other shoe is balancing precariously.

Go on. You do it too. Think back over your life and let yourself acknowledge how hard you've worked and how much you've accomplished. We'll go back to doubting ourselves soon but enjoy that feeling of pride for a minute.

Thank you to all of you reading my books. You've allowed me to live this dream.

Thank you to my wonderful family for always supporting me! You're the best cheerleaders a gal ever had. Thank you to my incredible critique partner C.R. Grissom, who has over the last seventeen years read everything I've ever written. She's a wonderful writer, funny, insightful, and terribly talented.

Thank you to Peter Senftleben, my extraordinary editor. He has the enviable knack of getting to the heart of the story and then helping me to see my own work through a different lens. Thank you to Susan Helene Gottfried, my exceptional proofreader who always knows exactly where the commas go (unlike myself).

Thank you to the remarkable team at NYLA! You've made every step of publishing a little easier with your wit, compassion, and expertise. Thank you to my incomparable agent Sarah Younger, the fabulous Natanya Wheeler, and the incredible Cheryl Pientka for working together to make my dream of writing and publishing a reality.

Dear Reader,

Thank you for reading *The Mermaid's Bubble Lounge*. If you enjoyed Sam and Clive's latest adventure, please consider leaving a review or chatting about it with your book-loving friends. Good word of mouth means everything when you're a writer!

Love,
Seana

Want more books from Seana?

If you'd like to be the first to learn what's new with Sam and Clive (and Arwyn and Declan and Orla and Owen and Dave and Stheno…), please sign up for my newsletter *Tales from the Book Nerd*. It's filled with writing news, deleted scenes, giveaways, book recommendations, first looks at covers, short stories, and my favorite cocktail and book pairings.

Sam's next adventure is **The Ferryman's Rest Inn & Grogshop.** It will be arriving in the fall of 2026. Stay tuned for more…

If you're a Sea Wicche fan, **Wicked Wicche** will be out March 31, 2026.

What else has Seana written? Well, I'll tell you...

The Slaughtered Lamb Bookstore & Bar
Sam Quinn, Book 1

Welcome to The Slaughtered Lamb Bookstore and Bar. I'm Sam Quinn, the werewolf book nerd in charge. I run my business by one simple rule: Everyone needs a good book and a stiff drink, be they vampire, wicche, demon, or fae. No wolves, though. Ever. I have my reasons.

I serve the supernatural community of San Francisco. We've been having some problems lately. Okay, I'm the one with the problems. The broken body of a female werewolf washed up on my doorstep. What makes sweat pool at the base of my spine, though, is realizing the scars she bears are identical to the ones I conceal. After hiding for years, I've been found.

A protection I've been relying on is gone. While my wolf traits are strengthening steadily, the loss also left my mind vulnerable to attack. Someone is ensnaring me in horrifying visions intended to kill. Clive, the sexy vampire Master of the City, has figured out how to pull me out, designating himself my personal bodyguard.

He's grumpy about it, but that kiss is telling a different story. A change is taking place. It has to. The bookish bartender must become the fledgling badass.

I'm a survivor. I'll fight fang and claw to protect myself and the ones I love. And let's face it, they have it coming.

The Dead Don't Drink at Lafitte's
Sam Quinn, Book 2

I'm Sam Quinn, the werewolf book nerd owner of the Slaughtered Lamb Bookstore and Bar. Things have been busy lately. While the near-constant attempts on my life have ceased, I now have a vampire gentleman caller. I've been living with Clive and the rest of his vampires for a few weeks while the Slaughtered Lamb is being rebuilt. It's going about as well as you'd expect.

My mother was a wicche and long dormant abilities are starting to make themselves known. If I'd had a choice, necromancy wouldn't have been my top pick, but it's coming in handy. A ghost warns me someone is coming to kill Clive. When I rush back to the nocturne, I find vamps from New Orleans readying an attack. One of the benefits of vampires looking down on werewolves is no one expects much of me. They don't expect it right up until I take their heads.

Now, Clive and I are setting out for New Orleans to take the fight back to the source. Vampires are masters of the long game. Revenge plots are often decades, if not centuries, in the making. We came expecting one enemy but quickly learn we have darker forces scheming against us. Good thing I'm the secret weapon they never see coming.

The Wicche Glass Tavern
Sam Quinn, Book 3

I'm Sam Quinn, the werewolf book nerd owner of the Slaughtered Lamb Bookstore and Bar. Clive, my vampire gentleman caller, has asked me to marry him. His nocturne is less than celebratory. Unfortunately, for them and the sexy vamp doing her best to seduce him, his cold, dead heart beats only for me.

As much as my love life feels like a minefield, it has to take a backseat to a far more pressing problem. The time has come. I need to deal with my aunt, the woman who's been trying to kill me for as long as I can remember. She's learned a new trick. She's figured out how to weaponize my friends against me. To have any hope of surviving, I have to learn to use my necromantic gifts. I need a teacher. We find one hiding among the fae, which is a completely different problem. I need to determine what I'm capable of in a hurry because my aunt doesn't care how many are hurt or killed as long as she gets what she wants. Sadly for me, what she wants is my name on a headstone.

I'm gathering my friends—werewolves, vampires, wicches, gorgons, a Fury, a half-demon, an elf, and a couple of dragon shifters—into a kind of Fellowship of the Sam. It's going to be one hell of a battle. Hopefully, San Francisco will still be standing when the dust clears.

The Hob & Hound Pub
Sam Quinn, Book 4

I'm Sam Quinn, the newly married werewolf book nerd owner of the Slaughtered Lamb Bookstore and Bar. Clive and I are on our honeymoon. Paris is lovely, though the mummy in the Louvre inching toward me is a bit off-putting. Although Clive doesn't sense anything, I can't shake the feeling I'm being watched.

Even after we cross the English Channel to begin our search for Aldith—the woman who's been plotting against Clive since the beginning—the prickling unease persists. Clive and I are separated, rather forcefully, and I'm left to find my way alone in a foreign country, evading not only Aldith's large web of hench-vamps, but vicious fae creatures disloyal to their queen. Gloriana says there's a poison in the human realm that's seeping into Faerie, and I may have found the source.

I knew this was going to be a working vacation, but battling vampires on one front and the fae on another is a lot, especially in a country steeped in magic. As a side note, I need to get word to Benvair. I think I've found the dragon she's looking for.

Gloriana is threatening to set her warriors against the human realm, but I may have a way to placate her. Aldith is a different story. There's no reasoning with rabid vengeance. She'll need to be put out of our misery permanently if Clive and I have any hope of a long, happy life together. Heck, I'd settle for a few quiet weeks.

Biergarten of the Damned
 Sam Quinn, Book 5

I'm Sam, the werewolf book nerd owner of The Slaughtered Lamb Bookstore & Bar. I've always thought of Dave, my red-skinned, shark-eyed, half-demon cook, as a kind of foul-mouthed uncle, one occasionally given to bouts of uncontrolled anger.

Something's going on, though. He's acting strangely, hiding things. When I asked what was wrong, he blew me off and told me to quit bugging him. That's normal enough. What's not is his missing work. Ever. Other demons are appearing in the bar, looking for him. I'm getting worried, and his banshee girlfriend Maggie isn't answering my calls.

Demons terrify me. I do NOT want to go into any demon bars looking for Dave, but he's my family, sort of. I need to try to help, whether he wants me to or not. When I finally learn the truth, though... I'm not sure I can ever look at him again, let alone have him work for me. Are there limits to forgiveness? I think there might be.

The Viper's Nest Roadhouse & Café
Sam Quinn, Book 6

I'm Sam, the werewolf book nerd owner of The Slaughtered Lamb Bookstore & Bar. Clive, Fergus, and I are moving into our new home, the business is going well, and our folly is taking shape. The problem? Clive's maker Garyn is coming to San Francisco for a visit, and this reunion has been a thousand years in the making. Back then, Garyn was rather put out when Clive accepted the dark kiss and then took off to avenge his sister's murder. She was looking for a new family. He was looking for lethal skills. And so, Garyn has had plenty of time to align her forces. When her allies begin stepping out of the shadows, Clive's foundation will be shaken.

Stheno and her sisters are adding to their rather impressive portfolio of businesses around the world by acquiring The Viper's Nest Roadhouse & Café. Medusa found the place when she was visiting San Francisco. A dive bar filled with hot tattooed bikers? Yes, please!

Clive and I will need neutral territory for our meeting with Garyn, and a biker bar (& café, Stheno insisted) should fit the bill. I'd assumed my necromancy would give us an advantage. I hadn't anticipated, though, just how powerful Garyn and her allies were. When the fangs descend and the heads start rolling, it's going to take every friend we have and a nocturne full of vamps at our backs to even the playing field. Wish us luck. We're going to need it.

The Bloody Ruin Asylum & Taproom
Sam Quinn, Book 7

I'm Sam, the werewolf book nerd owner of The Slaughtered Lamb Bookstore & Bar. My husband, Master vampire Clive, has been asked to go to Budapest to interview for a position in the Guild, a council of thirteen vampires who advise the world's Masters. The competition for the recently vacated spot is fierce. I worry about Clive, as it quickly becomes apparent that the last person to hold the position didn't leave voluntarily.

Ever the supportive wife, I'm tagging along. I researched Budapest and had a long itinerary of things to do. That is, I did. When we arrive, we find out that the Guild headquarters is in the ruins of an abandoned insane asylum. Awesome. If there's one thing I love, it's being hounded by mentally unstable Hungarian ghosts.

Let's just say this isn't the romantic getaway I'd been hoping for. With Clive in top secret meetings and a bunch of creepy Renfields skulking around corners, nowhere is safe. I want to help Clive because I know he really wants the job, but the other Guild members are ancient and scary powerful. Between you and me, I thought Vlad would be taller.

Wish us luck! We're going to need it.

The Mermaid's Bubble Lounge
Sam Quinn, book 8

The vampire Guild is in shambles. My husband Clive and I might have given more than a few Masters their final deaths—allegedly—so it's fallen on us to fix the problem. Mostly on Clive, that is, as he's the Master vampire. I'm Sam Quinn, werewolf book nerd and owner of The Slaughtered Lamb Bookstore & Bar.

Vlad (yes, that one) and Cadmael are the houseguests no one would want, but we're trying to grin and bear it because the Guild must be rebuilt, and we must make haste as rogue vamps are becoming a big bloody problem.

Finvarra, the fae king who had it out for me even before I helped cause his brother's death, is coming to do what none of his assassins have managed: end me in as painful a manner as possible.

In other news, Stheno and Vlad have been hooking up and we're all a little afraid of those two together.

The Ferryman's Rest Inn & Grogshop
Sam Quinn, book 9

Meg, or Megaera, is one of the Furies you probably read about in Greek Mythology. She's also been sitting on one of Sam's stools in The Slaughtered Lamb Bookstore & Bar since it opened, glaring into silence anyone who tries to strike up a conversation with her.

Sam, being Sam, eventually broke through Meg's walls and a tentative friendship grew—not a warm one, certainly. Meg doesn't do warm. She has, though, in a crisis situation, shown up to fight alongside Sam.

Until recently, that is.

Sam's getting more and more concerned about Meg's strange absences and then she and Clive receive a text that turns their lives upside down. Meg tells Sam and Clive it's their turn to help her... in Greece...in the Underworld.

Sam badgers her friend Stheno into coming with them. I mean, if you have to descend into Hades' realm, a Gorgon can be pretty handy.

Keep your fingers crossed. Things are about to get downright mythological around here.

———

Bewicched: The Sea Wicche Chronicles
Sea Wicche, Book 1

We here at The Sea Wicche cater to your art-collecting, muffin-eating, tea-drinking, and potion-peddling needs. Palmistry and Tarot sessions are available upon request and by appointment. Our store hours vary and rely completely on Arwyn—the owner—getting her butt out of bed.

I'm Arwyn Cassandra Corey, the sea wicche, or the wicche who lives by the sea. It requires a lot more work than I'd anticipated to remodel an abandoned cannery and turn it into an art gallery & tea bar. It's coming along, though, especially with the help of a new werewolf who's joined the construction crew. He does beautiful work. His sexy, growly, bearded presence is very hard to ignore, but I'm trying. I'm not sure how such a laid-back guy got the local Alpha and his pack threatening to hunt him down and tear him apart, but we all have our secrets. And because I don't want to know his—or yours for that matter—I wear these gloves. Clairvoyance makes the simplest things the absolute worst. Trust me. Or don't. Totally up to you.

Did I mention my mother and grandmother are pressuring me to assume my rightful place on the Corey Council? That's a kind of governing triad for our ancient magical family, one that has more than its fair share of black magic practitioners. And yes, before you ask, people have killed to be on the council—one psychotic sorceress aunt stands out—but I have no interest in the power or politics that come with the position. I'd rather stick to my art and, in the words of my favorite sea wicche, help poor unfortunate souls. (Good luck trying to get that song out of your head now)

Wicche Hunt: The Sea Wicche Chronicles
Sea Wicche, Book 2

I'm Arwyn Cassandra Corey, the Sea Wicche of Monterey. Want a psychic reading? Sure. I can do that. In the market for art? I have all your painting, photography, glass blowing, and ceramic needs covered in my newly remodeled art gallery by the sea. Need help solving a grisly cold case? Unfortunately, I can probably help with that too.

After more than a decade of being nagged, guilted, and threatened, I've finally joined the Corey Council and am working with my mother and grandmother to hunt down a twisted sorcerer. We know who she is. Now we need to find and stop her before more are murdered.

The evil the sorcerer and her demon are doing is seeping into the community. Violent crimes have been increasing and as a result Detectives Hernández and Osso have brought me another horrifying case. I'll do what I can, because of course I will. What are a few more nightmares to a woman who barely sleeps?

Declan Quinn, the wicked hot werewolf rebuilding my deck, is preparing for a dominance battle with the local Alpha. A couple of wolves have already left their pack to follow Declan, recognizing him as the true Alpha. Declan needs to watch his back as the full moon approaches. The current Alpha will do whatever it takes to hold on to power, including breaking pack law and enlisting the help of a local vampire.

And if Wilbur, my selkie friend is right, I might just be meeting my dad soon. Perhaps he'll have some advice for this wicche hunt. I'm going to need all the help I can get.

Wicching Hour: The Sea Wicche Chronicles
   Sea Wicche, Book 3

I'm Arwyn Cassandra Corey, the Sea Wicche of Monterey. My new art gallery is finally open, my boyfriend is the new Alpha of the Big Sur pack, and my sorcerer cousin is still on the loose. It's been a lot. I'm just sayin'.

Detectives Hernández and Osso are asking for my help again. Bodies have been found torn up in the woods in a manner that has those in the know thinking werewolf. Declan, as Alpha, will need to investigate his pack and help hunt the killer.

We're narrowing in on Calliope and her demon. She can't hide forever, and my uncle might just have the map to where she's been holed up. If it's the last thing I do, I'll make her pay for her treachery.

Did I mention there's a new podcast, hosted by a human, who is coming dangerously close to telling the kind of secrets the supernatural community kills to keep quiet? His latest season is about a certain artistic wicche.

Oh, and I finally met my dad. Like I said, it's been a lot.

Wicked Wicche: The Sea Wicche Chronicles
Sea Wicche, Book 4

Arwyn, our favorite artist and Sea Wicche, is trying unsuccessfully to deal with two new descriptors: murderer and mother.

The gallery is open, and the sorcerer is gone. Arwyn and the whole Corey clan should be celebrating. Instead, they're mourning a huge loss and now dealing with the Council of Wicches over a poisoning.

Lessons have begun with Dad. All the things a little faeling should have already learned, Arwyn is now being taught. And just in time, as the queen—cryptically and rather terrifyingly—told Arwyn that she has plans for her.

While trying to juggle all of that, and work on a huge order of glass octopuses, Arwyn is also drawn into another deadly police investigation. Send Arwyn your good thoughts because she really needs a nap.

About Seana Kelly

Seana Kelly lives in the San Francisco Bay Area with her husband, two daughters, two dogs, and one fish. She recently retired from her career as a high school teacher-librarian to pursue her lifelong dream of writing full-time. She's an avid reader and re-reader who misses her favorite characters when it's been too long between visits.

She's a *USA Today* bestselling author and a two-time Golden Heart® Award finalist. She is represented by the delightful and effervescent Sarah E. Younger of the Nancy Yost Literary Agency.

You can follow Seana on Twitter/X for tweets about books and dogs or on Instagram for beautiful pictures of books and dogs (kidding). She also loves collecting photos of characters and settings for the books she writes. As she's a huge reader of young adult and adult books, expect lots of recommendations as well.

Website: www.seanakelly.com

Newsletter: https://geni.us/t0Y5cBA

𝕏 x.com/SeanaKellyRW

📷 instagram.com/seanakellyrw

f facebook.com/Seana-Kelly-1553527948245885

BB bookbub.com/authors/seana-kelly

📌 pinterest.com/seanakelly326

Made in United States
Cleveland, OH
10 October 2025

24070025R00155